DELICIOUS

"One such as   's
delectation. Ho   ny
us the treat,"   is
around Rosema

"Let me go!" she demanded, trying to push him away with two clenched fists. She could feel the long, hard length of him pressing even closer, and it was making her dizzy.

"Presently," he said, in his normal voice.

She stared up at him, her eyes beseeching him to release her.

He shook his head in refusal, and then he bent and kissed her.

As his lips clung to hers, Rosemary was not aware that the fists she had made had opened, and her hands rested on his broad chest. She was lost in her first real embrace . . .

And if she did not find the means to resist, so much more would be lost as well. . . .

The Cloisonné Locket

(For a list of other Signet Regency Romances by Barbara Hazard, please turn page . . .)

The
Cloisonné Locket

Barbara Hazard

A SIGNET BOOK

NEW AMERICAN LIBRARY

NAL BOOKS ARE AVAILABLE AT QUANTITY DISCOUNTS
WHEN USED TO PROMOTE PRODUCTS OR SERVICES.
FOR INFORMATION PLEASE WRITE TO PREMIUM MARKETING DIVISION,
NEW AMERICAN LIBRARY, 1633 BROADWAY,
NEW YORK, NEW YORK 10019.

SIGNET TRADEMARK REG. U.S. PAT. OFF. AND FOREIGN COUNTRIES
REGISTERED TRADEMARK—MARCA REGISTRADA
HECHO EN CHICAGO, U.S.A.

SIGNET, SIGNET CLASSIC, MENTOR, ONYX, PLUME, MERIDIAN AND NAL BOOKS
are published by New American Library,
1633 Broadway, New York, New York 10019

First Printing, November, 1986

1 2 3 4 5 6 7 8 9

PRINTED IN THE UNITED STATES OF AMERICA

His face
Deep scars of thunder had entrenched, and care
Sat on his faded cheek, but under brows
Of dauntless courage, and considerable pride
Waiting revenge.

JOHN MILTON, 1608–1674

I

After almost a week of continuous rain, the weather had moderated at last, and the sun had appeared through racing clouds as if eager to dry the sodden earth that was just waking to another spring. Mrs. Joshua Fleming had given her daughter and her niece permission to walk to the village, ostensibly to purchase some ribbon to trim a bonnet, but in reality so she herself might enjoy a quiet visit alone with her old friend.

The two middle-aged ladies sat by the window of the morning room where the light was best, busy with their needlework. They had known each other for a long time, for they had grown up in the neighborhood, and married the same year. There all similarity between them ended. Mary Fleming had wed a man who lived only a few miles from her girlhood home, and she had seldom left the county since. Her guest, Lady Agatha Williams, married to a diplomat, had spent most of her life in various cities abroad. The two had kept their friendship intact by corresponding throughout the years, and when Mrs. Fleming had learned that Agatha was soon to go to Brazil for an indeterminate time, she had begged her to come down to Kent for a visit before she sailed.

Now Lady Agatha looked up to see her hostess serious and intent on her work, and she smiled. Mary had not changed much from the quiet girl she had always been. Her soft brown hair was graying now, and her sweet, plain face was acquiring a few wrinkles, but she was still the same person Lady Agatha remembered. As she took a stitch in her canvas, she realized that distance had been the salvation of their friendship, for if they had lived in close proximity all these years, it would have dwindled to mere acquaintance. Lady Agatha had been at Fleming Hall for only two weeks, but she was so bored, it seemed more like a month. In fact, she told herself as she set another stitch, not to put too fine a point on it, Mary herself was boring. Dear, of course, and worthy and pious, but placid and uninteresting as well. Lady Agatha was used to the diplomatic world, to the excitement of decision-making that could alter the course of the nation, to witty and learned conversation, and to consorting with those in power. The Flemings, concerned only with their crops and family and friends, and the relentless, ordered changing of the seasons, would have been astounded to learn how very tedious their guest found them. Indeed, Mary Fleming had remarked a number of times how restful this visit must be for her dear friend, and how very much she must envy her her ordered life. She had spoken in such a smug, righteous little voice that Lady Agatha had been hard put to conceal a smile.

Now this lady was reminded of something she had been meaning to speak to Mary about, and she put down her tambour frame and remarked, "Eleanor is a pretty girl, Mary. She reminds me of you at that age. She is twenty now, is she not?"

Her friend looked up, smiling. "Yes, that is true," she agreed.

"I am surprised you have not introduced her to society yet," Lady Agatha continued. "No doubt you plan her come-out soon?"

Now Mrs. Fleming frowned a little. "My mother-in-law's death forced us to delay the occasion," she explained. "But neither Joshua nor I believe in the London Season in any case. No, Eleanor will make her debut here in Kent. There are the local assemblies and parties, and I suppose we shall give a small dance to mark the occasion.

And in the fall, after the harvest, we plan to take her to Tunbridge Wells for a few weeks.''

Lady Agatha felt this hardly a plan fraught with much excitement or opportunity for the young lady, but being childless herself, she did not comment. ''May I make a suggestion, Mary?'' she asked instead.

Mrs. Fleming nodded, putting down her needlework at her friend's serious tone.

''I do not know what your plans are in regard to your niece, but may I say it would be most unwise for you to present both girls together?'' Lady Agatha said. ''Most unwise, indeed,'' she added in a firmer voice.

''Rosemary?'' Mrs. Fleming asked, as if perplexed. ''Why, of course she will go with us, for she is eighteen now. Why would it be unwise?''

Lady Agatha shook her head, and then she saw the two girls coming up to the house through the gardens. They were accompanied by the heir, Mr. Henry Fleming, age twenty-two. Lady Agatha waved a hand in their direction, and said, ''Do observe them now, Mary, and pretend you do not know either of them. How would you describe them?''

Mrs. Fleming leaned closer to the windowpane, looking confused, and her friend remembered that imagination had never been her longest suit. ''Why, just girls who appear to be very close friends,'' she said at last.

As Lady Agatha shook her head again, she added, ''Of course, they do not look at all like cousins, do they? I have often remarked it. But that is due to Rosemary's mother.'' She sniffed. ''To this day I have never been able to understand why Roger married a foreigner. Why, he was so besotted, he allowed his wife to name her Rosa Maria Barton. I ask you! Of course, when she came to us, we changed it at once. But it is from her mother's side that Rosemary has that awful complexion, that horrid black hair, and that large mouth. Poor girl, she is to be pitied!''

Now Lady Agatha laughed out loud. ''Poor girl, you say, Mary? Are you blind? Why, she is a beauty!''

Mrs. Fleming stared at her guest as if she thought she

had gone mad, and then she turned to inspect her niece again. The trio had paused to admire a bed of daffodils, and as she watched, her son stooped to pick one and present it to his cousin. A little frown lit his fond mother's brow, and Lady Agatha nodded.

"Yes, you are right to worry, for besides having such unusual beauty, there is something else about Rosemary, something that could be extremely dangerous. Without using a single wile, and even dressed as modestly as she is, she manages to attract every male in her vicinity. See there where your son is bowing as he gives her the flower, and do notice his eager smile. In an older man, I would be tempted to call it lecherous."

Mrs. Fleming was still staring into the garden, almost in horror now, as if a monster had suddenly appeared on her well-tended lawn. The April breeze blew Rosemary's cloak open and pressed the prim gown she wore against her body, outlining her voluptuous figure as if she were naked. Mrs. Fleming gasped.

"It is not only Henry," Lady Agatha persisted. "Your menservants' eyes follow her every move, your husband is well aware of her innocent sexuality—why, even the curate could not help staring at her in church on Sunday last. She is a temptress, in spite of her staid upbringing. To present both girls together will only ensure Eleanor's continued spinsterhood. Is that what you want?"

Mary Fleming forced herself to look away from her niece so she might study her daughter. Although she was two years older than her cousin, Eleanor appeared to be younger. Her skin was so pale as to be almost translucent, and in the past her mother had considered it her greatest asset. Now she saw that her daughter seemed almost wan next to the glowing complexion of her cousin, with the warm color coming and going in her cheeks as she laughed, and with her teeth very white against the deep rose of her generous mouth. Rosemary was so vibrant that Eleanor was only a pale, lifeless doll beside her. Her own mouth tightened.

"Yes, I see," she said slowly. "Strange, I have never

noticed it before, although I cannot admire such foreign looks myself. But surely you exaggerate, Agatha! Henry cannot be *épris* there, for they were brought up as brother and sister. And as for my dear Joshua and the curate . . . Well! I beg you to remember you are maligning both my sainted husband and a man of the cloth.''

Lady Agatha hid a sigh. She knew there was no point at all in explaining male susceptibility and lust to her sheltered friend. She herself had known a lot of good family men, as well as a few of the clergy, whose actions would have revolted Mary if she had been privy to them. Now she picked up her needlework again and said, ''Be that as it may, I do advise you to separate the girls at this most important time. Surely there must be someone else who could take Rosemary?''

Mrs. Fleming considered, as the trio in the garden began to stroll toward the house again. She saw her niece raise the flower to her face, and her son move closer to whisper in her ear, and she frowned again.

''No,'' she said uneasily. ''Of course, sending Rosemary to her Italian relatives is out of the question, and you know Roger and I were the last of the Bartons. But stay!''

She paused, deep in thought, and then she added, ''I forgot that there is someone else after all. My cousin, Emily Cranston. But the woman's a recluse. She lives alone in that great house in Berkeley Square, and I have not seen or heard from her in years. To my knowledge, no one has.''

Lady Agatha seemed to be trying to place the lady under discussion. ''Of course,'' she said at last. ''Lady Emily. Why, I have not thought of her this age. Wasn't she disappointed in love, or some such thing? I seem to remember some gossip, although the details escape me.''

''No one knows,'' Mrs. Fleming told her. ''She never married again after the untimely death of Lord Cranston, although there were whispers of some great love affair. I never inquired as to what that might be,'' she added, her voice disapproving.

Lady Agatha bit her lip. She knew she would have

inquired in a minute. Without a bit of remorse, she accepted the fact that she was nowhere near as saintly a person as her longtime friend.

"Recluse or no, I advise you to write to her without delay. If she lives in such a huge mansion, what will it matter if Rosemary comes to her? She will not have to take the girl about and present her, only house her. And after all this time, she might be glad of a young companion."

"Yes, I suppose I could do that," Mrs. Fleming agreed slowly.

"Be sure to tell her the whole truth, Mary," her friend urged. "There is no need to beat about the bush. It might even intrigue her if you explain the urgency of the situation, and tell her why Rosemary must be *in absentia* at this time. And then, after you have Eleanor safely established, Rosemary can return here."

Mrs. Fleming glanced out and saw her son holding the terrace door for both girls, his sandy head bent close to his cousin's dark one as he continued to whisper in her ear. Rosemary tapped him playfully with the daffodil in mock reproach, and laughed up at him, and her aunt stiffened. She would write today, and although she would explain the situation as Agatha had suggested, she had no intention of mentioning that the visit was to be of only short duration. No, indeed. Although she was fond of her brother's only child, and considered her care a Christian duty, she could see that Rosemary's return to the hall would be an act of the utmost folly. And where the welfare of either of her children was concerned, she was not a foolish woman.

In the days that followed, she observed her niece through new eyes, and she saw the truth of everything Agatha had told her. The footmen did stare at Rosemary, and they were quicker to answer her summons than either of the other two ladies of the household. And there was no denying that Joshua's smile was warmer for his niece than for his own dear daughter. As for the curate, she could hardly believe it! He called frequently, and on the slimmest of pretenses. Why, even Mr. Reginald Hanley-Jones, a widower she had considered a possibility for Eleanor if nothing more exalted offered, talked almost exclusively to Rosemary during a morning call.

And yet, although she watched carefully, she saw that Rosemary did nothing to encourage any of these attentions.

The girl had come to live with the Flemings after her parents died during a trip abroad when she was only ten. Once she ceased to mourn them, and began to feel at home, there had been an impulsive, almost reckless quality to her character that her aunt had not approved. Over the years, she had managed to curb such an undesirable trait, as well as an inherent gaiety—a quickness to laugh and sing—that she did not consider proper in a young lady. By now Rosemary was almost as quiet and demure as her cousin. This could come as no surprise, for Eleanor had been held up to her as an example of the perfect way a young lady behaved.

One evening shortly before Lady Agatha was to leave for London, the Flemings gave a small party in her honor, inviting those of the neighborhood whom she might remember from her girlhood, and their children as well. Elegantly gowned in maroon satin and wearing her diamonds, Lady Agatha sighed. It was not at all what she was used to, but she told herself it was an excellent lesson in diplomacy as she forced an interest in General Gate's gout and Mrs. Abernathy's gall bladder. She could hardly wait to reach Lord Williams in London so she could tell him all about her country experiences. How they would laugh together, as they always did!

Mrs. Fleming looked around her drawing room with satisfaction. She thought Eleanor looked lovely tonight, in a pink gown and with her soft brown curls arranged in a becoming style. But somehow Mrs. Fleming wished her eyes were not so pale a blue, and that she was less reserved and placid. Then she turned to watch her niece. Rosemary was standing beside Miss Bentworth, the neighborhood eccentric, who was her particular friend.

As she watched, Rosemary laughed at something Miss Bentworth was saying, and she bemoaned the gay sound and the toss of that sleek dark head. She had sent specific instructions to her niece, and she was pleased to see she had been obeyed. Rosemary was wearing a simple white gown that was adorned only with a quarter-inch of lace at the modest neckline, and she had brushed her hair back and braided it into a tight twist. But even dressed and coiffed as modestly as she was, there was that about her that made you constantly aware of the supple body under her demure gown. Perhaps it was the way she moved, her aunt mused, as Rosemary adjusted Miss Bentworth's slipping stole. Eleanor never looked like that, so . . . so *sensuous*. As she continued to watch, her son joined the two, and Mr. Hanley-Jones deserted Eleanor to hurry to Rosemary's side as well. Mrs. Fleming frowned. She had written to her cousin, but as yet she had had no reply. If she did not hear within the week, she told herself, she would be forced to take further steps, and then she turned to her guests again.

Fortunately, for her peace of mind, she had Lady Emily's reply the next day. Although her letter was hardly gracious, she agreed to the extended visit of her young relative. "I can tell she must be something quite out of common, Mary," she wrote to Mrs. Fleming. "And I understand completely why you do not wish her to put paid to any chances your own daughter might have. I can only infer from your letter that Eleanor is in no way outstanding. Does she look like you? No matter. Send the girl to London. No doubt she'll find it dull, for I do not entertain or indulge in any of society's pursuits anymore, but she will grow accustomed."

Lady Agatha, when told the good news, said she was agreeable to taking Miss Barton up in her carriage when she returned to town. That evening at dinner, Mrs. Fleming apprised her family of the visit in store for Rosemary. She thought Eleanor looked a little sulky that she was not to be included in the treat, and she reminded herself to have a quiet word about self-control with her. She noticed her son's face reddening with his disappointment, and the way he opened and closed his mouth several times in dismay, and she said a little prayer of thanksgiving that Agatha had been so perceptive.

Mr. Joshua Fleming's eyes were keen as he studied his wife's calm face, and then, after glancing at his niece, he nodded to himself. He saw the way Rosemary was clasping her hands tightly together lest she exclaim in a way she knew would bring censure on her head. But her dark blue eyes gave the game away, for they were sparkling with delight and anticipation. Not for the first time, Mr. Fleming pondered the dissimilarities that made up his niece's appearance. From her father, of course, she had inherited the blue eyes and good bones—that patrician nose and delicate jawline. And surely it was her father who had endowed her with that straight spine and elegant hands. From her mother had come the thick black hair that began in such a distinctive widow's peak at her brow, and the olive complexion, as well as her figure with its slim waist and voluptuous hips and bosom. From her mother, too, had come the graceful movements of a dancer. She was a study of delightful contradictions; a demure young lady of quality, all unconscious that she possessed the mannerisms of a born courtesan. He realized that he would miss her, and he hoped she would enjoy London and be happy with her reclusive relative, but after glancing at his son's downcast face, he could only applaud his wife's forethought. Rosemary Barton was a beautiful girl, but any liaison with her could only mean a storm of trouble.

Lady Agatha was anxious to be on her way, and she herself helped to assemble and pack Rosemary's clothes. After folding yet another girlish pastel gown, she was tempted to suggest they all be left at the hall. Mary had told her that her niece was a considerable heiress, so there was no reason why she should not replenish her wardrobe in town with something more suitable. Debutante colors did nothing for Rosemary. Her skin tones demanded a burning gold or amber or a deep, vibrant blue. She managed to hold her tongue, but she had every intention of mentioning it to Lady Emily when they arrived in town.

She did not comment, either, when Mary so often quelled

an excited remark or a cascade of laughter with a slight frown or little shake of her head, although she was amazed the girl obeyed so quickly. Surely there was nothing wrong with showing delight and enthusiasm; whatever was Mary thinking of? Then she realized that by trying to make Rosemary into a very pattern card of propriety, she was doing all she could to temper her exotic looks.

The two travelers and Lady Agatha's maid took coach one blustery April morning a week later. Up to the last, Rosemary had kept herself under tight restraint, kissing her relatives demurely, and promising to write in a soft, even voice. But as the carriage bowled down the drive, she bounced a little on the comfortable squabs of the seat and cried, "At last! We are away at last!"

And then she looked so conscious of her lapse of good manners that Lady Agatha laughed at her, not mentioning that she echoed these sentiments exactly.

"I do beg your pardon, m'lady," Rosemary murmured, demurely lowering her eyes to where her neat kid-gloved hands were clasped in her lap. "Whatever must you think of me?"

Lady Agatha chuckled, and patted those hands. "There is nothing wrong with showing pleasure, my dear child," she said. "I am delighted to see you are looking forward to the trip, as I am looking forward to getting to know you better. There seemed so little opportunity at Fleming Hall."

Blue eyes opened wide for a moment, and then were hidden by dark, curling lashes. "Aunt Mary does not believe in girls pushing themselves forward, ma'am. I did so want to ask you about your travels, and all the places you have seen, but . . . but it was not allowed. Aunt Mary said I would bore you with my enthusiasm."

"My dear Rosemary!" the lady exclaimed. "People are never bored when asked to talk about themselves and their experiences. There is nothing more flattering! I shall endeavor to do so these next two days, although I shall have to speak quickly. What a shame that Mr. Fleming does not live in Scotland, for then we would have plenty of time to cover all the many years I have spent abroad."

She waited, and was rewarded by the little chuckle that escaped her companion's lips before it was quickly stifled by that neat kid glove.

She saw she would have quite a bit of work to do to get the girl to forget the stiffness and propriety which had been ingrained in her by her upbringing, even for this little while. As the afternoon wore on, however, she found that the things she told Rosemary about Rome and Paris and St. Petersburg soon had her asking questions as naturally as if she had never heard the precept that well-behaved young ladies should be seen and not heard.

"How exciting it all must have been!" the girl enthused, leaning her head back against the squabs and sighing.

"Miss Cord would not agree with you," Lady Agatha said, smiling at her dresser, who sat facing back. "I can still remember her face when we lost the Battle Round the Crossroads and the French were expected in Brussels at any time. Isn't that so, Betty?"

The maid nodded, and then to Rosemary's astonishment, told a story of her own. Rosemary's eyes grew thoughtful. Lady Agatha was the grandest lady she had ever met, yet still she did not feel it was beneath her to converse with her maid, and laugh with her as well. Rosemary remembered that the only time Aunt Mary spoke to servants was to give them orders or a quiet reprimand, and she was puzzled.

By the time the outskirts of London were reached the following afternoon, Lady Agatha had given Rosemary a great many such things to ponder. The lady herself was delighted with her young companion, and promised her she would be glad to help her with her shopping. "It may be that Lady Emily will not care to do so," she explained to Rosemary as the carriage rumbled through Merton Upon Thames. "Did your aunt mention that Lady Emily does not go out much?"

Rosemary shook her head, looking a little troubled, for she had been looking forward to seeing the sights, and perhaps even attending the theater. "No, she did not, ma'am," she answered. "She only told me to be a good girl and try to please her. As of course I shall," she added, biting her lip and looking resolute.

Lady Agatha had discovered the girl's quick wit and warmhearted nature by now, and she was able to reassure her. "No doubt you are just what she needs to cheer her up and make her wish to join the world again," she said. "And since Lord Williams and I do not sail for a month or so, I can come and see how you go on."

Rosemary took her hand and pressed it as she said, "You are too good, dear ma'am! I am so glad I was able to travel with you, for it would have been sadly flat by myself."

"And with Betty, too," Lady Agatha reminded her. "To think you might have missed her hair-raising tales of Cairo—why, it does not bear thinking about!"

As the carriage entered the crowded London streets, Rosemary grew very quiet. Her interest was intense as she stared at the crowds milling about, and the mean streets and alleys. There were so many carts and hackneys and carriages, so many horses and dogs, and darting, poorly dressed children. And then there were tradesmen calling their wares, and disabled soldiers begging, and old crones— why, there were more people here than she had ever imagined existed in the world. And over the strident, noisy scene, the air was thick with a hundred smells, most of them unpleasant, that emanated from the refuse in the gutters and the piles of rotting vegetables and manure, to the smoke from a multitude of chimneys. She had never seen a metropolis, and she admitted to herself that London frightened her. Betty Cord leaned forward and twitched at her gown to get her attention.

"Here now, miss, not to worry," she said stoutly. "Lunnon's nowhere near as bad as Cairo, just you wait and see."

Rosemary smiled, but it was not until the poorer sections were left behind and the carriage entered Berkeley

Square that she was able to relax. She was glad to see the magnificent town houses that marched around the perimeter, and the fenced-in park in the center of the square with its grass and tall trees and gravel walks. It was not very large to a country-bred miss, but it seemed a little bit like home, and she began to feel better.

2

Lady Agatha's carriage pulled up before a large, solid house made of gray stone. As Rosemary waited for the groom to let down the steps, she looked up at the mansion with a little chill of apprehension. There was something about it, something that made it appear that no one had lived there for years. Her eyes went up the four stories seeking the chimneys as the groom handed her down to the flags, and she was relieved to see a thin thread of smoke coming from three of them. But even so, she was not completely reassured. Lady Agatha climbed down beside her, asking Betty to oversee the unloading of Miss Barton's trunks.

Rosemary stared up at the massive front door. It was painted black and had a brass knocker, but the paint seemed dingy and the knocker had not been polished for a long time. And then she saw that the ground-floor windows were all shuttered, and she could not restrain a little shiver. She looked up to the next story. On one side of the front, a shutter was a little ajar, and she thought she saw a flash of light.

Lady Agatha took her arm and led her to the steps. "Come, my dear, I will go in with you to make sure Lady Emily is expecting you."

As they climbed the short flight, she commented, her voice tart, "Wouldn't you think she would open the shutters? It must be dark in there on the brightest day!"

Her voice was matter-of-fact, and before she raised the

knocker, she turned to Rosemary and said quietly, "I know from Mary that a Miss Bentworth was one of your dearest friends in Kent. As I understand it, Miss Bentworth was considered an eccentric, was she not?"

She waited until Rosemary nodded, and then she smiled. "In that case, my dear, you should have no trouble with Lady Emily, for she is, I have been told, the queen of eccentricity. Just go on as you were used to with your older friend; you will soon grow accustomed."

She nodded, and then she banged the tarnished brass knocker with authority. Although she was determined to hide it from the young girl, Lady Agatha was more than a little perturbed, and she had no intention of going away until she had seen Emily Cranston and made sure she would be a suitable guardian.

It seemed to Rosemary that they waited for a very long time before they heard measured footsteps and the door was opened a few inches.

"Yes?" a surprisingly firm male voice inquired.

Lady Agatha was not about to stand for an interrogation on the doorstep as if she were a tradesman selling silver sand or tallow candles. "We are expected. Open the door at once!" she commanded, and assisted the reluctant guardian of the door by pushing it as hard as she could.

To her surprise, she was obeyed at once, and she almost fell into a massive front hall, closely followed by her young traveling companion. It was dark in the hall, and airless, and she could not restrain a slight *moue* of distaste for the musty, unused feeling that seemed to hover over it like some miasma.

She peered intently at the man who stood before them, bowing. He was young, in his middle twenties perhaps, with a sturdy build, and he had dark blond hair and bright blue eyes. In his fashionable town dress, he did not look as if he belonged there any more than they did. Lady Agatha saw his eyes go to her companion's face and figure, and linger there in a careful inspection, and she frowned.

"I am Lady Agatha Williams," she said. "This is Miss Rosemary Barton, who has come to stay with Lady Emily."

There was no response from the young man, and she tapped his arm. "Are you in Lady Emily's employ, my good man?" she asked, her voice indignant now.

At her tone, he dragged his eyes from Rosemary to smile down at her chaperon. "No, indeed, ma'am. I am Lady Emily's nephew. But since I knew it would take forever for old Fallow to reach the door, I took over his duty myself. I am so glad I did," he added more softly, his eyes sliding back to Rosemary again.

Lady Agatha saw her tentative smile, and she said hastily, "And what might your name be, Lady Emily's nephew?"

"Forgive me, m'lady. Ronald Edson, at your service," he replied, bowing once again.

Lady Agatha moved forward. "And where might your aunt be? I wish a few words with her before going on to join my husband at Grillon's Hotel."

She removed her pelisse as she spoke, and laying it over a chair, motioned Rosemary to do the same.

"She assured me that she will receive you presently, ma'am," Mr. Edson said, his blue eyes keen as he inspected Rosemary's figure in its neat traveling gown.

Lady Agatha was about to ask if they were to be kept standing in the hall until such time as their hostess would deign to receive them, when a slow footstep sounded at the back of the hall. She turned to see an elderly butler shuffling forward, the candle he held quivering as he shook his head and muttered to himself.

"No doubt this is whom you were expecting to see at first, ma'am?" Mr. Edson inquired, his pleasant baritone amused. "I often tell Aunt Em that Fallow is almost too perfect for the part of elderly retainer to a recluse. And wait till you see his wife, the housekeeper! The manager of the Drury Lane could not cast better."

His matter-of-fact words seemed to bring a sort of normality to the hall, and Lady Agatha found herself relaxing. She and Rosemary were introduced to the butler, and he bowed a rusty inch or so and muttered, "So you say!"

Lady Agatha was astonished, and would have spoken,

but he went on in his querulous way, "Well, come along then to the green salon. You're to wait there until milady can see you."

"I shall escort the ladies, Fallow," Mr. Edson said as he lit a branch of candles that sat on a mahogany side table.

The old man cackled. He had given Lady Agatha no more than a cursory glance, but his rheumy old eyes lingered on Rosemary's young face. "Aye, surely you will, Mr. Ronnie. Escort 'em, and wish you could do a great deal more besides, I'm thinkin'," he added. Mr. Edson ignored him as he offered his arm to Lady Agatha, and motioned Rosemary to follow. She stayed close behind, for she had no wish to be left here with the old butler, who was almost bent over in his mirth, his chortles interspersed with fits of coughing.

As he took the ladies upstairs, Mr. Edson remarked, "Do not be distressed by Fallow, ladies. Of course he should have been pensioned off years ago, but Lady Emily could not bring herself to do so. He is of little earthly use, but my aunt employs a sturdy footman and three maids as well, so her aged and decrepit retainers are unimportant."

Rosemary looked around in some curiosity as they climbed the stairs and reached the upper hall. In the flickering light of the candles Mr. Edson held high, she could see very little, and the darkness beyond the small circle of light seemed somehow threatening. Her spirits sank, and she wondered if she would ever be happy here. As the young man ushered them into a large salon that fronted the square, he smiled at her again. Somehow it made her feel better prepared to meet this eccentric recluse with whom she had come to live.

Lady Agatha wasted no time. She moved quickly to the heavily shrouded windows and flung back the draperies, and then she opened the shutters. Late-afternoon sunlight streamed into the room, illuminating the floating dust motes that had been disturbed by her actions.

Rosemary was able to look around more easily now, although Mr. Edson seemed uncomfortable. "I beg you will not open any more curtains, ma'am,'' he said, his voice concerned. ''My aunt does not care for too much light. Her eyes are weak.''

For a moment Rosemary thought her companion would argue the point, but at last she nodded and came to take a seat beside her charge. ''I am not a bit surprised,'' she said. ''Anyone who lives in perpetual gloom must of necessity suffer from weak eyesight. But at least we can see where we are now.''

She looked around as she spoke, and she did not seem pleased by what she saw. The salon, although furnished in an elegant style popular in the early Georgian period, looked as if it had not had a single thing changed, or even moved, since then. Rosemary looked around too. When she saw a tripod facing a still-shrouded window, she rose to investigate it.

As Lady Agatha continued to question Mr. Edson behind her, she inspected the long telescope that was fixed to the tripod, its lens facing a crack in the shutters through which a tiny beam of light managed to enter the room. How strange, she thought to herself. Whatever is it doing here, and what purpose does it serve? She was about to bend and peer into the scope when she heard a cold, stiff voice inquire, ''So this is Roger's girl, is it? And who might you be, madam?''

Rosemary whirled, one hand going to her throat. Standing at the door was a tall, thin lady dressed all in black. She appeared to be of a great age, for her hair was completely white, but as Rosemary drew closer to her, she saw her face was nowhere near wrinkled enough, nor her supposedly weak eyes dim enough, to maintain the illusion.

Lady Agatha rose from the sofa and came forward, holding out her hand. ''I am Lady Agatha Williams, a friend of Mary Fleming's,'' she said. And then, with all the diplomacy she had learned over the years, she smiled and added, ''And this, of course, as you so correctly surmised, is your kinswoman, Miss Rosemary Barton.''

Rosemary dropped a curtsy, her eyes lowered. When she straightened up, it was to see her hostess peering at her and then beginning to laugh. Rosemary shivered a little, for the lady's laugh seemed dry and rusty, as if she seldom had occasion to employ it.

"Of course!" her hostess said at last. "I quite understand why you had to be removed from Kent, Miss Barton, especially if your cousin Eleanor looks anything like her mother. Oh, my, yes! You are a beauty, and one not quite in the common style, either."

She walked into the room and motioned them both to be seated. "We will be delighted to excuse you, Ronald," she told her nephew. "What we are about to discuss can be of little interest to you, and you have been here long enough."

For a moment Lady Agatha thought the young man would protest, but then he bowed in submission. "Very well, dear aunt, I shall go away—for now."

He bowed to Lady Agatha then, and smiled at Rosemary as Lady Emily said tartly, "There is no need for you to make any polite morning calls, asking how the young lady goes on. I do not want you continually on my doorstep now, any more than I have wanted you there in the past. I trust I make myself clear, sir?"

Mr. Edson looked a little discomfited, but he agreed in a calm voice. Lady Agatha saw the way his eyes lingered on Rosemary's lovely face, and she was glad Lady Emily was so unwelcoming. Ronald Edson might be an unexceptionable young man, good-looking and wellborn, but she could not like the eagerness in those bright blue eyes when he turned them in Miss Barton's direction.

Lady Emily waited until he had closed the double doors behind him and they could hear his footsteps going down the stairs before she turned to Rosemary and said, "You *can* speak, can you not, miss?"

"Certainly, ma'am," Rosemary said. "It is very kind of you to allow me to visit you. Thank you."

"She doesn't sound Italian," Lady Emily remarked to no one in particular.

"Rosemary has lived in Kent since she was ten, m'lady,"

Lady Agatha reminded her. "She has been most carefully raised by her aunt, Mary Fleming."

"Pity, that," Lady Emily remarked in a voice that brooked no argument. "She probably ruined the gel, trying to make her all meek and mild and as spineless as she is herself."

"She did not entirely succeed," Lady Agatha replied, for once not thinking before she spoke.

Suddenly the older lady leaned forward on her chair and pointed a thin bony finger at her new houseguest. "Here, now, you're not with child, are you, miss? I'll have a straight answer, if you please!"

Rosemary gasped. Fortunately, Lady Agatha was quick to reply for her, her voice indignant. "Of course she is not! Whatever can you be thinking of, ma'am?"

Lady Emily did not look in the least contrite for her lapse of manners. "It would be just like Mary Fleming to send her up here, after her fall from grace, and expect me to house her until the bastard was born. And with her looks, surely there is no reason for me not to suppose that someone has not tried to seduce her. Unless, of course, there are no men in Kent anymore, or they are all blind." She paused, and then she smiled thinly at her own humor.

Rosemary sat very still, shocked by the older lady's assessment of her character. When Lady Emily saw how upset she was, she said, 'You must not mind my blunt tongue, child. I am all too familiar with the ways of the world, especially the true nature of men. No doubt that was why your Aunt Mary was so eager to have you leave her household."

"Eager, ma'am?" Rosemary managed to get out, sounding confused.

"Of course! Her daughter probably can't hold a candle to you, and that son of hers is no doubt mad with love for you. In sending you to me, she makes sure you will not only be out of their way, you will be kept safe by the very way I live here in seclusion."

"As to that, I am sure you must agree that there is no need for Rosemary to adopt your particular habits, ma'am,"

Lady Agatha interrupted, sounding a little militant. "I intend to take her about while I remain in London. I can assure you she needs to be outfitted with clothes more suitable for town, and I see no reason why she should not enjoy the sights, attend the theater, and meet some of her social equals under my chaperonage."

"I care very little what she does, so long as she behaves herself," Lady Emily said dryly. "I am not fond of company—or the young."

She moved a little as a sunbeam struck her face. "Adjust that curtain, if you please, girl," she ordered. Rosemary rose quickly to do her bidding.

Behind her, she could hear Lady Agatha telling her all the news of her relatives in Kent, and after she had pulled the offending drapery across, she wandered back to the telescope that was placed nearby. She could not resist bending to put her eye to it. It was trained on a doorway across the square that seemed so close she felt she was standing right before it. The tall door was imposing. It was painted a smart charcoal gray, the surrounding woodwork a glistening white, and its brass knocker, unlike her elderly relative's, gleamed with polish. A set of well-scrubbed white marble steps led up to it, edged on both sides with an intricately curved wrought-iron railing.

And then she heard Lady Emily say, her stiff voice peevish, "You must go away now. I'm tired of talking to you!"

Rosemary turned quickly to see Lady Agatha's face grow red, and as if she felt a little ashamed of her ungracious order, Lady Emily added, "I have a heart condition that requires I remain as serene as possible."

Lady Agatha rose, her lips in a thin line. "I will return tomorrow, Rosemary, to see how you are getting on," she said. "Perhaps we can begin shopping then, if Lady Emily can spare you."

Rosemary tried to make her smile warm, as Lady Emily said in a tone of disgust, "She will have all the time in the world. I have no desire to have her about me constantly. In fact, I shall be most distressed if she even makes the attempt. No, my girl," she said as she rose to her feet and straightened her shoulders, "I beg you to put from your mind any notion you might have cherished of serving as a *companion* to me." Her words were rich with scorn, and Rosemary tried not to cringe. "I have no desire for a companion, nor do I want you to run errands for me, or read to me, or chatter gaily to amuse me. Nothing would upset me more, and my doctor warns me to avoid upsets. Do you understand?"

"Of . . . of course, ma'am," Rosemary said, her hands tightening in the folds of her gown. She could not help feeling miserable that she had to live with such a difficult, unpleasant woman. As if she understood, Lady Agatha came and gave her a kiss and a little hug to reassure her.

"We will meet tomorrow, my dear," she said, and then she winked. Rosemary smiled as she thanked her for all her kindness.

After she left, Lady Emily was quick to close the draperies that had been opened. Rosemary remained standing in the gloom, uncertain of what she should do now. Her hostess stared at her, and, trying to think of some way to break the uneasy silence, Rosemary said, "Who lives in that imposing mansion across the square, ma'am? I could not help but notice that your telescope was trained on its door."

Lady Emily walked to the tripod and bent for a quick look. And then, as she rose, an alert, speculating expression came over her face, and she studied Rosemary very carefully, her eyes moving slowly from her head to her toes.

"Hmmm . . . I wonder . . . ?" she asked herself in a musing voice. Her eyes seemed to look beyond Rosemary then, and her lips tightened. In a moment she recalled her guest, and she said in a harsher voice, "That is the town house of the Duke of Rutland."

Ignoring her cold, stiff tones, Rosemary said, "A duke lives right across the square? How exciting!"

"Dukes are no better than other men, my girl," Lady Emily told her over her shoulder as she walked to the drawing-room door. "In fact, in many cases they are a good deal worse. But come, I will show you to your room so you might begin your unpacking. Dinner is served at seven, and until that time I do not care to see you."

Rosemary nodded and tried to act as if this were quite the common way for a hostess to behave. She followed the lady up another flight of stairs to a large bedroom facing the square. She saw that her trunks had been brought up, and a young maid was already beginning to unpack them.

She turned to her hostess, expecting her to introduce the maid, but Lady Emily was already disappearing into a room across the hall. The door closed behind her with a decisive snap. Rosemary could hear a dog barking, and Lady Emily's voice ordering him to be quiet, before there was silence again.

Turning back into her room, she said, "I am Rosemary Barton. Who are you?"

The maid bobbed a curtsy. "I'm Maggie McGuire, please, miss."

"Thank you for helping me unpack, Maggie," Rosemary said with her warm smile. Then she went to all the shrouded windows and threw back the draperies. The maid gasped.

"Lady Emily says we must always keep the curtains closed, miss," she told her.

"But this is my room, and here I refuse to stumble around in the dark," Rosemary said firmly. "The curtains will be drawn only at night, is that understood?"

Maggie grinned and nodded, as if they shared a secret. Rosemary smiled back. She thought the little maid very attractive with her brown curls and the golden freckles on her round, cheerful face.

Now she bent to lift another gown from the open trunk. As she shook it to remove the creases, she said, her voice admiring, "What a pretty pink, miss!"

Remembering her shopping trip with Lady Agatha on the morrow, and thinking she might make the maid an ally in this strange household, Rosemary said, "Would you like to have it, Maggie? I am about to buy a great many new gowns, and even though you are smaller than I am, perhaps you could make it fit."

The maid's eyes were shining. "Oh, thank you, that'd be prime, miss," she said.

She laid the pink dress aside carefully before she continued to unpack. Rosemary came to help, and the two were soon chattering together as if they had known each other for years. By asking a few questions, Rosemary was put in possession of a great many facts about the household. She found out that Maggie had come to work for Lady Emily only a few months ago, but nothing in the house seemed to have escaped her notice. Not a bit reticent, she told Rosemary a number of stories about the Fallows, the elderly couple who nominally held the reins of the household in their hands, about Ada, the cook, and Willa and Mabel, the other maids, and about Bert, the footman, as well. Rosemary saw how she blushed when she mentioned Bert, and stole a glance at her new pink dress, and she sensed a romance in the offing.

"That's all there is, miss," Maggie concluded. "But I almost forgot! There's Prinny, too, of course."

"Prinny?" Rosemary asked, as if she could not believe her ears. Surely the Prince Regent was not an intimate of this house!

"Her dog," Maggie explained, cocking her head in the direction of the room across the hall. "Ugly old mastiff, he is, but she treats him like a baby, she does. You'll meet him tonight, for he always lies at her feet at table." The maid's brown eyes twinkled. "You must hope he takes to you, miss, for ugly and old or not, he could make a meal of you if he wanted to. He weighs all of eight stone, he does, and he eats like a horse!" She chuckled, and then she added, "Lady Emily says he's a watchdog, although what she needs one for, I couldn't say. No one ever comes here for him to watch, no one at all."

She sounded disappointed that such was the case, and remembering Lady Emily's nephew, Rosemary said, "But I met a gentleman here this very afternoon. A Mr. Edson."

Maggie's shrug was eloquent. "Him! He's the only one

who ever comes, and Fallow says it's just so Lady Emily will leave him all her money when she goes. He's one, Mr. Edson is, who knows what side his bread's buttered on, if you take my meaning. And he's not one I like to be caught alone with in a dark hall, neither.''

As if afraid she had said too much, the maid bit her lip and fell silent, and Rosemary changed the subject. She had thought Mr. Edson very attractive, although no more than Lady Agatha had she liked the eager look in his eye, nor the way he inspected her figure with such lingering intensity. Perhaps it was just as well his aunt did not want him underfoot in her house, she thought as she put a pile of modest chemises away in a drawer.

Rosemary was only too aware how men reacted when they were near her, but in her innocence, she thought all girls were treated the same way. Having been brought up to hide her figure and disguise her beauty as much as possible, and discouraged from spending much time in front of her glass, she never gave it a thought. Besides, she knew from what Aunt Mary had let drop time and time again, it was Eleanor who was the true English beauty.

After Maggie had gone to fetch her some hot water, Rosemary wandered over to the window and stared out at the square. It was amusing to see so many people about: a nursemaid throwing a ball to two toddlers in the park, two fashionable ladies deep in conversation on one of the benches, a couple of darting footmen intent on some urgent errands, and several gentlemen swinging their canes as they made their way down the street, the sunlight gleaming on their shining top hats. Horseback riders and carriages clattered by.

As she watched, an elegant open landau drew up at the house Lady Emily had told her belonged to the Duke of Rutland. She moved closer to the window and watched as the two liveried grooms sprang into action. One opened the carriage door and let down the steps, while his counterpart ran to sound the knocker. The first groom assisted a middle-aged lady to descend, and then he reached into the carriage and picked up a slim girl about Rosemary's age.

He carried her into the house behind the other lady, and the charcoal-gray door closed behind them.

As if a curtain had fallen on the act of a play, Rosemary sighed. Going to brush her hair, she wondered why the girl could not walk, and then she thought how nice it would be if she could meet the young lady. It would be such a comfort to have a friend her own age to talk to and confide in in this huge, bustling metropolis. Despite its numerous population, it seemed to her that London was going to be a very lonely place indeed.

3

Rosemary came downstairs a few minutes before seven. She had been alone in her room for over two hours, for although she would have liked to investigate this house where she was going to live, somehow she could not bring herself to do it. If Lady Emily should discover her wandering around, she might think she was prying; besides, she had made it very plain that she had no desire to see her guest before the dinner hour.

No one had come near her after Maggie had finished the unpacking, and although she listened carefully, there was not a sound anywhere. It was eerie, and not at all what she was used to. Even with such well-trained servants as her Aunt Mary employed, there had always been some little noise in the house—footsteps going up and down the stairs, the sound of a door closing, or someone giving a quiet order. But here there was only a thick, unbroken silence. Even the dog didn't bark. It was almost as if everyone had gone away and left her here, completely alone. Rosemary tried to laugh, telling herself she was being fanciful, but still she was relieved when she reached the bottom of the stairs and found the elderly butler waiting to show her to the dining salon.

She wished him a good evening, but he only snorted and shuffled away, impatiently motioning her to follow him. When he opened the double doors, he did not bother to announce her, but that would have been unnecessary in any case, for as she entered the room, a huge dog leapt to his feet and began to bark.

Rosemary was not in the least afraid of dogs, but she admitted she found this one intimidating. His coat was a mixture of brindle and fawn, and he was very large, with long legs and a heavy, powerful frame. His head seemed especially massive and ugly as he bared his teeth at her.

"Quiet, Prinny!" Lady Emily ordered from where she sat at the head of the table, and after a few more token barks, the dog subsided. Rosemary noticed he still watched her carefully, and she could hear a rumble deep in his throat. She stood, hesitating, just inside the door until her hostess said, "Come here, girl! He won't bite you, not now."

At that, she took a deep breath and moved gracefully into the room. She sensed that these first few moments were important and that she must not show any fear. As the dog continued to watch her, she curtsied and said, "Good evening, ma'am."

Lady Emily nodded. "Good girl. Never show animals you are afraid of 'em, for if you do, they will never forget it, and make your life a misery. Prinny is my watchdog, and until he is sure you are acceptable to me, and an inmate of the house, he will be on his guard. Make no sudden motions near him; he is quite fierce."

"Should I pat him?" Rosemary asked, trying to keep her voice cool.

Lady Emily smiled a little. "I would not advise it, not yet." Then she turned to the dog and said, "It is all right, Prinny. Down, sir."

The dog stood uncertainly for a moment, and then he returned to his place under the table. He stretched out at her feet, his ugly, wrinkled muzzle resting on his paws.

Lady Emily indicated the chair at her right, and Rosemary took her seat. She could feel the dog's warm breath on her thin stockings, and, trying to ignore him, she studied her hostess. Lady Emily was still dressed in old-fashioned black, but this evening her gown was adorned with jet, and she wore diamonds in her ears and on her fingers. Rosemary was a little surprised to see that at her throat she wore a small cloisonné locket on a fine gold chain as well. It did not seem to go with her other jewels, but perhaps it was a family keepsake, she thought as she picked up her napkin.

And then she was absolutely astounded as Lady Emily took a book from her lap, opened it to the page she had kept marked with her finger, and calmly began to read. Rosemary could not help the feeling of anger that rose in her breast and made her dark blue eyes sparkle for a moment. She took a deep breath and reminded herself that since she had always been alone before this, the lady probably read at every meal.

To occupy herself, she looked around the dining salon. It was poorly lit, except for the branch of candles directly before her hostess, and she could see very little.

She was glad when a door opened at the back of the room several minutes later and a tall young footman came in bearing a tray. He was followed by Fallow, who was still mumbling to himself. Rosemary knew this must be the "Bert" the maid had told her about, and when he bowed to her, she could see why Maggie was attracted to him, with his open, friendly face.

As dinner progressed, she found herself wanting to laugh in spite of the silent treatment she was receiving from Lady Emily. The old butler followed the footman about as he served them, muttering orders which Bert completely ignored. Even when he left the room, Fallow trailed after him, still muttering. This behavior continued throughout the meal, which was plainly cooked but plentiful. It was obvious that although the footman was more than capable, and willing to do all the work unassisted, Fallow still considered himself majordomo here.

After the dessert of fruit compote had been served, Lady Emily dismissed the servants. Then she laid her book down at last, and turned to study her guest.

"At least you are not a chatterbox, and for that I must be grateful," she said. "No doubt you think me a rude old woman, but I refuse to change my ways simply because you have come to stay.''

''I see no reason why you should, ma'am,'' Rosemary told her, for the lady's voice had held a trace of belligerence, almost defiance. Beneath the table, Prinny stirred at the alien sound, and he growled a little.

''Quiet, Prinny!'' Lady Emily ordered, a little absent-mindedly. She nodded to Rosemary and said, ''You will soon grow accustomed. And if you go on as you have begun, I do not see any reason why we should not deal very well together.''

Rosemary did not know what to say. Since the lady's idea of dealing together seemed to comprise an almost complete refusal to acknowledge her presence, she did not think they would have any difficulty either, but she could not help feeling a pang of regret that there was to be so little camaraderie.

''You are very lovely,'' Lady Emily said, still inspecting her guest. ''At least you would be if you were dressed more suitably,'' she amended.

Rosemary looked down in confusion at her plain white evening gown. The modest neckline covered her collarbone, and everything about it proclaimed the debutante. She had dressed her hair as her Aunt Mary had always insisted, in tight braids coiled in a bun low on the nape of her neck.

''Just look at you,'' Lady Emily said, waving a disdainful hand. ''That gown might have been chosen for a thirteen-year-old, and it is much too loose. Besides, white makes you appear sallow, and with your hair skinned back in that ugly bun, you look just like an upstairs maid!''

''But Aunt Mary thinks my appearance most suitable for a young lady my age,'' Rosemary protested.

''I am sure she does,'' Lady Emily said, smiling a little thinly. ''But even all her attempts at disguise cannot hide your quality. Let us hope this Lady Agatha has better taste, and that she knows a fashionable hairdresser.''

Reminded of the lady who had promised to befriend her, Rosemary felt somewhat better. Then her hostess said,

"Do not worry about the expense. Mary tells me you are a considerable heiress, and she gave me the direction of your father's man of business. He will take care of your bills, and you may have Maggie to maid you."

She rose then, and her guest was quick to follow suit. As she did so, the dog came out from under the table and took up his position on Lady Emily's right, standing so close to her it was obvious he was guarding her from this intruder he had not accepted as yet. He put his muzzle into his mistress's hand and whined. She patted him absently and said, "Prinny is quite unlike the pretty prince he is named for, isn't he? But unlike his namesake, he is faithful. It is always wise to value faithfulness over a handsome face, my girl."

She sounded stern, but before Rosemary could wonder at it, she resumed their earlier conversation by saying, "After you have been properly gowned and coiffed, we shall see. Perhaps there is some way you can be of service to me after all."

Rosemary hastened to say she would be delighted to help any way she could, and Lady Emily chuckled in genuine amusement before she led the way from the room.

"I generally sit in the library after dinner," she said, her voice grudging. "You may join me there, but I'll have no chattering, do you hear?"

Her black-clad back led the way down a long hall, the dog padding at her side. After she took her seat in a comfortable wing chair near the fire and opened her book again, Rosemary went to inspect the shelves. Prinny watched her every move. He did not relax until she had chosen a book of etchings to study and had taken a seat a little way apart from the two old companions.

It seemed a very long time before the footman brought in the tea tray. He was followed by his elderly shadow, who still mumbled instructions. Rosemary was glad to hear even his quavering, whiny voice, for not a word had been exchanged since she and Lady Emily had sat down. The only sounds in the house had been the crackling of the fire and the dog's soft snores when he fell asleep at last.

Tea was drunk in perfect silence as well. When she had finished, Lady Emily rose and went to the door.

Rosemary stood and curtsied to her stiff back. "I wish you a very good night, ma'am," she said clearly.

Lady Emily did not bother to answer, or even look back, although Prinny seemed to sneer as he turned his massive head for a final inspection of this intruder.

Rosemary stayed in the library for some time, looking into the dying flames and wondering how she was to bear the life she saw stretching before her. If Lady Emily was right, and Aunt Mary had sent her away because Henry was behaving in such a silly way, she would not welcome a letter from her niece begging to be allowed to return to Fleming Hall. She still did not understand the bit about her overshadowing Eleanor. She knew she was too dark, too foreign-looking, to rival her cousin's English fairness. It was something she had resigned herself to years ago. And now she saw she must resign herself to staying in London, no matter how unhappy she might be. Suddenly she remembered Lady Agatha, and she smiled to herself. She would ask her tomorrow if what Lady Emily had said was true, even though she herself had a suspicion it was. Henry had been very persistent in his attentions lately, and he had tried to fondle her and kiss her a number of times, although she was sure Aunt Mary knew nothing about that!

As she went up to her room, she tried to cheer herself up by thinking of all the new clothes she was to have, and the events Lady Agatha had promised to take her to as well.

Rosemary had a message from her early the next morning. She was seated at the breakfast table, quite alone, when Fallow shuffled in to present it to her on a silver salver.

"I see what it's goin' to be like," he muttered as she tore her note open to scan it quickly. "The knocker soundin' every other thing, and comin's and goin's, and confusion and noise, and I don't know what-all! Well, I'm too old for it, and Lady Em oughtn't to ask it o' me, nor my good wife neither. It's not fair, but o' course, what does a young chit like you care about that? Ha! Not a groat, I'd wager, not a groat.''

All the time he had been speaking in his whiny voice, he had been making his slow way to the door, and now he passed through it and closed it with a snap. Rosemary did not even notice.

Lady Agatha wrote that she would call at eleven and that she had made arrangements for them to visit one of London's finest modistes. She also asked Rosemary to join her and her husband at Grillon's for tea so they might make future plans. Rosemary smiled. Now that she had this expedition to look forward to, she felt immensely better. She knew she would not see Lady Emily until evening, for Maggie had told her the lady never left her rooms till afternoon. Rosemary was relieved to escape another silent confrontation. There was something about Lady Emily—she could not put her finger on it, but it made her a little uneasy every time those supposedly dim eyes searched her face.

She finished her breakfast, and then she whiled away the time by writing a letter to the Flemings to tell them of her safe arrival in town.

She was peeking through the shutters when the familiar carriage pulled up at the front door, and she almost flew down the stairs. As she climbed into the carriage before Lady Agatha could get down, she said, "How glad I am to see you, ma'am!"

Her voice was full of such heartfelt relief that the lady had to smile before she gave her coachman an address in Bond Street. Turning to Rosemary, she said, "I have seldom been greeted so fervently! Tell me, things are not going well? Is there anything wrong?"

Rosemary told her everything that had happened after her departure the previous day, and Lady Agatha shook her head and frowned. But she laughed when Rosemary described the elderly butler, so jealous of his authority, and the young footman who just ignored him as he went about his duties.

She frowned again when she learned Lady Emily had

read a book throughout dinner and had not spoken a word all evening, not even to say good night. "I see you will have much time for reflection, my dear," she tried to say lightly. "I beg you will keep your sense of humor intact, however. This sounds more like a bad farce than real life."

"I suppose I will grow accustomed," Rosemary agreed, trying to sound cheerful.

As the carriage stopped before a shop and Lady Agatha gathered her belongings together, she said, "Let us forget the woman for now, Rosemary. We have a great deal to do today."

Rosemary followed her up the steps, and it was not very many more minutes before she was able to put Lady Emily completely from her mind. The dressmaker was all smiles when she saw the young lady she was to dress, exclaiming over her supple waist and delectable curves. She begged the two ladies to be seated until she could bring her patterns and fabrics.

It was well over an hour later before Rosemary had had her measurements taken, had been persuaded that a royal-blue evening gown and a soft gold silk trimmed with pearls were perfect for her, and had chosen several other gowns and ensembles as well. The modiste recommended a hairdresser, and sent the delivery boy running to make an appointment. Fortunately, there was a scarlet walking dress, with a matching capelet and bonnet that fit Rosemary so well, Lady Agatha insisted she wear it out of the shop.

Rosemary was both delighted and alarmed. She knew her Aunt Mary would throw up her hands in horror, not only at her extravagance, but at her daring as well. The scarlet gown clung to her so tightly, it outlined every curve, and, not being used to it, she was very uncomfortable. When she protested, the modiste threw up her hands and broke into impassioned speech. Lady Agatha laughed before she patted Rosemary's hands and said, "You are not in Kent now, my dear. If you appear in town in those horrid little dresses your Aunt Mary considered proper, you will be a laughing stock. Trust us! You look stunning!"

The modiste was fervent in her agreement, and assured the ladies that her staff would have the other outfits ready in a very short time. She promised to send word to Berkeley Square as soon as it was time to begin fittings.

As they left the shop, Rosemary saw a young man on the opposite side of Bond Street stop dead in his tracks when he saw her. As his mouth dropped open in astonishment, she could not help blushing and giggling a little at the sight of his comical face. Lady Agatha followed her gaze, and she nodded. "That's Freddie Archibald, the silly thing. Pay him no mind, Rosemary. But you must admit I was right, wasn't I? Even such as he would never have given you a second glance in that insipid sprigged muslin you wore when we began our shopping."

As she took her seat and arranged her skirts, she added, "And when you see how the other young ladies are decked out, you will be glad for your new clothes. London is the center of fashion. To be caught looking provincial is to condemn yourself to scorn and ridicule. But you will see."

Rosemary did see, that very day. She took special notice of all the ladies she saw as the carriage went from one shop to another. She observed the dashing bonnets and stylish gowns, some cut so narrowly she wondered that their owners could walk in them, and all of them, it appeared to her, designed to expose rather than conceal their charms. She wondered if Aunt Mary had any idea that ladies dressed this way, or if she were only old-fashioned and prim after all.

By the time Rosemary had been to a milliner's, a sandal shop, and a fascinating emporium that sold ribbons and laces and lingerie, the back seat of the carriage was piled high, and her dark blue eyes were sparkling in delight and wonder. She had hesitated when the hairdresser brushed her tight braids out, exclaiming as he did so, but when her worried eyes met Lady Agatha's, she had been reassured by her friend's wink and the nod she gave her.

When the hairdresser was done at last, she turned her head this way and that in astonishment as she stared into the mirror. Was this really her, Rosemary Barton? She did not even look like the same girl! The tight bun was gone, and in its place had come a riot of dark curls and little tendrils that curled over her ears. She thanked the hairdresser in a small, wondering voice, hardly hearing Lady Agatha telling her about the more elaborate hairstyles she might wear in the evening.

By the time they entered Lady Agatha's suite in Grillon's Hotel later that afternoon, Rosemary felt transformed, almost as if some benevolent fairy had sprinkled her with stardust. She wondered if she were imagining the stares she received as they crossed the lobby, and realized she was being foolish to think that the low bow a gentleman coming from the other direction made was for her. Of course not, she told herself stoutly. He is doing the pretty to Lady Agatha, of course, for she is a grand lady.

Lady Agatha kept her face schooled to polite indifference, but inside she was chuckling at the attention Rosemary was receiving. When her husband joined them a few minutes later and had been introduced to her charge, he signified his amazement by cocking an eyebrow at her. They had been married for so long, Lady Agatha was able to interpret it at once. George Williams had told her, as clearly as if he had spoken, that he had seldom seen such a piece of perfection, and asked her if she was quite sure she wished to befriend this gorgeous creature who he was positive would attract all kinds of attention and possibly cause them endless problems. Her nod assured him that she did, and he sighed and took a seat, accepting the teacup Rosemary handed him with a noncommittal smile and a word of thanks.

Rosemary tried very hard to behave quietly and modestly, as her Aunt Mary would have wished her to do, for she knew a young girl must not push herself forward. Lady Agatha would have none of it, however, and before long she was chattering to Lord Williams as if she had known him all her life. As he sipped his tea, the gentleman realized that the girl was completely unaware of her power over his sex. He wondered cynically how long that state of affairs would last, deciding that a week would be quite long enough to show her how she would be regarded by the male half of the *ton*, no matter what their age.

When she rose to go at last, he found himself offering to take her to the carriage himself, for he was not at all sure she would be able to traverse the lobby without being accosted by some eager beau. Lady Agatha rose and kissed her good-bye, waving away all her stammered thanks.

"It was nothing, Rosemary, nothing at all," she said. "I enjoyed myself very much. Now, don't forget that in two days' time you are to join us here for dinner before the theater. I shall have the carriage sent for you, and be sure to wear the nile-green gown the modiste promised to alter first. I never want to see you in any of the gowns you brought from Kent, ever again."

Rosemary promised before she took the arm Lord Williams was extending and let him lead her down the stairs, across the lobby, and out into the bright spring sunlight. She thanked him with a smile as he helped her into the carriage. He smiled in return, but he was wearing a little frown when he rejoined his wife.

"There is no need to say a word, dear George," Lady Agatha told him. "Yes, no doubt you are right, and there are storms and troubles ahead. But the poor child! Hidden away in Kent and scolded every time she laughed or chatted, dressed in die-away droopy gowns with her glorious hair pulled back in a tight bun . . . Well! I could not leave her to that fate, now could I? And even here in town she is not to have an easy time of it. That Lady Emily! I am very apprehensive—she is so strange."

Lord Williams demanded an explanation, and his wife told him about the elderly recluse, her shuttered mansion, and her lack of concern or even conversation with her young houseguest.

"Until we sail, I intend to befriend Rosemary Barton," she concluded. "At least I can make sure she meets some suitable people, sees the sights, and is properly attired."

Her husband shook his head, but he did not try to dissuade her from her task. He knew that little militant light in Agatha's eyes that told him there was nothing he could do to get her to change her mind. His wife had always regretted that they were childless, and this was not the first time her frustrated maternal feelings had been aroused.

"Beg you to do exactly as you please, m'dear," he said easily as he rose to go and change. They were to dine with some fellow diplomats home on leave, and he was already forming the questions in his mind that he wished to ask them.

Rosemary drove home in a happy daze, barely seeing the handsome streets the carriage was passing through. She looked down at her smart new scarlet dress and gently smoothed the fabric with her hand. Perhaps she would not find Lady Emily so hard to bear after all, not if she had Lady Agatha to befriend her, she thought. She put from her mind what her life would be like when that lady left for Brazil, determined to enjoy every moment until that time.

When the carriage pulled up before Lady Emily's house in Berkeley Square, she lingered while the groom unloaded her purchases and carried them into the house. It was late afternoon now, and the slanting light that came through the large trees in the park reminded her of home. Rosemary took a deep breath and glanced around the square, reminding herself that that part of her life was over, perhaps forever.

Suddenly her gaze was attracted to a smart sporting carriage that had pulled up before the Duke of Rutland's house across the square. Rosemary had never seen a perch phaeton before. With its sleek, streamlined body and its seat so high above the cobbles, it did not look like a particularly safe way to travel. It was painted a glossy black, picked out with gold accents on the wheels and shafts. As she watched, a liveried tiger jumped down from his perch at the back and ran to hold the horses' heads. They were black too, a perfectly matched set. For some reason, Rosemary held her breath as her eyes went up to where the driver was seated. He was staring straight ahead, his face expressionless. She studied that masculine profile in some awe. The gentleman had dark hair under his glossy top hat, and dark brows to match, and for a moment she admired his strong nose, lean cheeks, and firm jaw before he tossed the reins down and left his carriage.

Still Rosemary could not look away. She wished she were closer, wondering what he would look like if she were standing near him. She watched him climb the marble steps to the front door, noting his broad shoulders and the muscled legs so clearly displayed in skintight breeches. Then he turned to give some orders to his tiger. As if aware he was being spied on, his eyes lifted and seemed to burn into hers where she stood across the park.

Rosemary blushed, and hoped he could not see it as she picked up her skirts and hurried inside. How rude she had been, staring like that, she thought. She must have looked just like a country bumpkin come to town to see the sights.

But as she climbed the stairs to her room, she smiled. It had been worth it, for if she were not mistaken—and she really did not think she was—she had just seen the first duke of her life. There had been something about him, even at that distance, some quiet air of assurance, the proud tilt of his head, his stern, unsmiling mouth, that proclaimed his rank as clearly as if he had worn a badge telling the world that he was not as other men, for he was indeed the Duke of Rutland.

4

Dinner followed the same pattern as before, although this evening Prinny seemed to accept her presence, if not with glee, with a certain amount of resignation. He did not bark at her as she entered the dining room, and he made no objection when she took her seat next to his mistress. Lady Emily read throughout the meal again, and the two adjourned to the library to spend another long, conversationless evening.

Rosemary did not mind tonight. Although seemingly engrossed in a book about travel, she was reliving her exciting day and trying to decide which of her new clothes she liked the best. She was a little startled when, much later, her hostess put down her book and began to question her. Lady Emily listened carefully as Rosemary told her what they had done, and how she had been invited to dinner and the theater, and then she nodded.

"You look vastly different already, girl," she said in her harsh, rusty voice. "That hairstyle is becoming."

Rosemary smiled, but when she would have thanked her for the compliment, Lady Emily raised her long thin hand. "No conventional phrases, if you please," she ordered.

Rosemary saw her opening her book, and she hurried to say, "If I might ask you something, m'lady?"

Lady Emily did not look best pleased, but she nodded curtly, and Rosemary went on, "I do wish there was something I could do for you, ma'am. I cannot like to spend my days in idleness. Perhaps I could help your housekeeper? Aunt Mary taught me everything about domestic matters, and I would be glad to be of assistance, since I understand Mrs. Fallow is as elderly as her husband.''

She was surprised to see a grim little smile on Lady Emily's face. ''You have my permission to try, girl, but do not be upset if Mrs. Fallow refuses,'' she said. ''She is just as jealous of her authority as her husband.''

Rosemary was thinking hard. ''Then I have your permission to give some orders in regards to the housekeeping, ma'am?'' she asked.

Lady Emily waved her hand and opened her book, and Rosemary subsided, taking the gesture for consent.

The following day, Rosemary set about investigating the town house and meeting the other occupants. After she had been through all the rooms except those belonging exclusively to her hostess, she went to the housekeeper's room. She had thought a long time about how best to approach Mrs. Fallow, for she did not want the woman to refuse her, nor did she care to have her trailing after her, mumbling and whining as her husband was prone to do behind the footman. The door was slightly ajar, and Rosemary tapped and waited politely. No elderly voice bade her enter, and she was about to go away when she heard a long, noisy snore that ended at last in a series of little snuffles. At the homely sound, Rosemary smiled to herself, and rapped even louder. The snoring, which had commenced again, stopped abruptly.

''Yes, yes? Who's there? Willa, I told you I wasn't to be disturbed! Silly wench! Just you set about preparin' the veg cook ordered, and don't be botherin' me every other thing!''

Rosemary waited, but nothing more was heard but a rocker squeaking, as if its occupant was moving it impatiently. Waiting no longer, Rosemary pushed the door open and stepped inside.

An elderly woman sat before the fire, staring into the flames. She was so tiny, she had to have a footstool at her feet, and her plain face, as she turned it indignantly in Rosemary's direction, was covered with wrinkles. She wore a black dress and a white cap on her gray hair, and when she saw her visitor, her mouth dropped open so far, it was plain to see she had lost more teeth than she had kept over the years.

"And 'oo might you be?" she asked sharply, peering at her unwelcome visitor.

Rosemary introduced herself, smiling as she did so, and then she begged the housekeeper to keep her seat. Mrs. Fallow did not return that smile, and she looked as if she had never had any intention of rising.

"Well, what can I do for you then, miss?" she asked, hitching one shoulder in annoyance.

"Nothing at all," Rosemary assured her in a cheerful voice. "I have come to see what I might do for you, Mrs. Fallow. If I might sit down?"

The old lady indicated a straight chair on the other side of the fire, seemingly bemused by the young lady's statement.

Rosemary took the seat and folded her hands in her lap with composure. "You see, Mrs. Fallow, I am not used to being idle," she began. "So Lady Emily has given me permission to help you with the household."

"Help? Help?" Mrs. Fallow said in a testy voice. "I don't want any help!"

Rosemary smiled again. "You are too good! But I am sure you could use some assistance, for this is a very large mansion, is it not? Then too, there are only three maids and a single footman to do all the work. It is too bad!"

She shook her head as if commiserating with her on such a skimpy staff, and Mrs. Fallow peered at her in suspicion.

Suddenly the housekeeper nodded, and she leaned forward as if to take Rosemary into her confidence. "It is true there aren't enough to do the work well, but m'lady don't care for that. As long as the food is hot, and served on time, and her own rooms kept up, what's it matter to her if the rest of the place gets dustier and dingier?"

Rosemary could see that Mrs. Fallow didn't care either,

but she made herself say, "How distressing for you, ma'am. I am sure it is not what you have been used to."

"No, indeed," Mrs. Fallow replied, her voice swelling with pride. "Time was, years ago, when this house used to shine! Ah, those were the days! Parties and balls and soirees, the good china used every day, and the knocker never still." She sighed, and then seemed to recall herself to present company. "But that's all long past now. And there's no need to polish and clean. No one ever comes here, and no one will."

Rosemary cocked her head to one side as if considering. "But I have come, and so will my friends," she pointed out, neglecting to mention she hadn't even one to her name at the present time. "Perhaps things will be more lively here again," she added.

The old lady chortled, and slapped her knee, reminding Rosemary forcibly of the butler. "That I should live to see the day!" she said when she could speak again. "No, young lady, that will never be. Not while Lady Em's alive."

"Whether it does or not, I still intend to see to the cleaning," Rosemary told her. "For example, I am sure you would wish me to set the maids to scrubbing the hall and drawing room, and I see no reason why Bert cannot polish the door knocker while Maggie scrubs the steps. My friend Lady Agatha Williams will be calling here often, and I am sure you would not care for her to see such neglect, especially since it reflects directly on you."

Mrs. Fallow bridled a little, and then she raised her hand to stifle a yawn, before she waved it in dismissal. "Do what you like," she said in a long-suffering voice. "It makes no matter to me."

Rosemary rose and turned to the door. "Thank you, Mrs. Fallow," she said, but the housekeeper had closed her eyes and leaned her head back, and as Rosemary quietly closed the door, she could hear the snores beginning again.

Smiling, she made her way to the kitchen, where she found Willa and Mabel, the two middle-aged maids, enjoying a cup of tea. They rose to curtsy, somewhat flustered at Miss's invasion of their domain. In a short time they were hiding their chagrin, when Rosemary explained that they were to begin earning their keep with a vengeance. Rosemary thought Willa especially looked disgruntled. She was tall and thick-set, with heavy red arms now akimbo in defiance. Mabel, a spare, faded woman, only looked frightened.

"Lady Emily has given me permission to see to the household," Rosemary said, looking from one to the other. Willa sniffed until she added, "And Mrs. Fallow has agreed."

Both maids curtsied again, and promised to set to work at once.

Rosemary smiled at them. "Finish your tea first," she said. "And if there is too much to do, we shall see about hiring more help."

Willa nodded, looking a little brighter. She would be delighted to have others to lord it over, for bossing the timid Mabel had lost any charm it might once have held for her.

When Rosemary was safely out of earshot, she turned to her fellow servant and said, "Drink up, Mabel. You're to begin in the hall at once. I'll be along to help as soon as I've fixed the veg for dinner."

Mabel went to fetch the bucket and scrub brush, shaking her head as she did so. She knew it would be a long time before Willa made an appearance, if she ever did so at all.

Rosemary spoke to Bert, who agreed to polish the knocker at once. His cheerful compliance made her feel a great deal better, as did Maggie's quick nod when she was told about the grimy front steps.

By evening, a small part of the mansion looked much better, although Rosemary was discouraged it had all taken such a long time. She had helped herself until she had to go by hackney with Maggie for a fitting on her new gowns, returning with several boxes, one of them containing the nile-green dress she planned to wear to the theater the following evening. As the maid took the boxes to her room, Rosemary inspected the hall and the stairs. She wished they had been able to open the shutters, for surely it was hard to clean what you could not see, but she had not dared to suggest it, lest Lady Emily be upset at her meddling and rescind her permission.

That evening, she wore one of her new gowns to dinner, and although Lady Emily did not mention it directly, Rosemary was disconcerted when she looked up several times to find her hostess studying her, her book for once neglected. When that lady rose at the end of the meal, she put a firm hand on her dog's collar and ordered Rosemary to come and make Prinny's closer acquaintance. At her instruction, Rosemary patted his massive head. The dog growled at her, until a sharp word from his mistress quieted him.

At the end of the long evening, Lady Emily told her to pat the dog again. Rosemary did not understand, but she called Prinny a good dog as she obeyed. He stood very still, not growling now, but Rosemary noticed he did not wag his tail, either.

"Very good," Lady Emily said. "I have decided that you will take Prinny out for his walk from now on, girl. My footman has too much to do as it is. Prinny has accepted you; you won't have any trouble."

"But I don't know if I can control him," Rosemary protested. "He is so big!"

Lady Emily peered at her. "Nonsense!" she scoffed. "Of course you can! Prinny is a perfect gentleman, aren't you, boy?"

The dog looked up, his tail wagging furiously now, and Lady Emily scratched his ears. "You did say you wished to help me, did you not?" she asked her guest. At Rosemary's nod, she went on, "Very well. You shall begin tomorrow at teatime. The square will be quieter then."

She turned to leave the library, and then she said over her shoulder, "Be sure to wear the scarlet walking dress. It is vastly becoming."

Rosemary nodded, still looking a little troubled. She was not looking forward to the walk at all, but Lady Emily did not seem to doubt her success, and she did not like to protest, especially when it was the first time she had been asked for assistance.

With some trepidation, Rosemary set off at the time Lady Emily had specified the following afternoon. She managed to keep a tight grip on the leash that held Prinny, praying he would not see a cat or another dog, for she knew she would never be able to hold him. To her surprise, he behaved almost like the perfect gentleman Lady Emily claimed he was, only pausing much too long once to investigate an intriguing smell in the gutter. When he did not try to break free of her grasp, Rosemary relaxed, looking around her in interest as they made their way to the end of the square.

It was almost deserted this early in the evening, and she amused herself by looking into those windows she passed that were as yet undraped. In one house she could see a servant lighting the candles, and in another some children playing around their mother's chair. The scene touched her heart. They looked so happy, so content! She told herself it was almost as good as a play, trying to stifle the regrets she always felt when observing family groups. How different her life must have been if her lively, gay mother and adored father had not been killed while traveling!

Prinny tugged at the leash when she would have lingered, and putting the little tableau from her mind, she walked on again.

At the foot of the square, she had a little trouble with the dog. He did not seem to realize that they must wait until the roadway was clear, and would have charged across the street, ignoring both a hackney and a large closed carriage. Rosemary ordered him to sit. The huge mastiff looked up at her almost as if he were weighing his chance for a successful escape.

"Behave yourself, Prinny," she told him in what she hoped was a firm, authoritative voice. Fortunately, he did as he was bidden, and Rosemary felt greatly relieved. Lady Emily might tell her the dog had come to accept her fully, but in her mind she kept hearing Bert say, as she left the house, that he was a proper 'andful.

As they started up the other side of the square a few minutes later, the dog suddenly became impatient with the measured pace, and he tugged at his leash as if to spur her to a run. She spoke to him again, but this time he was not so quick to obey. Instead, he turned his massive head. Rosemary was sure he was sneering at her, for in a moment he quickened his pace to a lope, dragging her along behind him.

Rosemary was frightened. She did not wish to contemplate the scene there would be if she had to tell Lady Emily that her beloved Prinny had escaped her and was lost somewhere in the crowded London streets.

Wrapping the leash in another turn around her hand, she hurried after him, trying to look as if she always took the air at a dead run. She was forced to lift her skirts with her other hand, lest she rip the narrow scarlet gown. A lone footman, out on an errand, jumped aside to give them free passage, whistling at her as he did so.

And then, after a particularly vicious tug, she saw a streetlight ahead. The lamplighter had not made his rounds as yet, for it was only early dusk, but Rosemary eyed the wrought-iron standard as if it were a beacon shining the way to safety. When she drew abreast of it, she quickly loosened the leash and wrapped it around the pole, keeping a firm grip on the end. Prinny, bounding ahead, was brought up short. Rosemary leaned against the lamppost that had saved her, taking deep, gulping breaths. And then the dog, after several abortive tries to free himself from this new and stronger restriction, began to bark.

Rosemary tried to shush him, but every order of hers was met with another bout of deep, frenzied yelping. She looked around wildly. A door behind her opened, and an elderly footman stared out in amazement, and across the square two ladies stood stock-still, pointing accusing fingers at her. It was obvious that huge barking mastiffs were not much admired in Berkeley Square.

Rosemary felt very warm under her new scarlet walking

gown. She had no idea what she was to do now, or how she was to get the dog home. Every moment he was confined seemed to anger Prinny further, and she prayed he would not turn on her. She looked longingly at Lady Emily's door. It was so close, and yet so very far away.

Suddenly the dark sporting carriage she remembered rounded the corner and made its way to the Duke of Rutland's door, two houses ahead. The horses seemed to take exception to the large, noisy mastiff, and tried to rear in the traces. The driver had his hands full until the tiger came to hold their heads, calling for a footman's assistance as he did so.

Rosemary watched in horror as the stern man she was sure was the duke climbed down and strode toward her, whip in hand. Several other doors were open now, with people calling back and forth, asking each other what the matter was. One red-faced butler informed her he had a good mind to call the watch.

Prinny tried to lunge at the duke as he came within range, but the gentleman issued a sharp order, reinforcing it by raising the horsewhip he held. Prinny subsided.

In the sudden blessed silence, Rosemary could hear the excited chattering of the servants behind her as she looked up into his dark, unsmiling face with a small quiver of trepidation.

"What the deuce do you think you're doing, ma'am?" he asked in a cold, harsh voice. "You've set the entire neighborhood in an uproar with that beast of yours!"

Rosemary wished the pavement would open up and swallow her, but she made herself say, "I beg your pardon, sir. Prinny is very strong, and I have had to tie him here, for I was afraid I would not be able to hold him."

"The dog is named Prinny?" the duke asked in a bemused voice. And then he inspected Rosemary's face, and his eyes narrowed. Rosemary stood very still, her own eyes locked on his face. She wondered why her heart was beating so fast. He looked very stern, with his firm jaw outthrust and those dark brows drawn together in a ferocious frown. Rosemary saw he had cold, almost icy gray eyes, and she marveled that she still thought him the handsomest man she had ever seen.

"I asked you a question, girl," the duke reminded her.

Rosemary swallowed. "Yes, that is what Lady Emily calls him," she said.

"And who might Lady Emily be?" he asked, coming a little closer to lean against the lamppost. Rosemary could not retreat, not without letting go of the leash, so she was forced to stare up into his grim face from a much closer distance than her Aunt Mary would have considered proper.

"Lady Emily Cranston," she whispered, wishing she could look away. "She lives across the square at Number Fourteen."

"Ah, that Lady Emily," he replied, a little grimace twisting the corner of his mouth. "I do believe I have seen a burly footman exercising the animal at times. But why were you given the task? It is obvious you are not strong enough to hold him."

As he spoke, his eyes wandered from her face. He inspected her high bosom for a long moment, before he considered her neat waist and round hips. Rosemary felt her hands tightening on the leash until she was sure her knuckles were white.

She put up her chin. Although she was used to being stared at, no one had ever made such a thorough, leisurely inspection before. And in her new, flimsy, tight-fitting gown, she felt almost naked before him. She could feel a flush beginning in the pit of her stomach, and she knew it would be only a matter of seconds before her face showed her embarrassment.

"I . . . I am staying with Lady Emily, sir," she got out past dry lips. "She is a distant relation of mine, and she asked me to walk Prinny twice a day."

The duke shook his head. "May I suggest you bring the footman with you from now on, ma'am? Or perhaps two bruisers from the prize ring? The gentry that live around the square are not used to such a racket at teatime."

Rosemary lowered her eyes at last. She did not know what she was supposed to say to this pleasantry, but before she could try, he added, "May I ask how you intended to get the beast from his captivity at Number Twenty-four, back to Number Fourteen?" His voice was sarcastic again.

"I . . . I didn't know how," Rosemary told him, sure her face was as scarlet as her gown now. "I supposed I would have to wait until the footman noticed I had not returned home, and came to help me."

"How trying for you," the duke murmured. "Chained to a lamppost for what might have been an hour! It certainly is fortunate I came along when I did, isn't it?"

He reached out calmly and took the leash from her hand. "You must allow me to assist you, ma'am," he said, his polite words managing to sound both sarcastic and supremely bored.

Before Rosemary could speak, he had unwrapped the leash and tapped the butt of his whip on the pavement. "Up, sir!" he ordered Prinny. "You are about to return to your home now."

The huge dog rose, never taking his eyes from the duke's face. He shook himself before he set off, as if to show his indifference to this new, authoritative figure, and then he tried to break into a run. The duke was much too strong for him, however, and Prinny was held to a sedate walk. Flustered, Rosemary walked along beside the duke. As they passed his carriage, he called over his shoulder to his servants, "Take 'em back to the stables, Albert . . . and, Harris, inform my sister I shall return in a moment."

Both the tiger and the footman grinned as they nodded, their young faces impudent with concealed glee. Rosemary was sure they were laughing at her, and she tilted her chin again.

She had to marvel at how easily the duke held the huge dog in check. Even at the corner, Prinny was forced to wait until his handler was ready to cross. As they stepped up on the opposite curb, the duke remarked, "This is a poorly trained animal. In fact, his behavior is a disgrace. Dogs should be taught to obey."

Although Rosemary could not have agreed with him more, she felt it would be disloyal to Lady Emily to say so. Besides, the duke had sounded as if there were other species who should be taught obedience as well. Rosemary thought she had never heard such a cold, disapproving voice.

And then he startled her by asking, "Why are you here in town? I have been told Lady Emily is an eccentric, a recluse."

"She does live by herself, yes, but she was kind enough to take me in when I had to leave my aunt and uncle's in Kent."

"One does not even have to wonder why that must have been so," he remarked, his sideways glance raking her face and figure again. "How are you related to Lady Emily?" he added.

Rosemary frowned a little. "It is hard to say. My Aunt Mary and my father were cousins of hers, but what that makes me, I am not sure."

"From what I have heard of her, it is better for you that there is no closer relationship," the duke told her. He stopped as they reached Number 14, and inspected the mansion. Absurdly, Rosemary was glad the knocker had been polished and the marble scoured.

The duke climbed the steps and banged on the door with the butt of his whip. They waited together in perfect silence. Even Prinny was still subdued.

It seemed to take forever before the door opened, but the duke made no attempt to speak again. Rosemary noticed that the long fingers of his free hand beat an impatient tattoo on the railing.

At last Bert opened the door wide, bowing when he saw her escort. The duke held the leash out to him. "You will inform your mistress that this lady is not to walk the mastiff again," he ordered harshly.

Bert nodded, speechless, as Prinny bounded past him into the house.

Rosemary curtsied. "Thank you, sir," she said with as much dignity as she could muster. "I am very grateful for your assistance."

The duke stared down at her with those wintry gray eyes

until she lowered her own eyes in confusion. "It was a clever ploy, and one I have not encountered before," he said. "My congratulations. But although I will concede your cleverness, and your beauty and desirability as well, I am afraid that your performance has not been a success."

"I do not understand you, sir," Rosemary said, wondering if she had heard him correctly.

"Don't you?" he asked in his cold voice, that little grimace twisting his mouth again. Rosemary stared at him, but he only tipped his hat and turned away, and in a moment he was striding back the way they had come.

5

Berkeley Square had resumed its customary sedateness when the duke crossed it, returning to his own house. All those who had come out to investigate the uproar had disappeared into their respective dwellings, and with the doors shut behind them, it was now perfectly peaceful once again. The only person who could be seen was the lamplighter making his rounds, for the windows the duke passed were discreetly curtained, as the inhabitants settled down to enjoy their tea or make preparations for the evening's festivities.

As the duke strode along, he pondered the episode that had just occurred, and a grim little smile lifted the corners of his firm mouth. He would be the first to admit it had been a cunning trick. And so timely, too! The girl must have spent some time spying on him to know how often he returned home at just this hour to change for the evening, and perhaps dine with his family, before going on to a party or an evening of cards at his club.

And he had to admit as well that she was lovely, the loveliest girl he had seen in many a day. She was also a fine actress. He recalled her look of distress when he had come to help her, the way those dark blue eyes had pleaded with him, the color coming and going in her cheeks in her supposed embarrassed affliction. How fortunate he was no green young man, he told himself in congratulation. Only a few years ago he would have succumbed in a moment. Now, however, at twenty-nine, he was well aware of the traps that were set for him, and he despised them all.

Mark St. John William Halston, Duke of Rutland, had come into his title at his father's death two years before. But even when he had been only the Marquess of Landover, he had been assiduously pursued, not only for his future title and present fortune, but for his tall, handsome self as well. Many a young lady had said a fervent prayer of thanks that she had come out while such an attractive lord was still unattached, not that anything had ever come of their prayers. The gentleman was pleased to smile and dance and flirt, but he could not be brought to a proposal, no matter what stratagems they employed.

The duke's father had warned him over and over that he must be very circumspect when he came to choose his bride, and he had suggested his son wait until he reached the age of thirty before he even considered entering that holy estate.

Since the former duke had been so assiduous in instructing his heir in what was correct for Rutland, Mark Halston understood clearly that love played no part in marital arrangements. His own parents, although seemingly content in their marriage, had not been in love. He knew that well, for his father had told him so without a trace of embarrassment or apology. Their marriage was a business arrangement, nothing more. Everet Halston had been forty before he took a wife, and when he finally settled on the tall, handsome Lady Catherine Wheeling, she knew very well it was not because he was swept away with emotion. Oh, no. He had made it very clear what he expected of her, and although she was disappointed that it must be so, she had swallowed her regrets and agreed. The birth of a daughter first had been her only mistake, but she had remedied this fall from grace quickly, by producing the heir less than a year later. With the succession safe, the duke lost most of his interest in the marital bed, and it was a complete surprise ten years later when she produced another daughter.

At the duke's knock, the door of his mansion opened at

once, and he stepped inside to hand his hat, gloves, and whip to his bowing butler.

"Mark, I am so glad you have returned!" a gentle voice cried, and his face softened as he looked up the stairs to where a footman was carrying his younger sister down the stairs. Immediately he came to take the servant's burden into his own arms.

As she put her arms around his neck and nestled close to him, she asked, "What was all that confusion about? I could hear the uproar even in my room."

The duke carried her into the drawing room and put her down on a sofa there, covering her legs with a light throw against any chill she might feel. "Do you remember that huge ugly mastiff, Belle?" he asked as he arranged a pillow at her back. "The one that lives across the square with the elderly lady no one ever sees?"

His sister leaned forward eagerly, her thin face aglow with interest. Crippled as she was, her imagination was her mainstay, and she had spent many a long hour wondering about the lady, and making up stories about her and her self-imposed seclusion.

"It seems that Lady Emily Cranston has acquired a houseguest," the duke went on, his face cold again. Belle did not notice in her eagerness to hear the tale. "The young lady was walking the dog, and it tried to get away from her. She was forced to tie him to a lamppost, which, as you heard, he objected to most strenuously. At least that's what she claimed when I took her home," he added grimly.

"Claimed?" his sister asked, wrinkling her pale forehead. "But wasn't it the truth, Mark?"

The duke shrugged. "I very much doubt it, dear Belle. I think she was lying in wait for me," he told her.

His sister laughed at him, a silvery little peal, and he smiled ruefully as she shook her finger at him. "Oh, Mark, how very conceited you sound, to be sure," she scolded him. "It may very well have happened just as she said. I have seen the dog—why, he is frightening, he is so big and ugly!" She paused for a moment, as if to consider, and then she asked in an innocent voice, "But if you suspected a trap, why didn't you have one of the footmen help her, instead of walking her home yourself, my dear brother?"

The duke grinned down at her. It was amazing how the smile and the love in his eyes lightened his features and softened his customary stern expression. "That, my child, is none of your concern," he told her, going toward the door. "I must go and change, for all my gallantry has made me late. I see by your finery that you are all ready for your evening out, so I must make myself a worthy escort, must I not?" When she chuckled, he added, "I know Mama is engaged with friends. Will you be all right here, alone, until I return?"

When she nodded, he began to open the door, and then he turned and said, "To tell you the truth, Belle, I did it because I have never seen such a beautiful girl in my entire life."

He left the room to her delighted laughter, and he was smiling as he took the stairs two at a time. If there was anyone in all the world he loved, it was his little sister, Annabelle. For his mother and his older sister, now married and living in the country, he had affection, and he had felt only respect for his father, but the dark-haired, thin young sister with her big green eyes had his heart for more reasons than one.

She had not been born crippled, but when she was a small child she had run into the street from the park where her nurse had taken her to play, to capture a ball that had escaped her, and a carriage had run her down. There was nothing that could be done for her crippled legs, although many doctors had been consulted. The distraught nurse had never ceased to blame herself, but Mark Halston knew it was his fault, and his fault only. He had been playing with Belle, and he had thrown the ball over her head to tease her. He knew he would never forgive himself for it, for he had been fifteen then, and old enough to know better. He had vowed he would always care for her and make her life as comfortable and happy as he could.

Fortunately, now that she had attained her growth, her useless legs ceased to pain her, and he was able to take her out for drives and other amusements. Belle did not seem to regret her life. She had her books and her paints, servants to see to her every need, and a brother she adored. She remained sweet-tempered and kind in spite of her affliction, and there wasn't an occupant of Number 26 Berkeley Square who did not love her.

Across the square, Rosemary was dressing for the evening as well. She had hurried up to her room as soon as she entered the house, for a glance at the hall clock had told her Lady Agatha's carriage was due to pick her up in less than an hour. As she ran through the upstairs hall, she noticed the door to the drawing room was ajar, and the room was dimly lit, and she paused for a moment to peek inside. She was surprised to see Lady Emily bent over the telescope at the window, but she did not stop to ask what she was doing there. Prinny was safe; there would be time enough tomorrow to tell the lady of her adventure, if she had not seen it for herself.

As she went up the next flight, she told herself her hostess must have been so concerned for her beloved dog that she had watched her every move. For some reason, this thought made her shiver a little.

As she washed, and then sat at the dressing table so Maggie could do up her hair, she tried not to think of the Duke of Rutland either. He had been so cold, so enigmatic! And she still did not understand his last cryptic comments, although she had every intention of asking Lady Agatha what he possibly could have meant, the very first chance she got. He was handsome, that was true, but he was also cold and arrogant, and Rosemary was not at all sure she cared for him. But as Maggie buttoned her into the low-cut nile-green evening gown, she had to admit he was everything she had always imagined a duke would be.

Lady Agatha had invited some other people to her theater party, and when Rosemary arrived at Grillon's, she was introduced to Mr. and Mrs. Baskins, a middle-aged couple who were friends of the Williamses', and their daughter and her husband, Lord and Lady Mannering.

By the time the delicious dinner was over and the ladies had retired to prepare for the theater while the gentlemen lingered over their port, Lady Agatha was inwardly shaking her head. It was obvious to her that, newlywed or not, Lord Mannering was much taken by the beautiful young lady she was befriending, and that his wife was all too well aware of it. Lady Mannering was a very pretty blond, but she could not hold a candle to Miss Barton's dark, exotic beauty. And so all Rosemary's artless overtures of friendship were met with cold stares and thinned lips. Even Mrs. Baskins was haughty and unapproachable.

Rosemary looked confused, and more than a little hurt, and Lady Agatha put her arm around her for a moment before they went out to the carriages.

The first theater she had ever seen made Rosemary forget the snubbing she was receiving. Her eyes were wide with interest as they entered the box Lord Williams had reserved for them. As she looked down into the noisy pit, Rosemary was astounded by the crowd, and the size of the hall. She did not notice that Lord Mannering was attempting to take the seat beside her, nor the way his bride drew him away to whisper to him in an angry undertone, nor the venomous glare Mrs. Baskins gave her. Lady Agatha placed Rosemary between herself and her husband, and over the girl's head she gave him a rueful glance. He shook his head as if to say, "I told you so, m'dear," and Lady Agatha was forced to admit he had been right.

Rosemary was unaware of this silent exchange, as her attention was caught by the Duke of Rutland, who was entering a box across the way. He was carrying the slight dark young lady she had seen the day she had arrived in town, and now she watched as he put her down gently in a chair and bent over her to speak to her at length. Rosemary saw her smile and nod, and she wished again that they might meet. The girl looked so kind and pleasant, so very unlike the unfriendly Lady Mannering.

Lady Agatha saw where she was looking. "That is the

Duke of Rutland, and his sister, Lady Annabelle Halston, Rosemary," she said. "He is such a devoted brother, why, he takes her everywhere."

"Why can't she walk, ma'am?" Rosemary asked. "Is she crippled?"

"From an accident when she was very young," Lady Agatha explained. "Poor child! There is no hope of recovery for her."

"How sad," Rosemary mused aloud. "And yet she does not look sorry for herself, nor sad that it must be so. I have seen her before in the square, and I would like to meet her."

Her hostess considered this statement, and she told herself it might be a very good thing. It had certainly been made clear to her this evening that Rosemary would have a hard time making any friends of her own sex, no matter how many gentlemen clamored for the privilege of knowing her. No girl with any sense would care to be seen constantly in company that cast her quite in the shade. But perhaps Lady Annabelle would be glad to be her friend, for there could be no thought of competition there. Lady Agatha knew she would never marry, for what gentleman would want a helpless cripple, no matter how sweet and gentle she was? She recalled herself to present company as Rosemary said in a tight little voice, "They live across the square from Lady Emily's house. I . . . I would like to ask you something about the duke, if I may, ma'am."

The houselights were dimming, and before the curtain rose and the play began, Lady Agatha had only time to whisper that she would be delighted to hear it at the interval.

But at the first interval, Lady Agatha came to see there would be no chance for any *tête-à-tête* with Rosemary that evening. Several gentlemen in the audience and the surrounding boxes had discovered the vision who had accompanied Lord and Lady Williams to the theater, and even those who had only the slightest acquaintance with them had hurried to make their bows. Rosemary had no idea it was she who drew them, even whispering to Lord Williams at one point that he was a lucky man to have so many friends.

"Some of whom I barely even know," he murmured in an aside to his amused wife as their young guest turned away to answer an eager gentleman's question.

The Duke of Rutland was not among their visitors, although his attention was called to the crowded box by his sister when he came back with an ice for her.

"What a beautiful girl!" Annabelle exclaimed, her big green eyes admiring. "Do you know who she is, Mark?"

The duke turned and searched the box opposite then, and his lips tightened. "That, my dear Belle, is none other than the young siren I assisted this very evening. My, my! Can it be that she has taken to following me about, do you think?" he asked.

"Of course not, Mark!" Belle said indignantly. "She is with a party. How could she know we were going to attend the theater tonight? This feeling you have, of constant persecution, is absurd!"

The duke sat down beside her, raising his opera glasses to observe the lady in nile green more closely. "No doubt you are right, Belle," he said almost meekly. At her suspicious glance he added, "But there is something about the lady that gives me pause, and a definite feeling of unease."

Before he could elaborate, Rosemary glanced across and caught his sister's eye, and shy smiles were exchanged. The duke frowned. "Here now, Belle, don't you even think of taking her up," he warned his sister.

"Why ever not, Mark?" she asked. "She is a neighbor, and if she lives with an old recluse, she might like to have a friend. And I . . . well, I could use a friend as well."

This last statement was spoken softly, with not a trace of self-pity, but it stabbed her brother's heart. It was true that Belle had few friends, for all the young ladies she had met did not appear to have time for an invalid. And then his frown deepened. "I beg you to remember the widow Chace, Belle," he said in warning.

His sister's forehead wrinkled in a little frown. Last

year, Mrs. Chace, whose husband had fallen at Waterloo, had been most attentive, calling on her several times a week, inviting her to attend those events that she was able to participate in, and generally behaving as if it were her fervent wish to be a bosom bow to the young girl. Belle had been deeply hurt when the pretty widow had abandoned her the moment the Duke of Rutland made it plain that he had no interest in any liaison with her, neither marriage nor even an affair.

"We shall see," his sister told him now. "I will be careful, Mark, but I think sometimes you have become absurd, seeing voracious manhunters behind every pillar and post. You may be handsome and wealthy and titled, but you are not a god!"

The duke laughed. "If I were ever to think myself one and become big with pride, you would be quick to puncture my conceit, would you not, my dear?" he teased, and then he laughed again as she nodded fervently.

Two of his friends knocked on the door of the box then, and their discussion came to an end. Annabelle Halston did not forget the young lady who lived across the square. She watched her as her brother and his friends discussed a prizefight that was to be held outside London in the near future, and whenever she could for the remainder of the evening.

When her brother carried her from the theater at the conclusion of the play, she smiled again when they came face to face in the lobby. The young lady smiled back at her, but her smile faded when she saw the cold, stern frown of the tall duke, who was carrying the girl she wished to meet. Without a single word, or even a curt nod, he turned his back on her. Rosemary's face grew white.

Lady Agatha could not help but notice this cut direct, and she wondered at it. The lobby was crowded with people waiting for their carriages to be brought round, so she was unable to question Rosemary. Before she took her home, she made arrangements to call the following morning. Rosemary agreed eagerly, trying to forget the scornful duke and his unrelenting manner, even though her heart was sore at his treatment of her.

Rosemary received Lady Agatha in the newly cleaned green salon the following morning, and ordered them both refreshments. Fallow shook his head and mumbled as he left them there, but for once, Rosemary was not amused. Lady Agatha did not think she looked as if she had slept very well, for her eyes were shadowed and her shoulders had an uncharacteristic droop.

She chatted of the play they had seen and the pleasant weather, until Fallow had served them, but as soon as he shut the door of the salon behind him, still grumbling about the extra work, she began her questioning.

Rosemary was quick to tell her what had transpired at dusk the evening before. Lady Agatha could not restrain a smile at her predicament with Prinny, but that smile faded when Rosemary asked her about the duke's last remarks.

"Whatever could he have meant, ma'am?" the girl asked, her eyes confused. "Why did he congratulate me on what he called a clever ploy? And why did he say it had not succeeded?"

Lady Agatha summoned up all her diplomatic powers. "I am afraid he thought you had set a trap for him, Rosemary," she explained.

"A trap, ma'am?" Rosemary asked in astonishment. "I don't understand."

"He appears to think that you lay in wait for him using the dog to get his attention," Lady Agatha said. "That there was no problem, and it was all nothing but a ruse to get to meet him."

Rosemary's face was indignant. "But it wasn't!" she exclaimed. "How dare he think that of me? Why . . . why, my Aunt Mary would be horrified at the very idea, and you must know ma'am, I would never, ever, do such a thing!"

Lady Agatha patted her hand. "I do know, Rosemary, but the duke does not. You see, he has been courted and pursued for so many years, it has made him leery of our sex."

"But that is horrid," Rosemary broke in. "And to think he even considers me in that light—good heavens, ma'am, what am I to do?"

She sounded distraught, but there was nothing Lady Agatha could say to reassure her. Rosemary Barton still had no idea that it was not only her unusual beauty but also her unconscious seductive grace that made men want her. She was young and chaste, and as proper a young lady as could be found anywhere, but what man would believe it of her from her exotic appearance? Short of dressing in a bag with a flour sack over her head, Lady Agatha was aware she would always have this problem. It was one many women would have sold their souls to the devil to acquire, but Lady Agatha could see it would not always be comfortable, or even welcome, to its owner. She sipped her tea for a moment while Rosemary looked at her in concern, and then she set her cup down and gave a decisive nod.

"There is something I think you should know, child," she began. "If you do not learn of it, you may find yourself in all kinds of trouble. And I shall be leaving England soon, and there will be no one to advise you. Please listen to me carefully."

Rosemary nodded and sat very still, her eyes growing more and more amazed as Lady Agatha told her of her seductive beauty in a cold, matter-of-fact voice. "It was why your Aunt Mary wanted you to leave Kent, my dear," she concluded. "Your cousin, your uncle, Eleanor's beau, the curate—all of them had been captured in your spell. Why, even Lord Mannering last evening was eager for you, and that is why his wife and mother-in-law were so cold. And I asked them especially, thinking a bridegroom of only three months was a safe addition to the party."

As Rosemary opened her mouth to protest, Lady Agatha raised her hand. "I know it is not done consciously, child, and you cannot help it, but it is there, and it draws every man like a lodestone attracts metal. I tell you this so you will be on your guard. Make sure that the gentleman in question is sincerely in love with you before you finally give your heart. There are ways to tell, Rosemary. Forgive me, my child, if I speak frankly. You must be especially wary, for although you are of good birth on your father's side, there are many Englishmen who would look at you askance because of your Italian mother. She was not noble, I believe?''

As Rosemary shook her head, Lady Agatha went on, ''You have wealth, and that beauty we have been discussing, but you have no one to protect you but yourself. Your Uncle Joshua never comes to London, and Lady Emily is a recluse. Test any man carefully when he professes his love. Try, if you can, to trick him into indiscretion. If he does not take the bait, you can be sure he loves you indeed. I am sure this is hard for you to understand, for you are a good, innocent girl, but I pray you will remember my words. I would not have you ruined by some man's eager seduction.''

Rosemary looked down at her lithe, ripe figure in the gay blue morning gown, and her vivid face paled.

''Is there nothing else I can do, ma'am?'' she asked in some despair. ''Is there no way I can convince people I am not a temptress?''

Lady Agatha shook her head.

''Perhaps it was wrong of me to buy these clothes and change my hairstyle,'' Rosemary said eagerly. ''Perhaps if I were to go back to the gowns Aunt Mary considered proper, and became very quiet and prim . . .''

''Do you want to, my dear?'' Lady Agatha asked softly.

There was silence for a moment, and then Rosemary put up her chin. ''No, I do not! I cannot help the way I look, but I do not see why I should have to make myself into a drab because of it, do you, dear ma'am?''

As Lady Agatha gurgled with laughter and shook her head, Rosemary smiled in relief. ''Then I shall go on as I have begun, but I thank you for your warnings, m'lady. You may be sure I shall be very, very careful from now on.''

Later that morning, after Lady Agatha had left her, two

large bouquets were delivered from gentlemen she had met briefly at the play.

Rosemary's full lips tightened as she read the effusive cards that accompanied these tributes. Here, if she was not mistaken, were two of the men Lady Agatha had warned her about. She was glad she had done so, for in her innocence she might well have believed their ardent praise was made in earnest sincerity.

6

Rosemary spent the remainder of the day first writing to her cousin Eleanor and then working with the maids. It was a lovely spring day, and she had intended to walk in the park in the center of the square for some exercise and fresh air. Now, of course, after hearing what the Duke of Rutland thought of her, she had no desire to wander those graveled paths, admiring the sunlight on the early tulips and daffodils, and amusing herself watching the children at play under the vigilant eyes of their nannies. If he should see her, he would be sure to think she was parading there to catch his eye.

The brass candlestick she was polishing received an extra hard buffing that made it shine as it never had, she was so indignant. To think that he dared consider her in that light, she thought darkly as she took up the other candlestick of the pair. It was more than distressing, it was insulting. Well, she told herself as she rubbed in the polish, he shall see. The next time we meet, I shall treat him to my haughtiest, coldest glare, and I shall turn my back on *him*. That will teach him that all women are not chasing him or trying to seduce him, the conceited man!

She was still at work when Ronald Edson came to call, and when he asked her to join him for a walk in Hyde Park that same afternoon, she was very cool in her refusal.

She seemed to be hearing Lady Agatha's warning as she listened to his teasing comments and imploring words. Now that she knew the reason for his intent stare as his bright blue eyes wandered over her figure in the old gown she had put on to work in, she could not help but feel mortified. Other girls might have preened themselves on their power, but Rosemary Barton could only deplore it. Mr. Edson was forced to take his leave with no appointment made for any future meeting, and his face was grim as he took his hat from a cackling Fallow and left the house without even attempting to see his aunt.

At dusk Rosemary asked Bert to take Prinny for his evening walk, and she could not resist peeking between the curtains of her room to see if the duke would make an appearance. When he did not do so, she told herself she was only disappointed because she had wanted him to see she was not pursuing him as he thought.

When she came down to dinner, she was surprised to find Lady Emily waiting for her at the table, minus her ever-present book.

She curtsied in silence before she took her seat, ignoring Prinny, who stared at her with his great dark eyes, his head on his paws as he lay at his mistress's feet.

"I understand you had some trouble with the dog last evening, girl?" Lady Emily remarked, ringing the bell for Fallow and the footman to commence serving.

"Yes, I am sorry to say that I did, m'lady," Rosemary told her as she unfolded her napkin. "He is much too huge for me to control, especially since he does not see any reason why he should have to obey my commands. I was lucky to get him home without incident."

And then, as Lady Emily nodded to the footman, who was presenting a tureen of soup, Fallow hovering at his elbow, Rosemary felt a little spurt of anger. "But surely you know of my predicament, ma'am," she said. "Weren't you watching us the whole time through your telescope?"

Lady Emily's head turned toward her quickly, and her eyes narrowed. For some reason, Rosemary felt a quiver run up her spine, and she lowered her own eyes to the table.

"So I was," the lady said at last. Her voice was harsh

and cold. "And I saw that you required assistance with Prinny. Who was the gentleman?"

Rosemary was positive she already knew, but she did not dare to accuse her of it. "I was forced to accept the Duke of Rutland's offer to see us safely home, ma'am," she said instead.

"What is he like?" Lady Emily asked, ignoring her soup to lean forward so she could peer into Rosemary's face.

"He is very cold and proud, ma'am," Rosemary told her. "And he was insulting as well."

She stirred her soup, determined to say no more, until Lady Emily demanded, "Whatever do you mean, insulting? Explain yourself, girl."

Rosemary waited until the footman and his shadow had left the room. "He seemed to think I was playing a trick on him, ma'am," she said. "Why, he even accused me of deliberately pretending to have trouble with Prinny so I could make his acquaintance. He is a conceited, arrogant person, and I do not care for him at all."

Lady Emily gave a rusty chuckle deep in her throat. "Most of 'em are, girl. His father was arrogant, too, and the apple never falls far from the tree."

As Rosemary stared at her where she sat fondling the cloisonné locket she habitually wore, Lady Emily suddenly snorted and picked up her spoon. "Eat your soup, girl, lest it grow cold," she ordered. "I am tired of talking."

Rosemary was delighted to apply herself to her dinner. She had not liked the look Lady Emily had given her when she dared to mention she knew she had been spied on. As she ate her veal and new spring peas, she wondered when her hostess had known the duke's father. Was it during the time Mrs. Fallow had told her about, when the house was filled with people and parties and gaiety? She did not dare to inquire, however, and the usual silence she was becoming accustomed to remained unbroken.

The two sat in silence in the library later as well, although every so often Rosemary would look up from her book to see her hostess staring into the glowing coal fire, her own book forgotten.

Early the following afternoon, Lady Agatha called for her in her carriage, to take her on a tour of London. They inspected the British Museum and the Royal Academy, and drove by the Tower and several government buildings. Later they joined Lord Williams for a stroll through Hyde Park. Rosemary enjoyed every minute. The park was lovely in the late afternoon, and crowded with the *beau monde*, either walking like themselves, or driving in dashing carriages. She thought the Serpentine a delightful stretch of calm water, surprising in its size here in the heart of the metropolis. Lady Agatha assured her it was perfectly proper for her to walk here unaccompanied, as long as she had her maid or the footman with her. Lord Williams was quick to remark he thought such a course would be most unwise, even at an unfashionably early hour. Now that she knew what his remark meant, Rosemary blushed a little.

A short time later, she saw the Duke of Rutland go by in an open landau. He was seated facing back, and across from him were his sister and an older lady she assumed was their mother. They were all in animated conversation. Rosemary was glad the park was so crowded that the duke could not possibly have noticed her.

As they were driving home, Lady Agatha told her about an invitation she had obtained for Rosemary so she might attend Countess Norwell's ball in a few days' time. "Peter Truesdale and his wife are in the forefront of society, Rosemary," she said. "I am sure you will enjoy it."

As Rosemary thanked her, her blue eyes sparkling with anticipation, Lady Agatha continued, "It will be an excellent opportunity for you to meet others your own age, and perhaps expand your acquaintance. I do so hope you will have many friends by the time I sail, for I would hate to think of you here alone and lonesome."

Rosemary could not resist giving the lady a kiss on the cheek and a hug before she stepped down from the carriage. "You are too kind to me, ma'am, too good," she said.

Lady Agatha shook her head. "Run along, Rosemary," she said. "You refine on it too much, for I am delighted to help such a dear girl as you."

As Rosemary waved good-bye, she thought what a good friend Lady Agatha had turned out to be, even to making sure she went to her first ball. She ran up the stairs to her room to spend an exciting hour with Maggie discussing which ball gown she would wear to this most important event. The maid thought the royal-blue gown became her to perfection, but Rosemary preferred the softer gold silk for her first appearance. She had her mother's pearl set to wear with it, and although the dress was cut just as low in the bosom, and narrow in the skirt, somehow she felt it the less dramatic of the two. And with Lady Agatha's explanation ever present in her mind, she did not care to call attention to herself any more than she could help.

She wondered if Lady Emily would ask her about her afternoon when she joined her for dinner, but her hostess was already reading as she entered the dining room, and the evening was marked only by the complete absence of a single word of conversation.

Rosemary spent a great deal of time on her toilette for the ball. She had bathed and had Maggie wash her hair that afternoon before the hairdresser came to style it. He brushed it back from that distinctive widow's peak and fastened it high on her head with pearl combs before he arranged it in a rich cascade of ebony curls. Rosemary was delighted with the result. It was ladylike, and she thought it made her look older and wiser as she tilted her head this way and that before her glass.

When Maggie helped her into the gold gown, she could only deplore the way it clung to her figure, until she remembered that she had no intention of playing the dowd, not even to keep men eager for dalliance at bay.

As she went down the stairs to dinner, she carried her long white gloves, her fan, and a new gold embroidered sarcenet stole. Lady Agatha was coming to take her up in her carriage just before ten, and she did not want to keep her waiting.

Rosemary thought Lady Emily seemed very interested in her turnout, for she caught her staring many times throughout dinner. And then she wondered what the lady found amusing, for every so often she would surprise a fleeting smile on those wintry lips, and a strange, delighted gleam in her eyes. It made her very uncomfortable, although she was somewhat reassured when, at the conclusion of dinner, Lady Emily rose and said, "You look stunning, girl. Yes, you will do, and do very well."

Rosemary thanked her with a smile.

"Turn around," Lady Emily ordered. Slowly Rosemary complied. Her hostess was smiling openly now, and nodding. "Remember to stand tall, with your shoulders back," she told her. "It gives you dignity and presence."

When she was introduced to her in the receiving line at the ball, Rosemary thought Countess Norwell a stunning woman, so tall and vibrant. It was obvious that her husband, the earl, thought so too. His harsh-featured, unsmiling face softened whenever he looked at his wife. As Lady Agatha presented her, the countess held out her hand and gave her a warm smile. "I am delighted to meet you, Miss Barton," she said. "I do hope you will enjoy yourself this evening."

"Of course she will," the earl murmured, nodding to George Williams as he did so, as if to ask for that gentleman's agreement. Lord Williams chuckled.

As Lady Agatha led the way to the ballroom, Rosemary tried very hard not to stare. She had never imagined such splendor. The crystal chandeliers all sparkling with more tapers than she had ever seen, the flowers and other decorations, and the liveried footmen standing against the wall were an impressive sight. It was so rich and grand! Why, it even smelled rich, Rosemary thought as she breathed the warm air scented with dozens of perfumes. But it was the gloriously attired throng of guests that made it hard for her to appear natural and easy. And the jewels the ladies wore, glittering in the candlelight, made Rosemary feel as if she were watching a play. It was almost as if the *beau monde* were *en fête* this soft spring evening for her enjoyment, and hers alone.

Rosemary stayed very close to Lady Agatha, who introduced her to several dowagers and a few middle-aged ladies with their daughters beside them. No one asked them to linger or take seats nearby, and Lady Agatha moved on.

It was not long before the gentlemen present noticed the beautiful newcomer in their midst, and as before, they hurried to her side. Her dance card was filled in a very short time, and Rosemary relaxed now she was an accepted member of the throng.

Sometime later, she saw the Duke of Rutland joining her set. At the time, she was engaged to dance with Lord Greene, a young peer who was distinguished only by his height and beak of a nose. He stared at her unceasingly, as if he could not believe his good fortune in attaching this heavenly creature, who, by some intervention of a benevolent spirit, had decided to decorate the Truesdale ball this evening.

The music began, and Rosemary commanded her rapidly beating heart to behave itself. The duke was stunning in his dark evening dress; Rosemary was sure he was the handsomest man in the room. He was partnering an attractive brunette who was dressed in a demure white gown. She looked cool and refined, and Rosemary longed to emulate her. When she was forced to take the duke's hand in the dance, she refused to look anywhere but at his right lapel. His hand tightened for a moment, but she was determined not to give him the satisfaction of even a small social smile.

"How graceful you are, ma'am," he murmured. "You dance like a flower swaying gently in the soft spring breeze."

Rosemary tried not to stiffen, sure he was comparing her with his own partner, to her detriment. She had noticed that only the young lady's feet moved; the rest of her body remained still. She was hurt by this taunt, and she was careful to hide her dark blue eyes under her long curly lashes until the movement of the dance allowed her to turn away.

When the dance was over, it made her feel better to know she had been successful in letting him know how little she cared for him, and she forced herself to laugh and chat with her new admirers with a degree of animation she knew her Aunt Mary would deplore.

Sometime later, when she heard music in three-quarter time begin, she explained to her current partner, Sir Reginald Wallingford, that she was not approved for the waltz, and so must sit out the dance. Sir Reginald did not seem at all disappointed as he led her to a small sofa set somewhat apart from the crowd.

"But I should be delighted to talk to you instead, Miss Barton," he enthused. Rosemary tried to ignore the way his Adam's apple moved up and down in his throat as he swallowed in his excitement. "This way we can get to know each other," he went on. "I have often found it difficult to converse when I am minding my steps. Don't you agree?"

Rosemary smiled and nodded, and he excused himself to fetch some champagne punch.

"Paltry, my dear," said the sarcastic voice she remembered only too well, from behind her. She turned to see the Duke of Rutland leaning against the wall nearby, a most sardonic smile on his stern lips. "You can do much better than Reggie Wallingford, you know," he went on, coming closer as if to share a confidence. "My, yes. He is only a baronet, and you must not underestimate your . . . mm, considerable charms."

Rosemary forced herself to stare at him as his gray eyes inspected all the glowing skin her gold evening gown exposed. The warm color in her cheeks deepened but she waited until he had completed his leisurely inspection before she put up her chin and turned her shoulder on him, opening her fan to wave it before her heated face in seeming nonchalance.

The duke sat down beside her, taking the fan from her fingers to ply it for her himself. "I am sure you will find it an easy matter to ensnare an earl, perhaps even a marquess," he told her in his cool drawl. "You must not be discouraged because the highest rank did not fall into your net."

Rosemary lost her temper, and she whirled in her seat, her blue eyes gleaming with anger. "You are mistaken, your Grace, as mistaken as you were in Berkeley Square. I set no snares, nor was my misfortune with Lady Emily's dog preconceived. I had no idea you would arrive home when you did, and now, in spite of your very welcome assistance at the time, I regret that you offered it," she said. And then she added, as coldly as she dared, "I do not intend to entrap anyone, and if what I have learned about dukes is consistent to the breed, I do assure you I would rather marry the lamplighter!"

"And you would have me believe that that is whom you came out to meet the other evening?" he asked, sounding amused. "Good gracious, how very democratic of you, ma'am!"

Before she could think of a reply, he went on, "But of course you would deny that you are husband-hunting. Everyone does. I realize, however, that like so many others, you are on the lookout for title, wealth, and position. Why does my knowledge of your intent anger you? It is only what every other unmarried female in the room is after too."

Sir Reginald returned then, a footman in tow bearing champagne. He looked from Rosemary to the duke with a little frown, and he was glad when the duke rose and excused himself. He knew he could not compare to Mark Halston; it was too bad if Miss Barton had captured his discerning eye! He began to talk to her with great vivacity, glad that the duke was strolling away, and he felt considerable relief when he saw that the lady's eyes did not follow that tall, arresting form with its dark head held so arrogantly high.

When the duke left the ball a while later, Rosemary told herself she was delighted to be spared any more of his insulting comments. She had noticed that he had danced again with the lady in white, and spent some time with her between sets. Rosemary wondered who she was. In spite of her air of breeding, and an assurance that told you she was not a miss in her first Season, she did not look at all the type most men would admire. She was too slim, too elegantly handsome, instead of being enticing and beautiful. But perhaps, Rosemary told herself sadly, that is what the duke prefers. How I wish I could appear so cool and contained, such a perfect lady.

Lord and Lady Williams did not set Rosemary down in Berkeley Square until after three in the morning. As she went up to bed, she imagined she could see the beginning of a faint gray dawn, and she wondered what her Aunt Mary would say about her keeping such decadent hours.

Rosemary did not wake up and ring for her maid until past eleven the following morning, and she felt a wave of guilt when she saw the time. At home in Kent, she had always risen at seven, along with the rest of the household, and that she had wasted four perfectly good hours of the day seemed wicked to her.

She fully intended to spend the rest of the day helping Fallow and Bert polish the silver in atonement, but when Maggie brought in her chocolate, there were a number of cards and invitations on the tray. Rosemary's eyes widened in delight as she propped up her pillows before she began to read them.

The maid bustled around straightening the room, but her eyes went often to Miss Rosemary's face. She thought it was just like a fairy story as she took the girl's evening sandals and the gold gown to the dressing room to put away. But she's so lovely, she told herself, no wonder everyone admires her and wants her company.

When Rosemary finished her last note and sank back on her pillows, a little smile playing over her full lips, Maggie said, "There's three bouquets and a nosegay belowstairs as well, miss. You must have had a good time!"

Rosemary could see how anxious the girl was to hear all about the ball, and as she was dressed for luncheon with Lady Agatha, she told her everything she could remember.

At last, wearing a pale aqua muslin walking gown, with matching sandals and a saucy little hat that tilted over one eye, she picked up her reticule and gloves and ran down the stairs.

Until the carriage came, she amused herself by admiring her posies. The nosegay was from Lord Greene, and two of the bouquets had come from Sir Reginald and a Mr. James Kay, who had been most attentive last evening. And she had just received an invitation from this last gentleman's mother, asking her to honor them at a small dance she was giving the following week. Several others of her notes this morning had been invitations too, and Rosemary could hardly wait to tell Lady Agatha of her success. The Williamses were to sail in two weeks, but now that Rosemary had been accepted by the *ton*, and was to be included in many of its festivities, she did not feel so sad to be losing her first London friend.

She picked up the note that had accompanied her last bouquet, starting as she opened it. There was no signature. Instead, there was only a drawing of a streetlamp and the words "I pray you will curb any base desires, ma'am. It would be less than just to bestow your charms on anyone below a viscount."

Rosemary crushed the card between her fingers, tempted to crush the deep red roses that had accompanied this missive, as well. But when she bent to inhale their sweetness, she told herself she was being foolish beyond belief. She did not know why the duke had sent her flowers, feeling as he did about her, but she would not scorn them as she scorned him. No, instead, she would arrange them in a low bowl as soon as she returned home, and place them in the drawing room with the others.

The time spent with Lady Agatha passed quickly, for she had so much to tell her. Her friend was relieved to hear of all her invitations, although she was quick to note they came only from mothers with sons. She wished she could do more for Rosemary, but her acquaintance in the *ton* was not extensive enough. What with her years spent abroad on the various diplomatic missions her husband had undertaken, she had few close women friends herself. The people she knew best were those involved in world affairs, and while she had always considered their company more stimulating than that of any society lady, she could see they would be of little use to her young protégée.

She was still thinking of Rosemary's dearth of feminine companionship when her carriage turned into Berkeley Square later that afternoon. Glancing idly at the scene before her, she saw Lady Annabelle Halston being pushed in a wheeled chair through the park by a tall, heavily built maid. Quickly she signaled her coachman to pull up.

Rosemary looked at her, somewhat surprised, for Number 14 lay directly opposite, on the other side of the square.

Lady Agatha indicated the slim young girl as she said, "Here is a perfect opportunity for you, my dear. I shall drop you here. It is such a lovely day, I am sure you will wish to stroll for a while before going in. And you may, just may, make Lady Annabelle's acquaintance as you do so."

Rosemary would have liked to protest, but Lady Agatha made shooing motions as she said, "Run along, now, Rosemary. I shall be in touch with you in a day or so."

Obediently Rosemary climbed down after the groom had let down the steps. She looked around nervously, but the tall figure of the Duke of Rutland was nowhere in sight. She had not told Lady Agatha about his comments the evening before, nor the insulting message he had sent this morning, so the lady had no idea why she wished to avoid any semblance of putting herself forward, making friends with his sister to catch his eye. And although she had thought at one time that she would like to be friends, now she saw that that would not be possible. She could just imagine the duke's acid comments if she attempted it.

Rosemary waved as the carriage drew away, and then she entered the park. Lady Annabelle was a little way ahead of her, her chair motionless now as she watched two little boys rolling hoops along the gravel path.

Rosemary started forward, determined to pass the lady as quickly as she could. But as she drew abreast of the girl's chair, the smallest boy's hoop escaped him and rolled toward her. She put out a hand to hold it for him until he could run up on his chubby little legs.

"Thank the kind lady, Master Tom," his nanny admonished him.

The boy's lower lip pouted, but he dropped her a jerky bow, his blond hair falling over one eye as he did so. Rosemary smiled at him, and he grinned before he turned and ran back to his play.

Behind her a soft voice said, "I beg your pardon, ma'am, but don't you live here in the square?"

Rosemary turned to see Lady Annabelle Halston leaning forward in her chair, a tentative smile on her face, and her big green eyes a little wary. For a moment Rosemary wondered why. It was almost as if the lady thought that any overture of friendship by her might be met with a barely concealed shudder or a direct snub. Rosemary's heart went out to her. She knew there were people who could not bear to look at cripples, and who turned their heads away from anyone who had an infirmity. From her expression it was clear Lady Annabelle had been treated this way before.

She smiled back at the girl, therefore, the duke's disapproval gone from her mind, and she was glad she had done so when she saw how relieved and happy Lady Annabelle looked now. "Yes, I am Rosemary Barton," she said, coming closer. "I live at Number Fourteen with the Lady Emily Cranston, a distant relative of mine, m'lady."

"You know who I am?" Lady Annabelle asked.

"I have seen you before, driving in the carriage with your mama and . . . and your brother," Rosemary admitted.

Lady Annabelle indicated a bench nearby. "Won't you sit down and talk to me?" she asked a little diffidently. "It is such a nice day, and I would enjoy making your better acquaintance."

Again Rosemary was sure there was a hesitant note in her voice, and, forgetting what the arrogant duke would think if he saw them together, she said warmly, "I should like that. I know only a few people in London, and not a single girl. It has been lonely since I left Kent, for my cousin Eleanor and I were used to do everything together.''

Lady Annabelle's thin face brightened again. "Just push me nearer the bench, Patsy," she told her maid. "And then you may go home. Send one of the footmen for me in half an hour or so, if you would be so good."

"I'll come back for you myself, milady," the tall, sturdy maid assured her as she easily positioned the chair and bent to arrange the light throw that covered the lady's legs. Her voice was full of affection for her mistress. Rosemary noticed her muscled arms and glowing complexion, sure she had been chosen for her ability to lift Lady Annabelle unaided.

As she sat down on the bench, she said, "I would be glad to push the chair back to your house, m'lady, when you are ready to go in."

She did not notice the shrewd, suspicious look the maid threw in her direction, for Lady Annabelle was clapping her hands in delight.

"What a good idea!" she enthused. "Yes, do run along, Patsy. I shall be quite all right here, since Miss Barton is so kind."

7

It was nearly an hour later before Rosemary pushed the chair back to the Rutland town house, and she knew that if a little breeze had not come up, Lady Annabelle would have been delighted to remain longer. She herself had enjoyed their conversation immensely. They had talked easily of everything under the sun: London, Rosemary's former home and all her relatives, Lady Agatha's kindness, and the play they had both seen. It was as if, perfectly attuned to each other, they had become instant friends.

As Rosemary bent to release the brake of the chair, Lady Annabelle said, almost as if she had read her mind, "How delightful this has been! I have not enjoyed myself so much this age!"

"Nor I, m'lady," Rosemary agreed, giving her another warm smile. Encouraged, the lady said, "I feel I know you so well already. I would be pleased if you would call me Annabelle, or better yet, Belle. That is what my dear brother, Mark, calls me."

"I should be happy to, Belle, and you must call me by my first name, too," Rosemary said, going behind to push the chair. She had forgotten the duke in their warm conversation, but now she realized by the long shadows falling across the square that it was almost the time he generally came home. She looked around a little nervously, pushing the chair faster as she prayed she would not be forced to meet him.

At Lady Annabelle's direction, she went up the steps to summon a footman to carry her new friend inside.

"I do hope we will meet soon again," the lady said wistfully as they waited for this servant to appear. "Perhaps you would care to join me for a drive in Hyde Park tomorrow, Rosemary? If it is fine, that is?" she asked.

As Rosemary hesitated, she added, "I shall understand if you are engaged. You must have many invitations, you are so lovely. I . . . I did not mean to presume."

Rosemary took her hand and pressed it. "I would love to drive with you, Belle," she assured her. "I was just regretting how quickly this hour has passed, myself."

A time was set, and then Lady Annabelle waved goodbye as the footman carried her into the house, another one busy bringing in the chair. As soon as the door closed behind them all, Rosemary turned and almost ran back across the street and through the deserted park. Even though she had enjoyed their meeting, she knew all too well how the duke would react when he learned of it. The sneer on his dark face, which she could picture, had almost made her claim another appointment for the morrow, but Lady Annabelle's pleading green eyes had been her undoing.

"Well, I don't care what he thinks," she told herself stoutly as she waited for a hackney cab to pass so she could cross the street. "I know I have no ulterior motives, and Belle is such a dear! Even if he does make some disparaging remark, I shall ignore him. It is so good to have someone my own age to talk to again."

Just before she stepped onto the cobbles, something made her raise her eyes to the drawing-room window where the telescope was located. She saw no flash of light, no movement of any kind, but still she shivered. She was positive that Lady Emily had been there throughout her visit in the park; that she had watched her push Lady Annabelle home, and seen their smiling camaraderie. As she lowered her eyes and crossed the street, Rosemary knew the lady would be pleased by her new friendship, and then she wondered why she was so sure that this was so. She told herself it was because Lady Emily seemed to have an interest in the Halston family that did not extend to any of the others who lived around the square. It was a mystery, and one she knew she might never solve, for even as the days passed, Lady Emily made no move to relax her distant formality, nor did she talk to her at any greater length than she had employed from the beginning.

Rosemary was not engaged that evening, and it was with some regret that she took her usual seat in the library with her hostess after their mute dinner. She had searched the shelves carefully, and found a romantic novel that had been published some years ago. Soon she was immersed in the adventure, and able to forget her silent, enigmatic relative.

She spent the next morning directing the maids in the cleaning of the library. Maggie was cheerful and willing, and Mabel too meek to question her orders, but she could tell Willa resented the extra work she was forced to do, now Miss Barton had taken charge of the household. She sniffed often, and worked as slowly as she dared, obviously aggrieved. No new maids had been employed, for Lady Emily would not hear of it. At last Rosemary was forced to speak to Willa sharply, and the maid's eyes gleamed for a moment with hatred before she lowered them in token submission.

The smart open landau that Rosemary remembered came around the square that afternoon at the appointed time. As she ran down the steps, Rosemary could see that Lady Annabelle was alone, except for her maid. She told herself that the little flutter she felt in the vicinity of her heart was only relief that the duke was not accompanying his sister.

By the time the carriage had passed through the Stanhope Gate, Rosemary was able to put Mark Halston from her mind, for she was deep in another animated conversation with Lady Annabelle. She had happened to mention the book she was reading, and as Belle had also read that particular novel, she was able to discuss it at great length. They discovered that although they both considered the heroine brave and lovely, they were identically impatient with the handsome hero, who, as Lady Annabelle tartly pointed out, seemed a perfect idiot not to be able to understand his lady's motives from the beginning.

"In fact, my dear Rosemary," she said, shaking her head, "I think him perfectly muttonheaded, don't you? What can the fair Miriam see in such a dolt?"

Rosemary laughed, and in a moment Lady Annabelle joined her. Even Patsy, her maid, smiled a little to see her mistress happily amused.

They were so busy talking that Lady Annabelle missed the signal she received from another carriage that was pulled off to the side of the roadway. As her maid called her attention to it, Rosemary was surprised to hear her little sigh, even as she gave her coachman an order to stop.

Seated in the carriage, also with her maid beside her, was the lady Rosemary had seen dancing with the duke at the Truesdale ball.

"My dear Annabelle, how delightful to see you taking the air," she remarked. Her voice was well-modulated and quiet, only her brows lifting a little as she gave Rosemary a cursory glance. "I would have asked you to drive with me this afternoon, if I had felt you were up to it. It is a trifle cool; I wonder if your decision was wise?" she continued, ignoring the dark, vibrant beauty she did not know, as if she were not even there.

Lady Annabelle refused to comment on her concern, as she said, "May I present a new friend of mine, Margaret? This is Miss Rosemary Barton."

The lady inclined her head an inch, but her rather thin lips, set in a narrow, well-bred face, were stern and unsmiling.

"Rosemary, this is Lady Margaret Malden," Annabelle continued, her own voice completely devoid of any animation.

"M'lady," Rosemary said, and then she smiled.

Lady Margaret did not seem to have any interest in conversing with Lady Annabelle's new acquaintance. Turning a little, as if to shut Rosemary out, she said, "I understand the duke has gone out of town, my dear? I do so hope you will send me a message when next you wish to drive out, so we may go together. I am sure the duke would prefer to have you in my company, for he knows my affection for you, and my concern. Indeed, he asked me specifically to look in on you often, and so I shall.''

Rosemary thought Lady Annabelle seemed to be trying to look pleased. ''You are very kind, Margaret, but there is no need for such devotion. My dear mama looks after me very well, and there is no one more concerned for me than my faithful Patsy.''

Perhaps feeling this had been a less-than-gracious reply, she added with her wistful little smile, ''I would be glad to see you anytime you care to call in Berkeley Square, however. I do not expect Mark will be away long. He has only gone with a few friends to Grantham to see a prizefight.''

Lady Margaret shuddered delicately. ''How disgusting men are, are they not, with their prizefights and cockfights and all manner of low amusements? I have never been able to understand why such things fascinate them so. I shall call on you tomorrow morning, my dear, to see how you go on. I pray you will have a good night. Miss Barton,'' she added as an afterthought before she gave her coachman the office to start.

As her carriage drove away, Lady Annabelle sighed again.''She will be on the doorstep at ten, isn't that right, Patsy?'' she asked. The maid nodded, looking grim, and her mistress made herself laugh. ''I should be grateful to Margaret, I suppose, but sometimes it is hard to bear her never-ending solicitude. Somehow she makes me feel even more weak and crippled than I am! But that is unkind of me, I know. Let us forget her, Rosemary. I do hope you will call on me, too, tomorrow, for I have another novel I think you would like to read. Come at teatime. I will arrange for us to be quite alone.''

Rosemary promised to do so, feeling much easier in her mind now that she knew the duke had gone out of town. She was aware that he would find out about her friendship with his sister as soon as he returned, but until that time she would not have to worry about any meetings with him.

By the time the carriage set her down again in Berkeley Square, Rosemary knew a great deal more about the Lady Annabelle. She had spoken openly of her crippled legs, and the accident that had caused them, and she had treated the matter with such little concern that Rosemary was not at all uncomfortable. She then discovered that Belle enjoyed painting and music, as well as novels; that she adored her brother, was amused by her mother, and considered London the perfect location for anyone in her condition, since there was so much to see and do here.

As she climbed the steps of Number 14, Rosemary had to admire Lady Annabelle's spirit. In spite of her affliction, she was so involved, so accepting, and so kind. Rosemary was grateful they had met.

She refused to raise her head to the drawing-room windows as she waited for Bert or Fallow to open the door. Lady Emily had made no mention of seeing her with Lady Annabelle in the park the day before, but Rosemary was sure she knew of it. She had felt the lady's eyes on her many times the long, quiet evening before, and had once surprised such a smug, gratified expression on her face, it made her wonder what her hostess was thinking.

That evening, she was not at all astonished, therefore, when Lady Emily questioned her about Annabelle Halston. She wanted to know a great many things; Rosemary's estimate of her character, how much she liked her guest, and when they were to meet again. On hearing Rosemary had been asked to tea on the morrow, she gave her a wintry little smile. "Good!" she said. "I am delighted to see you are not put off by her infirmity, girl. She sounds a nice young lady; I encourage you to be her faithful friend."

Rosemary nodded, but she wondered why she felt that little tremor of unease. It seemed so out of character for Lady Emily to be at all concerned about a stranger, to say nothing of caring whether her relative made any friends or not.

Lady Emily nodded brusquely before she disappeared in her book again. Rosemary continued to ponder her strange behavior as she ate her dinner. She tried to ignore Prinny as she did so. This evening he had settled down heavily on her foot, but somehow she did not care to disturb him by moving it.

She told Lady Agatha all about the lady Annabelle Halston the next morning when she came to call. Her delighted reaction was reassuring. Unlike Lady Emily, she seemed happy just to know that Rosemary had made a friend.

Rosemary tried not to look around too obviously that afternoon when she entered the duke's house across the square. It was much grander and more luxurious than Lady Emily's, and well staffed with efficient servants. As she followed the butler up the wide staircase to Lady Annabelle's rooms, she could not help but admire the gleaming cleanliness, as well as the lightness in the atmosphere that was so different from her own dark, airless abode.

Lady Annabelle's rooms were large, and graciously, although scantily, furnished. There were no rugs on the gleaming parquet floors. This surprised Rosemary until she saw that it had been done deliberately, for here Lady Annabelle could wheel her chair easily from table to piano to desk, without having to call for assistance. Once again the two girls were soon in animated conversation. Rosemary wondered if Lady Margaret had come to call as promised, but Belle did not speak of her.

They were lingering over a second cup of tea when the door was thrown open and a tall, stout middle-aged lady surged into the room.

"*Dearest* Belle," she said breathlessly, and then, catching sight of Rosemary, she skidded to a halt. "Oh, I did not *realize* you had company, my dear. That's nice. You did not *miss* me, but still I must *apologize* for my delay. The card party went *on* and *on*. I would probably be there *still*, except Mrs. Fells remarked the time, and then, *well*, I just *flew* away! But since you have had someone to sit with you, I might have *stayed* after all. It is too *bad*. The cards were *definitely* running in my favor today, too."

As she spoke, in a high, breathless fashion that made it hard for Rosemary to keep her face expressionless, she removed her hat and her gloves, patted her daughter on the shoulder, and plumped herself down in a nearby chair.

"Who are *you*?" she asked Rosemary abruptly, bending toward her a little suspiciously as she smoothed her slightly wispy hair.

"Oh, Mama," Lady Annabelle said indulgently. "This is the young lady I told you about at dinner last evening. She is Miss Rosemary Barton who is staying with her relative, Lady Emily Cranston, across the square. We met in the park. Don't you remember?"

"Of *course* I remember," her mother said with an indignant toss of her head that undid all her smoothing. "But since I have never *seen* the young lady, for all I knew, she might have been a new *maid* you were interviewing. How-de-*do*, Miss Barton? I am *Catherine* Halston. You must tell me *everything* about Lady Emily. We have all been *consumed* with curiosity this *age* about the lady, she is so reclusive. You may speak *freely*."

As she edged forward on her chair and fixed her daughter's guest with an intent, eager stare, Rosemary wondered what on earth she was supposed to say.

"Mama!" Lady Annabelle protested. "That was not well done of you, not at all. Perhaps Rosemary does not care to speak of her hostess."

"*Pooh*!" Lady Catherine said inelegantly as she searched the plate of cakes for some particular favorite. "Why *shouldn't* she? And I cannot *bear* not to learn why Lady Emily positively *hides* herself away over there! Is she, by any chance, *insane*, Miss Barton?" she asked, turning to Rosemary again. "*I* certainly would be. One can only play so *many* games of patience, after all."

"No . . . no, ma'am," Rosemary stammered. "I think it is just that she prefers her own company." As Lady Catherine looked disappointed, she added, "Truly, I do not know why she will not go out, for you see, she has never told me. You do see that I cannot like to ask."

The duchess still looked disappointed, but then she said, changing the subject in her abrupt way, "You are a very *unusual*-looking gel. I do not think I have ever seen *anyone* quite like you. You are so *dark*, so . . . so. . . .''

She stopped as she caught her daughter's little frown, and Rosemary said quietly, ''My mother was Italian, your Grace. I have my dark hair and complexion from her.''

''Oh, *Italian*,'' Lady Catherine repeated. Rosemary listened hard, but she could discern no obvious distaste in her inflection. ''*That* explains it. But your *father* is of the *beau monde*?''

''Both my mother and father are dead, ma'am,'' Rosemary explained. ''They died when I was ten. I have lived with my aunt and uncle, Mr. and Mrs. Joshua Fleming, in Kent ever since. My father was Roger Barton.''

''Hmm, Roger *Barton*,'' the duchess mused through a mouthful of cake. ''I *believe* I remember him vaguely. Was he one of the *Wiltshire* Bartons?'' she asked.

As Rosemary nodded, she rose and smoothed her skirts. ''*That's* all right, then,'' she added, a little obscurely, as she bent to kiss her daughter. ''*Positively* I must *run* now, dear, *dearest* Belle. I am to play cards at Lady Augusta's this evening. Perhaps Miss *Barton* could stay for dinner and keep you *company*?''

''I have company already, Mama,'' Annabelle told her. ''Lady Margaret came to see me this morning, and somehow or other, she is dining here this evening as well.''

''Oh, how *nice*,'' Lady Catherine said. Her face was as expressionless as her daughter's. ''I know *Margaret* will not keep you up *too* late, my dear,'' she added, and then she moved with quick steps to the door. ''Toodle-*loo*, Miss Barton. So *good* to meet you.''

Even after the door closed behind her, Rosemary could hear her breathless voice calling for her maid. She glanced at Lady Annabelle, and saw her shaking her head, a fond little smile on her face.

''I hope you will forgive my mama, Rosemary,'' the girl said. ''We are used to her impulsive ways, but she can be startling to a stranger. You see, she always says exactly what she is thinking. If she ever asks you something you would rather not discuss, just tell her so. She will not be offended. In truth, she cares deeply only for her card games. She always has. Ever since I can remember, she has been rushing from one game to the next.''

She looked down at her hands and added softly, ''I do not think my Mama has had a very happy life.''

Rosemary was a little uncomfortable, hearing this revelation, and she was glad when her hostess changed the subject.

''Are you going to Mrs. Kay's dance, Rosemary?'' she asked. ''I have had an invitation, but I will not attend unless Mark has returned by then.''

Rosemary suggested they might go together, since she had received an invitation too. Lady Annabelle looked brighter. ''That would be such fun,'' she said. ''And I shall expect you to tell me every outrageous compliment you receive, and what each of your partners has to say while waltzing with you. It will make the evening so much more enjoyable if I can share your triumphs, even vicariously.''

''I should be glad to tell you, but I will not be waltzing,'' Rosemary said. ''You see, I have not been approved for the waltz, and even if I were, I could not perform it. My Aunt Mary thought that dance sinful, so I have never learned.''

Lady Annabelle's eyes twinkled. ''But how gothic of her, my dear,'' she said. ''You must learn it at once! In fact, when next you come, I shall tell you the steps, and play for you while you practice. I have made a special point of observing the waltz—it looks like so much fun! You need not think I will be a poor dancing master.''

''But . . . dance by myself?'' Rosemary asked, much surprised.

Lady Annabelle chuckled. ''I am sure you will find it easier if you do not have to be concerned about stepping on a gentleman's toes,'' she explained.

Unfortunately, Rosemary was engaged with Lady Agatha the following day, but she agreed to visit the morning after at eleven, for her first lesson. She pressed her new friend's hand as she took her leave, thanking her for the novel that Belle had lent her.

Rosemary was much happier in the days that followed. She was so busy, she did not have to spend much time in the quiet, gloomy mansion that was Number 14 Berkeley Square. She even agreed to a drive in the park with Ronald Edson when he called again and begged her to join him. Rosemary was much on her guard, but when she saw Mr. Edson was on his best behavior, she was able to relax. She knew she looked well in her new driving gown of navy silk, trimmed with braid and gold buttons. Mr. Edson was an amusing companion, for he knew all the latest *on-dits*, and did not seem to mind pointing out the various personages in the park to her.

The only time Rosemary felt any alarm in his company was at the very end of the drive. For the first time, his eyes caressed her figure in the tight navy silk, and a hot little gleam shone in his eyes as he lifted her down from the carriage and pressed her hand in farewell. She drew away to curtsy, her eyes lowered as she thanked him for the drive, and then she ran up the steps, feeling somehow as if she was making an escape.

She realized she really did not care for Mr. Edson, but she knew she must be polite to him since he was Lady Emily's nephew. She made herself a promise, however, that she would not spend any more time in his company than she could help. Lady Agatha's warning was still very much in her mind, and she did not think her intuition that Mr. Edson was one of the men Lady Agatha had warned her about was wrong.

As usual, the gloomy, deathly-still atmosphere of the house depressed her after the bright spring sunlight she had just enjoyed, and she was quick to go up to her own room for the remainder of the afternoon. She was glad now that she had been so quick to explain to Belle why it was not possible to return any of her invitations. She did not think Lady Emily would object if she asked the girl to tea, but somehow she did not care to have Belle in this somber atmosphere where only the ticking of the clocks broke the thick silence. Lady Annabelle had assured her she understood completely, before she pointed out how much easier it was for them to meet in her own home.

"That way, my dear Rosemary, I shall not have to throw the establishment into the upset that always occurs when I am going out," she said. "Mark's servants are such dears, but they worry about me over much. And James must be summoned to carry me downstairs, and Harris to fetch my chair, and Patsy to bring the rugs, and Mr. Filbert, the butler, to fuss over whether it is too hot or too cold or too windy—sometimes I feel like a fragile princess in a fairy tale! And they are even worse when Mark is not here."

Rosemary longed to ask if Belle had heard from her brother, but she made herself refrain. She knew this time alone with her was only an interlude, and that someday soon she would come face-to face with the duke on his own territory. She knew he would not be best pleased to see her here in his home, but she refused to worry about it, and any possible reactions and comments of his, until he actually returned.

8

The Duke of Rutland returned to town the very next day.

Rosemary was in Annabelle's rooms practicing the waltz while her hostess played the piano and instructed her, and neither girl heard the duke's impatient call as he climbed the stairs, still in his driving clothes.

He was about to knock when he heard the music, and then, smiling, he opened his sister's door and stepped inside. The warm smile he wore faded at once, to be replaced with a ferocious frown when he saw Rosemary in the center of the room, her arms uplifted as one hand rested on an imaginary gentleman's shoulder, while the other pretended to clasp his hand. She stood on tiptoe, and in spite of himself, the duke was forced to admire her graceful movements as she followed the beat. He closed the door softly and leaned against it, his arms crossed over his chest, and his gray eyes narrowed.

"Turn now, Rosemary," Annabelle ordered. "One and two and three, and one and two and three . . . excellent!"

Suddenly, as she turned, Rosemary caught sight of the duke, and she stopped dancing at once, one hand going to cover her rosy mouth in her confusion. Her instructress looked around, and when she saw her brother, she stopped playing abruptly.

"Mark! Oh, my dear!" she cried, wheeling her chair away from the piano and coming toward him across the gleaming floor as rapidly as she could. Mark Halston pushed his shoulders away from the door and went to meet her, his arms outstretched.

"Darling Belle, I trust I find you well?" he asked, looking deep into her eyes as he knelt beside her to kiss her soundly.

Lady Annabelle's thin hand caressed his face. "Of course, my dear," she told him. And then she turned toward the dark beauty standing in the center of the floor and said, "This is my brother, Rosemary, the Duke of Rutland. But I forgot, you have already met!"

"Your Grace," Rosemary said as calmly as she could. As he raised his head to stare at her, the smile he had worn for his sister faded.

"Miss Barton," he said coldly.

"No doubt you are surprised to see Rosemary here," Lady Annabelle said, a little frown between her brows for his stern, unwelcoming expression. "I have been teaching her to waltz, for we have become good friends."

"I am not surprised to see her here at all. It is exactly what I would expect from her," the duke remarked, rising to bow slightly to his unwelcome guest.

Rosemary knew what he meant by that statement, and her already glowing cheeks deepened in color. She made herself put up her chin and look him straight in the eye. She was not aware of the defiance that gleamed in her dark blue eyes and made them sparkle.

"You must excuse me, your Grace, Belle," she managed to say, feeling proud of her even voice. "I would not intrude when you have not seen each other for so many days. I am sure you must have a lot to say to each other."

"I know I have a very great deal to say, Miss Barton," the duke remarked in a grim voice. Rosemary ignored him as she picked up her stole and reticule, and then she came to her friend's chair and took her hand.

"I shall look forward to seeing you soon again, Belle," she said, trying to smile.

"My dear Rosemary! But of course I shall expect you at the same time tomorrow," Lady Annabelle told her, a hint of wild roses in her cheeks now, she was so happy to see her brother again. "Perhaps we can persuade Mark to partner you while you practice," she added a little mischievously, reaching up to pull Rosemary's face down so she could kiss her good-bye.

Rosemary noticed how the duke's dark brows soared at this intimacy, and she was not at all sorry to shut the door behind her and make her way down the stairs and out of the house.

Behind her, she left a silence until the duke said, "So, you have made her your friend after all, Belle, in spite of my warnings that she is apt to prove a most unsuitable connection."

Annabelle wheeled her chair to the sofa and beckoned him to take a seat there. "You are wrong, Mark," she said firmly. "Rosemary is a delightful, dear girl, nothing at all like you imagine. We have so much in common, and we enjoy each other's company completely. Why, I have been happier these past few days than I have ever been before. In fact, the only thing missing to make my joy entire was your presence."

The duke ignored the compliment. "But surely it would be more suitable for you to rely on Lady Margaret's friendship. I know that at least *she* has no ulterior motives. You cannot have been so bereft of companionship that you needs must take up with Miss Barton, for when I told her I was going out of town, Lady Margaret promised to call on you often."

His sister waved an impatient hand. "And so she did. Called and called and called." She sighed. "I am sorry, Mark, for I know you think her marvelous and a suitable friend for me, but I cannot value Margaret as I should. She is so conventional, so prim. She never speaks anything but platitudes and niceties, and that makes her dull."

"Dull?" the duke asked. "You never said that about her before, Belle. Perhaps it is Miss Barton who thinks her dull, and she has persuaded you to her side?"

"Rosemary?" his sister asked, a little bewildered by this cold accusation. "I don't know what she thinks of Margaret, for we have never discussed her. I only know that now I have made Rosemary's acquaintance, I find the Lady Margaret too bland to be a stimulating companion. And you know something, Mark? I have noticed that she never laughs. Just think of it! She never laughs, and she rarely smiles.''

The duke rose to pace the room. His sister thought his back looked stiff, as he said over his shoulder, ''I must change, for I have an engagement in the City. I shall return and join you for tea, unless, of course, that most unsuitable young lady is going to be present.''

His sister opened her mouth to protest, but he raised his hand and said sternly, ''We shall speak of this later, Belle.''

As the duke washed and changed his driving clothes for proper town attire, he continued to think of the audacious Miss Barton. To actually see her in his sister's rooms had been a severe shock. He had not thought she would be so bold as to take advantage of his absence to insinuate herself into Belle's good graces. And his sister was such a little innocent, she would never suspect that the lady's motives were not as pure as her own. Of course Miss Barton would be a congenial companion; she would make it a point to go out of her way to endear herself to Belle as a means of gaining admission to the house, and thus ensuring his attention. Belle did not see that, for she thought everyone as good as she was herself. Her crippled condition had kept her from becoming knowledgeable in the ways of the world, and she was generally so much under his watchful eye that all the ugliness and the shams and pretenses of the human race had never come her way.

Well, he told himself as he tied his cravat while his valet held his coat ready, Miss Rosemary Barton shall discover in short order that the Lady Annabelle Halston is not without a protector. And she shall discover, as well, that I am not to be caught in any trap of her making, and that all her conniving, caressing ways will come to nothing in the end.

He frowned then, and Dibble, his valet of many years' standing, cast a worried eye over his attire. No, he told himself, it could not be the breeches that fit like a second skin, nor the elegant coat that displeased him. His Grace looked complete to a shade, just as he always did. He must have lost a considerable wager on that prizefight to make him look so grim, the valet thought as he handed the duke his curly beaver and gloves and bowed him from the room.

Mark Halston ran lightly down the stairs, still thinking of this new problem he had come home to discover. Perhaps he should make a point of seeing his mother before he spoke to Belle. She might have some idea how he could separate them. And then he shook his head as he went out to his curricle. Mama would notice nothing amiss; what was he thinking of? All her attention was given up to aces and kings. She would not think a dark queen of any concern unless the lady spoiled a hand for her.

He looked around the square before he took his seat in the carriage. Miss Barton had disappeared, but he had expected that. His cold gray eyes went briefly to the house across the park, as he wondered if she were standing at one of the shuttered windows peeking out at him, and smiling victoriously at the success of her latest ploy.

His lips tightened, and he was quick to jump up and take the reins, nodding to his tiger to let 'em go as he did so. As he tooled the curricle in the direction of Chancery Lane, he told himself that his only regret was that Belle must suffer another disillusionment. Miss Barton, like Mrs. Chace, would be quick to cut the connection as soon as she learned that the Duke of Rutland was not to be had, in any way.

But as he threaded his way expertly through the traffic of Piccadilly, he realized he still felt a small quiver whenever he saw Miss Barton. It annoyed him that he had so little control over his breathing, or his heart. He had to admit she was something quite out of the common way, and although he knew her dark, sensuous beauty and her Italian mother made her completely unsuitable for any alliance with the Duke of Rutland, he could not help being attracted to her. He could not remember ever feeling this way about a woman before. He had had his affairs, of course, and some of his mistresses had been even more lovely than Miss Barton, but none of them had given off such an aura of sensuality, one that promised so much delight in her arms. Why, every movement the girl made beckoned and tantalized. And yet, supposedly she was an innocent, proper young lady of quality. Her father's birth was unexceptionable. Miss Barton could well expect to marry into society, although she had set her sights too high when she had decided on a duke. Any duke, he told himself, but especially not this one. His father would turn over in his grave if his son were ever to do such an infamous thing. He had raised Mark Halston to consider what he owed his name first and foremost, and he had plainly instructed him as to the type of lady he should choose for his future duchess.

He had been thinking for some time now that Lady Margaret Malden would be a perfect wife. She was the daughter of an earl, and she was a refined, quiet lady. Just as important was her liking of, and care for, his sister. He would never marry anyone who could not love Belle, or live with her, for he intended to keep her beside him always. But Lady Margaret had shown by her attentions and friendship that she understood this concern, and concurred with it.

He frowned a little then, as he feathered a corner expertly. It was unfortunate that Belle did not value the Lady Margaret as she should, that she thought her bland and uninteresting. Surely, when she came to know her better, she would like her more. And when she was separated from the encroaching, opportunistic Miss Barton, she would cease any comparison between them. And then his frown deepened as he remembered her comment that the lady never laughed, and only rarely smiled.

It was not a prerequisite in a wife that he had ever considered important. Marriage, for those of his rank, was not meant to be amusing or exciting. It was meant to produce the next duke, and respect and a little mild affection between the participants were all that was necessary to bring to it. He thought of his mother then, and he won-

dered if she had approved this type of arrangement throughout the years of her marriage. He did not know. She had
always seemed content, though not at all ecstatic. He
could not remember any discourse between her and his
father that had been more than a polite exchange, but
neither had there been any arguments or passionate storms
to mar the well-bred fabric of their marital relationship. As
he pulled up before his bank, he wondered irrelevantly if
his mother had always had her passion for cards, or if she
had fallen into the habit as a way to escape a lonely,
unfulfilled existence.

As he stepped down and gestured to his tiger to walk the
team, he told himself he was being absurd. His mother
was no different from many other noble ladies, and if
sometimes he had to rescue her when the cards did not run
her way, that was a small price to pay for her only
amusement in life.

Later that afternoon, when he joined his sister for tea,
he was more determined than ever to do all he could to
divorce her from her new, impossible friend. He found
Belle unusually stubborn. All through his well-reasoned
speech to her, she shook her head, and when he finally
finished, she was quick to protest.

"You are wrong, Mark," she said firmly, her green
eyes steady on his. "Rosemary is nothing like that. She is
a nice girl. She cannot help how she looks. Besides, I like
her!"

"Belle, Belle!" he said, shaking his own head now.
"You are such a little innocent! And now you will be hurt
when Miss Barton drops you, as drop you she will just as
soon as I make it clear to her she has no chance with me."

"How impossibly conceited you sound!" his hitherto
adoring sister exclaimed.

The duke nodded. "No doubt I do, but I have been
about the world, and women like Miss Barton are not
unknown to me. The widow Chace, Belle—remember?"

Seeing his sister still looked mulish, he added gently,
"But I can prove the truth of my words. We shall put Miss
Barton to the test, if you agree."

"The test?" she asked, looking perplexed.

"Yes. I shall flirt with her madly the next time we meet, and you shall see how she reacts. If she really is the nice girl you claim, she will be horrified, and repulse me, but if, as I suppose, she is cultivating your friendship as an avenue to me, she will betray herself at once."

Lady Annabelle looked at her brother in a considering way, as if she had never seen him before. His black brows rose a little as she continued to study him.

"Why do you look at me that way, Belle?" he asked at last.

"Somehow such a test seems unethical to me," she said. "Then, too, you are very handsome, Mark, especially when you smile and take the trouble to be pleasant. Rosemary has only recently arrived in town, and she is not up to snuff. Less, perhaps, than you say I am. I am not entirely sure such a test would be fair to her."

The duke laughed and rose to come to her side and give her a quick hug. "I shall not quite devastate her, you know," he promised. "Come, tell me the next evening party she attends. We will contrive to be there as well."

"She has been invited to Mrs. Kay's dance in two days' time," Lady Annabelle said slowly. "She asked me to go with her, if you had not returned to town by then."

"Excellent!" the duke said. "We shall most certainly attend, and there we shall discover whether Miss Barton is a lovely innocent or a tigress on the prowl."

As he walked to the door, he said over his shoulder, "Play fair, now, Belle! You must not warn her in any way of my plan."

"Of course I will not!" she said hotly. But as her brother threw her a kiss and left the room, she wheeled her chair to the window, a little frown on her face. She had never seen Mark in hot pursuit of any lady, but he was such a handsome man, and so polished and brilliant, she was afraid he would be able to wind Rosemary around his little finger with only a minimum of effort. As she stared across the park to Rosemary's house, she sighed. There was nothing she could do but wait and see.

Lady Agatha and her husband took Rosemary to the dance on the evening appointed. Rosemary had not seen the duke since his return to town, although she had called on Annabelle each day. She did not know the duke was purposely avoiding her, that he did not intend to see her until they met at the dance.

Lady Agatha was loud in her praises of Rosemary's gown, a float of soft blue crepe made up in the empire style so popular now. It was adorned with three flounces of old lace caught up with matching ribbons at the hem. Mr. Kay's eyes also admired her as she made her curtsy and thanked his mother for inviting her. Mrs. Kay hid a startled exclamation. She had not attended the Truesdale ball, and so had no idea what the young lady her son was so desirous of entertaining looked like. Now her heart sank at the girl's exotic beauty and her graceful, richly curved figure. How like James to choose someone so completely unsuitable, she thought, even as she smiled at Miss Barton. He doesn't even have enough in his brain box to consider the dance she would lead him, the men he would have to repulse, the silly boy!

Rosemary moved forward into the Kays' double drawing room with Lord and Lady Williams, looking around eagerly. Lady Annabelle beckoned to her from the sofa where her brother had placed her. He stood beside her, his dark evening dress emphasizing his striking masculinity and strong, muscled body. As Rosemary excused herself and went toward the two Halstons, she thought how lovely Belle looked this evening, in a slim green gown with her hair a mass of dusky curls. She felt a pang that her friend must only sit and watch, that she could never, ever, know the exhilaration of dancing. Because she thought it was so unfair, her smile was warm and loving when she reached her and curtsied.

"How beautiful you look this evening, Rosemary," Belle said, moving her skirts to one side so her friend could take the seat beside her.

"Very beautiful indeed," the duke agreed in a pleasant voice.

Startled, Rosemary looked up at that dark, stern face, and she almost dropped her fan at the smile he was giving her, the warm, intimate look in his eyes. She looked down at her lap in confusion. "Thank you," she managed to get out.

"So beautiful, in fact, that I must insist on a dance or two," the duke went on smoothly, coming to take up the little card that dangled from her wrist. "I do not believe any of the patronesses of Almack's are to be present this evening, but if by some lucky chance any of them should appear, I shall beg them to approve you for the waltz at once. And I shall insist, as payment for my intervention, on claiming two of them."

Rosemary stared at him for a moment, feeling safe in doing so now that that dark head was bent over her card. She saw Mr. Kay hurrying toward her, closely followed by Sir Reginald Wallingford. At another time she would have smiled a little at their identically eager expressions, but now she felt so confused, she could not even do that.

The duke stepped back as the young gentlemen made their bows and begged for a dance. Rosemary tried to ignore him as she chatted with her two admirers, but even when other men came up, including Ronald Edson, she was unable to put the mysterious behavior of the Duke of Rutland from her mind.

When the small orchestra began to play, Mr. Kay bowed. Rosemary was aware that this was a singular honor, as she took her leave of Lady Annabelle.

"Remember, my dear, every single compliment!" the lady whispered before she rose to take Mr. Kay's arm.

Rosemary smiled and nodded. As she moved away, the duke took the seat she had vacated.

"Aren't you going to dance, Mark?" his sister asked him. "I see Lady Margaret on the other side of the room. Surely she will wonder if you do not come to her."

"I prefer to remain with you, dear Belle," her brother

said, pressing her hand. "I would not leave you here alone."

"Nonsense, Mark!" Annabelle protested. "I shall do very well, for you know how I love to watch the dancing."

"It is too late, in any case. Lady Margaret has just had her hand solicited by Nigel Delincourt, and the sets are made up."

Annabelle saw that Lady Margaret and her partner had joined the same set Rosemary was in, and as the dance began, she compared the two. She was not aware that her brother was similarly engaged. Miss Barton looks so vibrant, so alive, he thought. Lady Margaret's quiet elegance seemed pallid when compared to her dark curls and warm complexion. And when Rosemary smiled a little at something Mr. Kay was whispering to her, her generous, rosy mouth opened to display dazzling white teeth. Her curls swung with the music, and he wondered what they would feel like under his hand. He admitted he was looking forward to their dance, even as he forced himself to admire the Lady Margaret's smoothly banded brown hair and discreetly covered narrow shoulders.

Rosemary returned to the sofa when the dance was over. She found the duke had gone to greet Lady Margaret Malden and others of his friends, and she was glad. She had spent the entire set wondering what on earth he was up to, why he had greeted her so warmly and given her so many compliments. She wished she could ask his sister, but she knew that was not possible.

All too soon she saw him excusing himself and coming back to her side. His bow was graceful, and as he held out his hand, Rosemary rose and took it, wishing her heart was not jumping in such a disturbing manner. She hoped he did not notice her agitation. As he put his arm around her, he smiled down into her face, his eyes caressing each feature as if to memorize them.

"I have admired your dancing from afar, Miss Barton," he said after a moment. "But now that I have you in my arms, I must admit I am stunned. How very graceful you are, how supple, and—dare I hope?—yielding, as well."

9

The duke's hand tightened at her waist, and Rosemary stifled a little gasp.

"If . . . if you please, your Grace," she whispered. "I do not understand . . ."

"What is there to understand, my dear?" he asked, bending his dark head closer. "You are a beautiful, exciting woman, and I, alas, am only mortal. How could I not be attracted to you?"

Rosemary could think of nothing whatsoever to say. Her mind was reeling with shock. She took a deep breath to steady herself, and forced herself to look up into those gray eyes so close to hers. They were not icy now. Indeed, there was a light in them that caused her heart to beat even faster. She made a sudden movement, as if to escape him, and he tightened his hands again.

"No, no, Miss Barton, you would not be so cruel," he said, laughing down at her. "To leave me when I have just captured you at last? I beg you to be kind."

"Kind?" Rosemary whispered again. Her mouth was dry, and she felt hot and cold by turns, all over her body.

"Why, yes. How happy I would be if you would only consent to be *kind* to me," he said, putting a wealth of meaning into the word. "I am sure you understand me, do you not?"

"No, I do not," Rosemary made herself say. "I cannot believe anything you are saying to me this evening, your

Grace, nor the way that you are behaving. Surely it is vastly different from your previous attitude toward me.''

"But perhaps I have been stricken by Cupid's arrow, Miss Barton, no matter how I fought it in the beginning,'' he insisted, still smiling down at her. His look was as intimate as a kiss.

Rosemary lowered her eyes. "That is ridiculous,'' she said. "You know you dislike me—why, you have from first meeting.''

"I will admit I was not very warm, was I, my dear? But you see, I could not maintain such an icy pose. Besides your beauty, my sister has been telling me of your kindness to her, and that alone must make me grateful to you,'' the duke said.

There was barely veiled contempt in his voice now, but Rosemary was so confused she did not notice it. "I refuse to accept any gratitude, sir,'' she said, glad they had left the dangerous subject of the duke's sudden impossible infatuation. "To be sure, there is no need for it. I am happy to be Belle's friend. I did not have a friend my own age in London, you see, until we met in the square one day.''

"Was it by any chance around lamplighting time?'' the duke asked, at his most urbane.

When Rosemary looked indignant, he gave a knowing chuckle. "Ah, if only you would feel as warm toward me as you do toward that lamplighter! What a fortunate man! How he is to be envied!''

"You know very well I feel nothing for the lamplighter!'' Rosemary could not help retorting. "You are teasing me.''

"Indeed I am, ma'am,'' he agreed. As he turned her expertly, Rosemary was sure that the hands holding her could tell how nervous she was. She ordered herself to behave, but somehow her body refused to obey.

"You are trembling,'' he remarked next, his voice softer. "Can it be that you are not indifferent to me either, my dear Miss Barton?''

"You frighten me,'' Rosemary said before she thought. His dark brows rose. "But I never meant to frighten you, my dear. No, no, I intend only to make love to you, in any way you will permit."

Rosemary gasped. "You . . . you must not say such things," she got out. For a brief moment he pulled her closer and dropped a kiss on her curls. It was done so quickly, Rosemary was sure no one had noticed. She began to pray that the dance would be over soon, and then she began to worry that she would fall when he let her go, her legs felt so shaky.

For all the duke's expertise, someone, unfortunately, did notice. Lady Margaret Malden, who was sitting out this particular set, had not taken her eyes from the handsome couple on the floor. For some time she had been sure of Mark Halston, positive from his attentions that it was only a matter of time before he asked her to marry him. Her mother had cautioned her to do nothing to try to hasten the proposal along. They had had a serious talk about the kind of marriage she could expect with him, and Lady Margaret, who was currently embarked on her fourth Season, had been happy to agree to it. She had no love for the duke, or any other man, but she knew it was her duty not only to marry but also to marry as well as she could. The Duke of Rutland was an admirable catch. And she planned on being an exemplary wife to him, housing his crippled little sister, and giving him his heir, even though the thought of physical intimacy filled her with revulsion. But to see him holding that foreign-looking Miss Barton so close in his arms, and smiling down at her, even kissing her quickly, caused a distinct tremor of foreboding, and another unfamiliar emotion as well. To her surprise, Lady Margaret's thin breast swelled with jealousy.

When the dance ended, she excused herself from the people around her and made her way to Lady Annabelle's sofa. A young man was sitting beside her, chatting, and Lady Margaret sensed his relief as he made his bow and escaped.

"How kind of you to rescue him," Lady Annabelle said with her wistful little smile. "He is new-come to town. He did not realize I could not stand, never mind dance, when he asked me.''

''Try not to dwell on it, Annabelle,'' Lady Margaret advised her as she settled down in the young man's place. ''I myself have often thought it would be so much better for you to abstain from these festive evenings, for you see where it has led. If you had remained quietly at home, you would not have been forced to endure such a slight. Besides, I am sure such exertion drains your puny strength. You should have more care for yourself.''

''Only my legs are crippled, Margaret,'' Lady Annabelle said a little sharply. ''The rest of my body, my eyes, and my mind are intact. Why should I not come? I enjoy it. Besides, quietly sitting here hardly taxes my strength.''

Before Lady Margaret could reply, the duke came up. At her whispered request, he had taken Miss Barton to Lady Williams. Now he nodded a little at his sister's look of inquiry, and then he smiled. Lady Annabelle thought he looked a little grim even so, and she wondered at it.

The three conversed until the music began again and the duke asked Lady Margaret to waltz. As they went onto the floor, he noticed Miss Barton shaking her head at Lord Greene, and indicating Belle's sofa.

Sometime later, as he turned, he saw her sitting alone with his sister, deep in conversation, and he wished he could hear what they were saying.

''You seem strangely abstracted this evening, Duke,'' his partner said. Her voice was as smooth and colorless as ever, and he forced himself to smile down at her. Holding her in his arms, he could not help but compare her slender figure to Miss Barton's ripe curves, and he wished she were not so thin, so brittle.

He made himself answer in his usual manner, but Lady Margaret was not deceived. She set herself to chat with him on a number of interesting subjects, and when the dance was over, she made sure he remained by her side throughout the interlude, by telling him about the slight his sister had received, and how much she regretted it. The duke pressed her hand in real gratitude.

He took her in to supper as well, after he had carried his sister to a quiet table. Of Rosemary Barton there was no sign. Belle chuckled as he lifted her, and told him of the four gentlemen who had insisted on sharing Rosemary's table.

"I could see she really wished to remain with me, but then, when she saw you coming over with Margaret, she was quick to agree to the scheme," Lady Annabelle said. "What outrageous things have you been saying to her, Mark? She would not even speak of you to me."

"I shall tell you later," the duke replied as he lowered her carefully to a chair. "As much, that is, as I think suitable for your girlish ears and tender age," he added with a grin.

Belle laughed again and shook her finger at him. "You are very bad, Mark, you know you are. I cannot wait to hear all about your success—or better still, your failure. Come, give me one hint!"

"But the evening is not yet over, dear Belle," he said, and as she pouted, he excused himself to go and fetch Lady Margaret. Their table was set somewhat apart from the noisy, crowded one where Miss Barton was ensconced. When he returned, the duke saw that she had taken a seat that put her back to them, almost, he thought, as if she did not dare to look at him. As he talked easily with his sister and Lady Margaret, he pondered Miss Barton's reaction to his flirting during their dance. He would be the first to admit that she had surprised him. He had not expected such innocent shrinking from a lady who looked as warm and knowing as she did. And yet, unless she were involved in a very deep game indeed, it was obvious that she had not enjoyed the experience.

His gray eyes narrowed as he studied her ebony curls and the rounded cheek that were all he could see of the lady. Yes, of course, that must be it! She was playing the role of innocent, to intrigue him and lead him on. He raised his wine and sipped it, admiring her round, satiny shoulders. Beside him, and well aware of his abstraction,

Lady Margaret tried not to stiffen as she continued to chat with Lady Annabelle.

When the duke came to Rosemary's side later in the evening to claim his second dance, he could tell by the way she paled that she had been awaiting it in some trepidation. As he bowed, the orchestra struck up another waltz. The duke thought her smile of relief most uncalled-for, and he felt an uncharacteristic anger.

"How unfortunate, your Grace," she said, sitting back again. "You must excuse me."

"I have no intention of excusing you, Miss Barton. And I consider it, far from unfortunate, a golden opportunity," he said.

Rosemary's questioning eyes flew to his face.

"Come, let us stroll about together instead," he said, offering her his arm.

"Can't we just stay here, or perhaps join Annabelle?" Rosemary asked, looking around the crowded drawing room.

"I have something to say to you, Miss Barton, and I prefer a more private setting," the duke told her. "Come!"

Rosemary studied the hands she had clasped tightly in her lap. "But I would prefer to remain in company, sir," she whispered.

The duke bent over her and calmly raised her chin. His hand was warm on her skin, and as she stared into his intent gray eyes, Rosemary felt another shiver travel quickly up her spine to stir the hair at the nape of her neck.

"I am afraid I must insist," he whispered back, and then he let her go and straightened. "Shall we?" he asked, his courteous words a cold command.

Helplessly Rosemary rose and took his arm, since she did not know what else she could do. She saw one corner of his mouth twist for a moment in a grimace as he led her from the room, and she wondered at it. She was glad that there were other guests in the hall, sitting and talking together, or admiring the family portraits that lined the walls. The duke did not pause to speak to anyone, however, as he led her toward the back of the house. He stopped before a door and opened it for her. Rosemary could see it was a small, empty salon, and she hesitated.

The duke was impatient, and he frowned. "Come, come, Miss Barton! I believe I am a gentleman, after all," he said harshly.

His words seemed to mock her timidity, and Rosemary put up her chin and walked by him. "I shall not remain long, your Grace," she said. "I do not understand why you have brought me here, for I am sure it is not at all the thing. Lady Agatha would be most upset if she knew, and my Aunt Mary would be horrified."

The duke did not comment as he indicated a sofa, but Rosemary made no move to sit down. For a moment they stared at each other, and then he strolled away to the fireplace, to lean against the mantel. Rosemary's heart resumed its normal beat.

"I must admit you are a puzzle to me, Miss Barton," he said, his gray eyes never leaving her face. "You are not at all what I expected."

"And what did you expect, sir?" Rosemary asked, gripping a chair back for support.

"An adventuress," he said. "A tempting, grasping adventuress. I am still not sure that you are not that woman, in disguise. If you are, you must allow me to congratulate you. Your acting is superb. You play the young girl in her first Season to perfection. Alas, that your performance has a serious flaw."

He paused, but since Rosemary refused to speak, he shrugged his shoulders and continued. "You see, you do not look at all the part. You are too voluptuous, too sensual and graceful, and much too tempting to be that frightened little girl from the country that you pretend you are."

"I cannot help the way I look," Rosemary interrupted, her blue eyes blazing with anger. "I am not a temptress!"

The duke strolled back to her, coming close to look deep into her eyes. She forced herself to remain still.

"Yes, my dear, you are, no matter how you continue to deplore the fact," he said calmly. "You do not have to even speak or move or smile, nor do a thing but stand before a man to tempt him."

He stepped even closer and took her chin in his hand again. "And what a shame if your looks are a lie," he said more softly. His breath stirred her hair, and Rosemary imagined she could feel his warmth even from a foot away. "One such as you was made for love, for a man's delectation. How unjust the gods would be to deny us the treat," he continued.

Rosemary tried to twist away, her breath coming unevenly, but he put his arms around her and pulled her nearer, making her his prisoner.

"Let me go!" she demanded, trying to push him away with two clenched fists. She could feel the long, hard length of him pressing even closer, and it was making her dizzy.

"Presently," he said in his normal voice.

She stared up at him, her eyes beseeching him to release her. As if she had spoken, he shook his head in refusal, and then he bent and kissed her.

As his lips clung to hers, Rosemary was not aware that the fists she had made opened and her hands rested on his broad chest. She was lost in her first real embrace. She had wondered what kissing a man would feel like, and whether she would like it or not, but none of her reading about it, nor any of her dreams, had prepared her for the reality, the tide of feeling that swept over her from the very tips of her toes to the top of her curls. And when she remembered her cousin Henry's inept gropings and hot, hurried kisses, she was even more amazed. As the duke's mouth moved more and more insistently, she ordered herself to remain untouched by his embrace, and she tried to ignore those strong hands caressing her back and her bare arms, the heady scent of his warm skin and the lotion he used, which teased her senses so.

When he raised his head at last, she could not even open

her eyes, they felt so heavy. Her whole body was languorous with sensation. She knew she would have fallen if he had not held her safe in his encompassing arms.

"You see?" he whispered. "I was right. You enjoyed that kiss, you know you did, my lovely temptress."

His last words brought Rosemary back to her senses, and she opened her eyes to push him away. The duke let her go. She could not tell from his rigidly controlled body and stern, unsmiling face what he was thinking, but she was sure that inwardly he was mocking her. He must think now, after her response, that she was what he had claimed she was, after all. And suddenly she was furious. Furious at the liberty he had taken, and his calm assumptions about her character and her motives. She wanted to scream at him, to pummel him with her fists. It was not fair!

She grasped the chair back again for support, wishing she did not feel as if she were about to burst into a storm of weeping. Still he waited, making no move to speak or touch her again. She drew a deep breath and stood as tall and straight as she could.

"You are mistaken, sir," she said, glad that her voice was cold and steady, in spite of her fury. "I tell you again that I am not what you imagine. You have insulted me, and if I had a brother or . . . or a father, I would be quick to tell them so they might call you to account for it. You may be sure I shall have nothing further to do with you, nor will I ever again be so naive that I will go apart with you or any other man. Lady Agatha warned me, but I thought a duke, because of his high rank, could be trusted."

She paused to draw a shaky breath, but Mark Halston only stared at her, one dark brow raised, almost as if he were astounded that she dared to criticize him.

"If you will excuse me, your Grace," she said. "We have nothing more to say to each other—ever."

Out of habit, she started to curtsy to him, and then warm color flooded her cheeks, and she checked herself. Her scornful glance told him clearly that she considered him unworthy of the courtesy.

She left the room, quietly closing the door behind her. The duke stared after her, a bemused expression on his face. It was several moments before he went to pour himself a glass of wine and dash it down, and several more before he remembered his sister, all alone in the drawing room. He put the enigma that was Miss Barton from his mind as he hurried back to Belle, but he knew he would not be able to sleep tonight until he had thought this puzzle through.

Although Belle teased him on the carriage drive home, Mark Halston would not tell her exactly what had happened between himself and Miss Barton.

"But, Mark, *you* are not playing fair now!" she said indignantly. "And although I was able to watch you together while you were dancing, later you took Rosemary out of the room. You were gone for such a long time! And then, when Rosemary came back, she was alone, and I thought she seemed distressed. She hardly came near me after that. What happened? I demand to know!"

"I was putting her to the test, as I told you I would, Belle," her brother replied.

Lady Annabelle stared at his dark, stern profile. Somehow he looked more formal and ducal than she had ever seen him look before. She reached out and took his hand and squeezed it, and he turned and gave her a little smile. It was not one of his better efforts.

"And did your test succeed, Mark?" she asked quietly. "Did Rosemary betray herself?"

He put her hand back in her lap and patted it before he answered. "She did . . . but then again, she did not," he said slowly.

His sister frowned. "I don't understand," she said.

"I believe Miss Barton is playing an even deeper game than I had supposed," he explained. "On one hand, she is the lovely young innocent she claims, a girl who only wants to enjoy your friendship. But on the other hand . . ."

His voice died away and his mouth tightened.

"On the other hand?" his sister prompted.

"I cannot tell you what passed between us in the salon, Belle, for that would not be the act of a gentleman," he said. "Let me say only that it showed Miss Barton's motives to be questionable. And that is all I intend to tell you."

Although his voice was calm and easy, Lady Annabelle heard the implacable note in it, and she subsided. She wished she did not feel so uneasy. But perhaps Rosemary would tell her more when she called in the morning, as she had asked her to do. As she stared out the carriage window, Lady Annabelle realized that Rosemary had not promised to come, not in so many words. She told herself she would send her friend a note, to be sure of her attendance. What could Mark have said to her? Done to her?

The duke himself carried his sister to her room and gave her into the care of her faithful maid. And then, going to his own rooms, he dismissed his valet for the night.

As Dibble bowed himself away, he was sure the sum the duke had lost at the prizefight must have been tremendous. What else could preoccupy him so, and cause such a dark frown after a pleasant evening out? he wondered.

Mark Halston sat down in a big wing chair before the fire and propped up his chin with one hand, to stare into the flames. He knew it would be a long time before he would be able to forget the kiss he had exacted from Rosemary Barton. It had made his head swim, and he was not at all sure he cared for the sensation. He was a man who prided himself on his control; he could not remember ever responding to a woman as he had responded to her. And then his frown deepened, and he knew why he felt uneasy. Although he was sure she had returned his kiss, there had been a sweet innocence about her lips, a sort of wonder, as if she were moving into uncharted waters hitherto unknown to her. He remembered now how he had wanted to kiss her even more deeply, caress her more passionately, but he had controlled his desires with a great deal of effort. It was as if he knew somehow that such an intimacy would not only shock her, but frighten her as well.

Yet how could this be? He would wager any amount you liked that she was no innocent. She could not be! And then his eyes narrowed. If she were not, why hadn't she pressed the advantage she must have known was hers after that kiss? Why hadn't she smiled at him, and been content to nestle in his arms? Instead, she had pushed him away and read him a lecture on morality that had left him feeling vaguely ashamed. It was not an emotion he had ever enjoyed. And her scornful look when she refused to curtsy had flicked him on the raw.

The duke rose to pace the room, his hands clasped behind his back. He wondered what she would tell his sister when they met again, and then he stopped short. If she were merely the young girl she claimed, would she ever come across the square again? She had said she wanted nothing further to do with him. Might not her reluctance to be in his company also extend to Belle? And if it did, Belle would be hurt beyond belief, and it would all be his fault. There would be nothing he could do to make it up to her.

For a moment he considered writing Miss Barton a note, begging her to come and see Belle as often as she liked, and promising to stay far away from her whenever she was in the house. Surely her affection for his sister would overcome any qualms she might have about stepping into the lion's den.

But he realized a note would be most unwise, if, as he still believed, she was involved in some intrigue. No, he could not write. He would just have to wait and see what the lady did now.

He went to the window and pulled aside the curtains. It was a clear night, although there was no moonlight to brighten the square. Below him the streetlights glowed, but he did not look down. Instead, his eyes went to her house. It was dark and still, as dark and still as it always was both night and day. Not even a tiny chink of light told him the location of her room. As he leaned his hands on the windowsill, he pondered again the mystery that was Miss Rosemary Barton.

Which was she? The lovely innocent young girl or the scheming, seductive wanton?

He shook his head. Even after all his efforts to unmask her this evening, he had to admit, he still did not know.

IO

One of the duke's liveried footmen ran around the square early the next morning, Lady Annabelle's note in hand. He had been instructed to wait for a reply, and he passed the time chatting with Bert, who was on duty in the front hall. The two men had struck up a mild friendship since Miss Barton and Lady Annabelle so often corresponded, but when Maggie tripped down the stairs with Miss Barton's reply, Bert stiffened. The other footman's admiration was so obvious, he was quick to show the man to the door. He and Maggie were fast coming to an understanding, and he had no intention of losing her to one of the duke's men.

Lady Annabelle was having her breakfast in bed, and she tore Rosemary's note open eagerly. But as she read it, her thin face fell. Rosemary had written to say she would not be able to visit that day, for she was indisposed. She sent her regrets, but Lady Annabelle thought the note very stiff, and most unlike her friend. She put it down on her tray, and sipped her tea, her eyes far away.

It was obvious to her that something serious had happened between Mark and Rosemary the evening before. She recalled again her friend's look of distress when she had returned alone to Mrs. Kay's drawing room, and the way she had stayed close to Lady Agatha for the remainder of the evening. But since Mark would not tell her about their meeting, she was left in the dark until such time as she could question Rosemary.

Lady Annabelle's big green eyes grew pensive. It could not be that Mark was right; no, she would not believe it! Rosemary was a dear girl and nothing more. She was sure she had no ulterior motives, that Mark in his concern that she might be hurt again was only making a mare's nest out of the situation. She would continue to refuse to believe any perfidy of her friend. Why, it was entirely possible that Rosemary was not feeling well this morning. As she rang for her maid, Lady Annabelle decided to write her another note, and send her a book to read as well. And maybe tomorrow, or the day after that, her friend would come and visit her again.

But in the days that followed, Rosemary did not come.

She had spent a sleepless night after the dance, thinking about what had happened, and what she was to do now, and she had come to see she must avoid the duke at all costs. It hurt her to refuse all Lady Annabelle's invitations, to say she was busy or tired or had a previous engagement, when often such was not the case. She missed their companionship, the gay conversations, and their laughter together so much more than she had ever missed her cousin Eleanor when she had first come up to town. But since the duke had sneered at her, and slandered her, as well as subjecting her to that passionate embrace, there was no other way for her to behave.

Rosemary wished she might discuss her problem with Lady Agatha, but all of a sudden that lady was much too busy. The Williamses' ship sailed soon, and she was involved in shopping and packing, letter-writing and saying good-bye to all her friends. She had invited Rosemary to a party she and her husband were giving the evening before their departure, but until that time Rosemary had no expectations of seeing her. And she did not feel, after all Lady Agatha's kindness, that she could beg for an interview, bothering her when she was so very preoccupied with her own concerns. She had given her time so unstintingly, it would not be at all fair to impose on her further.

To her surprise, Lady Emily was quick to notice that she

was no longer an intimate in the big mansion across the square. One evening, as the two were finishing their silent dinner, she had questioned her sharply about this falling-out. Rosemary had returned an evasive answer, her eyes lowered to her plate.

"Look at me, girl!" Lady Emily had commanded.

As Rosemary raised her eyes, she had to stifle a gasp. Lady Emily was leaning toward her now, her own eyes narrowed, and with such a look of anger on her face, Rosemary was stunned. Under the table, Prinny began growling softly at the harsh tones in his mistress's voice, but Lady Emily did not order him to hush. Instead she said, "This displeases me very much, girl! Very much indeed! And I am sure Lady Agatha would deplore it as well. Your very first friend, and you say you do not care to call on her again? What rot! Come, tell me your reasons at once!"

Rosemary twisted her napkin in nervous hands. "I cannot go there again, ma'am," she said, wishing her throat were not so dry. Her hostess looked more than displeased now, she looked almost menacing.

"Why ever not?" she demanded.

"Please, ma'am . . ." Rosemary began, but Lady Emily waved an imperious hand.

"You will have the goodness to tell me, and at once, miss, if you know what's good for you," she said.

Prinny's growls had grown louder, and under the table Rosemary edged her feet away from his massive head.

"I cannot go to the Duke of Rutland's house ever again, ma'am," she said when she realized there was no escape from the truth. "He has insulted me."

Lady Emily sat back in her chair, looking thoughtful, and even, Rosemary thought in amazement, a little pleased. She wondered if she were imagining such an emotion. "In what way?" she asked now. "He has tried to seduce you, embraced you, you mean?"

Rosemary nodded, speechless, and the lady's lips twisted in a little smile. "Well," she said more softly, as if she spoke to herself. "Well, well, well."

Rosemary waited, but her hostess only sipped her wine, her eyes far away. One hand crept up to fondle the cloisonné locket that she wore as usual.

Nothing more was said until the end of the evening, but then, as Lady Emily rose from her customary place in the library and put her book down before retiring to bed, she paused and turned to stare at her guest. Rosemary had risen politely as well, and now she faced her hostess in some trepidation. Lady Emily subjected her to a long stare, inspecting her from head to toe.

"I order you to resume your calls, miss," she said at last. Rosemary shivered. They had not exchanged a word for three hours, but Lady Emily spoke as if they were still involved in their earlier conversation. "In spite of the duke, surely it will be possible for you to see your little friend alone sometimes. He is not always at home. You have only to watch the house to discover when he has gone out. And then, in perfect, virginal safety, you can run across the square for a visit."

Her words mocked Rosemary, and she felt the color rising in her cheeks. "You do not understand, ma'am," she said. "He does not think I am a good girl. He thinks I am pursuing him, trying to entrap him in some way. If he learns I have resumed visiting his sister, he will be sure he is right. I cannot go, I cannot!"

Prinny growled, deep in his throat, at her passionate cry, and Lady Emily tightened her hand in his ruff. "And I say you shall," she ordered. "I do not care to have you moping about here. It disturbs me, and my doctor says I must not be upset—in any way. I shall expect your obedience, girl, as payment for my kindness in giving you a home in the first place."

Before her guest could reply to this order, she wheeled and marched away, accompanied by the huge mastiff. In some confusion, Rosemary watched her leave the room. Why was her friendship with Annabelle Halston so important to Lady Emily? Why did she insist the visits be resumed? Her explanation that she did not care to have

Rosemary moping about the house seemed very thin, almost lame. How was she even to know what her young guest did? She never left her room until late afternoon, and sometimes Rosemary did not see her until they met at the dinner table. And it was unfair of her to say that Rosemary was 'moping.' She still went out to an occasional party, called on those hostesses who had entertained her, or walked or drove in the park whenever she was invited to do so. Besides, since Lady Emily ignored her most of the time they spent together, it was not as if she would see moroseness or sullen silences, even if there had been any to notice.

Rosemary put both hands to her head, deep in thought. Lady Emily was frightening in a way she did not understand. It was not Prinny's growls that had raised the hair on the back of her neck this evening—oh, no. It was the look in Lady Emily's eyes. Almost, one might call it a fanatical gleam. And her harsh voice had been so impassioned, so determined, and about such a little thing, too. For the first time since coming to London, Rosemary wondered if her hostess was quite sane. And then she immediately shook her head, for such a bizarre thought was not to be considered for a moment. Being a recluse could be called an aberration, but just because you preferred your own company, it did not mean you were mad. She was only a little odd, and of course, used to getting her own way.

When Rosemary went to bed at last, she still had no idea what she was to do about the situation, and again she regretted Lady Agatha's preoccupation at this time. If only she could talk to her; if only she could have the benefit of her advice!

The next morning, she chanced to look out her window just as the Duke of Rutland was coming down the steps of his town house. He was pulling on his gloves as he greeted the four mounted gentlemen who awaited him. Rosemary saw him swing into his own saddle before the little troop rode away.

She dropped the curtain she had been holding, and took a deep breath. It certainly appeared that the duke was off on a riding expedition with his friends, and she realized this was an excellent time to obey Lady Emily and visit Belle again. Hurrying to change her clothes, she decided to chance an impromptu visit. If she waited for an exchange of notes, the duke might return. No, she told herself as she settled her bonnet on her dark curls, she could never take that risk. She would drop in on Lady Annabelle as she was used to do, returning the book the girl had lent her, and she would say she could not stay long because she had another engagement.

She was ushered up to Lady Annabelle's rooms as soon as she entered the house. She thought the butler seemed almost relieved to see her, and she wondered at it as she followed him up the stairs. She did not know how depressed her friend had been since her visits had ceased, and that all the duke's staff was aware of it, even though Lady Annabelle was as kind and thoughtful as ever. It was there in the droop of her mouth when she thought no one was looking, and in her silences. And whereas before, she had practiced her piano and her singing every morning, now not a single happy note came from her rooms. The staff had discussed it among themselves, and come to the conclusion that their young mistress was unhappy because her friend had ceased to call on her.

Lady Annabelle's smile as the butler announced her caller confirmed their conclusion, and Filbert nodded in satisfaction as he quietly closed the door behind him.

"Rosemary! Oh, my dear, how happy I am that you have come at last!" Lady Annabelle exclaimed as she wheeled her chair rapidly toward her friend. Rosemary bent and kissed her, suddenly glad she had come after all.

"I am sorry it has been so long, Belle," she said, trying to smile and act normally.

Lady Annabelle indicated a chair. "Sit down, and tell me what you have been doing, and more importantly, why you have not come to see me," she said. She saw a shadow cross her guest's face, and she added gently, "It is something to do with Mark, is it not Rosemary? Yes, I can see by your face that it is. I would not pry, but I know something happened the evening of the Kays' dance. What was it?"

"Your . . . your brother did not tell you?" Rosemary asked as she sat down and adjusted her skirts.

"No, he did not," his sister admitted. "He only said that telling me would not be the act of a gentleman."

She thought her guest stiffened for a moment, and she put her thin hand on her arm. "But whatever it was, Rosemary, I hate it for causing such an interruption in our friendship. Surely, that is a separate thing, is it not?"

Her voice seemed to plead, and Rosemary relented. "You are right, Belle. And I have been wrong. But I must ask for your understanding when I tell you I cannot come here when the duke is at home. I do not care to see him, and if he discovers me here, he will think he is right about me after all. Please understand why I cannot do it!"

Lady Annabelle could see how upset Rosemary was, and she knew she could press her no further. For a moment she felt a deep regret that her dear friend and her beloved brother had had this falling-out, but since it was a *fait accompli*, she must make the best of it.

She pressed Rosemary's arm and made herself smile. "Of course I understand, my dear. But there are many occasions when Mark is from home. I will send you word when he will be away. For example, he is gone to Richmond with a riding party today. I do not expect him to be back much before late afternoon."

At these words, Rosemary removed her bonnet and settled down happily for a long visit. To her relief, Lady Annabelle did not question her further about that fateful evening. Instead, she asked her to fetch the folder of papers that she would find on her writing desk. When Rosemary had brought them to her, she squared them up, and then she held them out a little shyly.

"I wish you would read this, Rosemary," she said.

"Oh, not now, of course! Sometime when you are alone. It . . . it is a new venture of mine, and I would like your opinion of it."

Rosemary looked down at the thick sheaf of paper, wondering what on earth it could be. "Of course I would be glad to, Belle," she said. "But what is it? You are very secretive."

Lady Annabelle's grin transformed her face. "I have begun a contemporary novel, my dear," she explained. "I have wanted to try one for some time. You see, since I am only an observer of society, I have a great deal of time to watch the *ton*. I can hear their conversations, see how they behave, and speculate on their motives. From that it is an easy step to writing down my impressions. But I have no idea if my scribbling is any good. That is what I hope you will tell me, and, mind now, I expect honesty from a friend. Honesty, and reticence as well, for I would not care to have anyone know of this as yet. I have not even told my . . . mother."

Her little pause brought the duke back into the room, but Rosemary did not comment. "How very exciting, Belle," she said instead. "I shall read it this very day. I can hardly wait to begin!"

"It is, of course, a work of fiction," Lady Annabelle explained. "But I am sure you will recognize some of the characters, even though I have tried very hard to disguise them. Be sure to tell me if I did not succeed, or if I have been too blatant! I would not like to be sued."

"You mean to publish?" Rosemary asked, her eyes wide.

Lady Annabelle nodded. "If it is good enough, and anonymously, of course," she said. "We shall have to think up an exciting name for me, unless you think it might be better to call myself only 'An Unknown Lady.' But what do you think of Mrs. Elizabetha Parkinton? Or perhaps Lady Deirdre Dewhurst? Too flowery?"

Lady Margaret Malden heard the gay laughter coming from Lady Annabelle's rooms as she followed the butler up the stairs, and her lips tightened. So, the most unsuitable Miss Barton had resumed her calls, had she? she thought grimly. She herself had been delighted when days passed and nothing more had been seen of the girl in the duke's home, and she had made it a point to drop in on Lady Annabelle often. Unlike Rosemary's current plan, she always called when she knew the duke would be home, and thus able to notice—and applaud—her solicitude for his sister. Somehow, no one had mentioned his riding expedition to her today, or she would have come at another time.

She thought both girls looked a little self-conscious as she entered the room, and she wondered about the folder that Miss Barton was so quick to put out of sight. As she greeted Lady Annabelle and asked in her most dulcet tones if she had spent a good night, she continued to wonder. If the marvelous Lady Margaret had any fault at all, it was her insatiable curiosity, which bordered perilously on nosiness.

Lady Annabelle was forced to ask her new caller to join them, but conversation could not be said to flourish. Lady Margaret managed to treat Rosemary to a cold contempt without actually being rude. She spoke to Lady Annabelle as if they were alone, refusing to acknowledge Miss Barton's presence except when she was forced to do so. Since she was so determined to outwait the earlier caller, it was not long before Rosemary began her good-byes. As she did so, Lady Margaret rose as well.

"You seem distraught, a little overpowered this morning, Annabelle," she remarked as she collected her stole and reticule. "I shall not remain either, for it is obvious that your caller has tired you. I beg you to rest and compose yourself. You must remember that too much excitement is not good for someone in your fragile state."

Rosemary thought Belle looked mutinous at this sisterly concern, but she did not refute it directly as she wished them both a good day. Thus it was that the two antagonists went down the stairs and out into the square together.

Rosemary would have curtsied and left Lady Margaret then, except the lady detained her.

"A moment of your time, if I may, Miss Barton," she said, her cool, aristocratic face expressionless. As Rosemary paused, she went on, "I do not know if Lady Annabelle has spoken to you about her condition in any detail. Those of us who are closer to the family and have her concerns very much in our hearts know that she is even frailer than she appears. Your visits excite her, and such excitement is not good for her. I had hoped that your disturbing calls had ceased, but I see that is not to be the case. I must ask you, however, to at least limit your attendance on the lady, and the length of time you spend with her, if you are not prepared to give it up completely."

As Rosemary searched her mind for a reply, Lady Margaret continued smoothly, "And if, as I suspect, you think these calls will lead to an even greater intimacy with another member of the Halston family, I must disillusion you lest you waste your time. You see, Miss Barton, the duke and I are much closer to an understanding than we appear to be in public. Our engagement has not been announced as yet, that is true, but that is due to matters that are none of your concern." For the first time a faint color washed her cheeks, and she lowered her eyes. "I am sure you must take my meaning and thank me for my honesty; there is no need to say any more on this head."

Rosemary bit back a retort that as far as she was concerned, the duke might be as close to her as he cared, for she had no interest in the man herself. Instead, angered by the cold lecture given in such a superior way, she made herself say as calmly as she could, "But I do not understand your words, or your motives, m'lady. And until Belle or her mother ask me to moderate my visits, I shall go on as before. I see none of the signs of weakness in Lady Annabelle that you mentioned. Why, haven't you seen how easily she propels her chair about her rooms? And how delighted she is with any social intercourse and offer of friendship? No, I do not believe you have the right of it at all."

Lady Margaret's lips tightened, and a pair of red blotches burned high on her cheeks. Rosemary did not think the color improved her looks.

"Now I understand, Miss Barton," she said in a constricted voice. "You are playing a deep game, but you will not win that game. I shall see to it. You think your overabundant charms will win the duke from my side, but I tell you, he will never marry the like of *you*. Men of high position may dally with the Rosemary Bartons of the world, even make them their mistresses, but when they marry, they choose a lady born and bred."

Rosemary gasped, but without another word Lady Margaret stepped up into her carriage, where her maid awaited her. Rosemary watched her drive away, and then she began to walk in the opposite direction, back to Lady Emily's house. She was deeply hurt. She could not help but wonder why both the duke and the disagreeable Lady Margaret insisted on attributing all kinds of ulterior motives to what was, after all, only a desire for a close friendship with Lady Annabelle. As for Lady Margaret's remarks about her own future liaison with the duke, Rosemary had suspected it all the time. She felt a little pang when she thought of their engagement, and then she called herself sharply to order. Whom the Duke of Rutland married was none of her concern, and as for any dalliance with him, or any other man, she would never consent to it. Regardless of the lady's opinion of her, she knew she was just as much a lady—perhaps even more so—for she would never treat anyone as Lady Margaret had just treated her. Furthermore, she was welcome to her duke. Perhaps they even deserved each other, for they were both rude and arrogant. Indeed, she told herself as she climbed the steps of Number 14, the sooner they are engaged, the happier— and safer—I shall be. She was glad when Bert opened the door so promptly, for somehow this bracing thought was not as satisfactory as it should have been.

She smiled at the footman, and lingered to exchange a few words with him before she went up to her room. The folder of sheets that Lady Annabelle had given her was tucked under her arm, and she could hardly wait to settle down to an intent perusal. Imagine, writing a novel! She herself would never have dreamed of attempting it, but then, she did not have the least idea how to go about it in any case. No, she did not think she would ever tackle such an onerous job that would entail spending all those hours at your desk, writing and writing and writing. How confining it would be, how tiresome!

Before she could mount the stairs, Fallow shuffled in from the back of the hall to tell her his wife wanted a word with her. His request was hardly phrased politely, but Rosemary, used to his sullen ways by now, only nodded and went back to the housekeeper's rooms.

It was some time before she was able to get away. Mrs. Fallow had a number of complaints, each one of which had to be dealt with at some length, and with great patience. Willa had complained of overwork; what did Miss Barton have to say about that? And Mabel was not happy either. All those lamp chimneys to polish every morning! All that sweeping and dusting and scrubbing! Perhaps she would have to disturb Lady Em? Mrs. Fallow told her she was most reluctant to do so, looking indignant that her morning nap had been interrupted in such a cause. And Cook had taken exception to Miss Barton's orders for meals. She did not see why Miss should take this chore upon herself. Lady Em had never had any complaints about how often she was served boiled mutton or huntsman's soup. And as for herself and her husband, they were becoming exhausted by all the activity and confusion.

Rosemary dealt with the angry old woman as best she could, soothing and agreeing, until she was in a happier frame of mind. But she shook her head ruefully as she left the housekeeper's room at last. It was true her orders made more work, but the house showed her care now. Although it was still dark and airless and without cheer, it was at least cleaner, and the meals were better.

She settled down in a chair by the window in her room,

and it was not long before the unhappy domestic situation at Number 14 disappeared from her mind. To her surprise and delight, Lady Annabelle had written a gay, quick-paced story of the *beau monde*. It centered around the numerous adventures of a lovely young lady named Marielle Montclief, and it had, besides a dashing and handsome hero, a number of minor characters who lent sparkle and amusement to the whole.

It was late afternoon before Rosemary had finished the last page, and she found herself disappointed that that was all there was to read at the present time. She sighed and put her head back, a smile on her lips. Mr. D'Aubrey was Lord Alvanley, of course, and Lady Guenivere had to be Lady Jersey. Prince Roberto must be Beau Brummell, and she was sure the forbidding Mr. Augustus Reginald Stanwood was Peter Truesdale, Earl Norwell. The ballroom scene had had her laughing out loud in delight. She could hardly wait to see Belle and ask her what she planned to write in the next chapter.

She jumped up, wondering if there were enough time to run around the square right then. But as she looked out the window, she saw the Duke of Rutland walking up his front steps as his groom led his tired horse away to the stables in the mews. She dropped the curtain and shook her head. Now he had returned home, she would have to wait at least until the next morning.

As she went to her dresser, she realized how much she hoped the duke planned another excursion or a long shopping trip then. Perhaps he needed more snuff, some wine, or a new team? Or perhaps he had a fitting on a new coat from Stultz or Weston? She hoped that was the case, for she knew gentlemen spent as much time, if not even more so, than ladies did, having their clothes fitted.

Lady Emily made no mention of her visit to Lady Annabelle Halston when they met at dinner that evening. Rosemary was sure she knew of it somehow, by the very absence of any questions as to whether her orders had been obeyed.

When Bert removed the huntsman's soup with a platter of boiled mutton and limp vegetables, she was reminded of Mrs. Fallow's complaints that morning, and she made a little *moue* of distaste and tried not to sigh too noticeably. She foresaw an unpleasant morning in the kitchens before she would be free to see Belle, even if the duke did chance to go out.

II

When Lady Margaret Malden called at the duke's town house the following afternoon, she was surprised to be denied. Filbert was most apologetic when he told her Lady Annabelle was not receiving—so apologetic, in fact, that Lady Margaret's suspicions were aroused.

"I trust it is no sudden indisposition, Filbert," she said quietly, her expression full of her solicitude. She was not at all concerned for Lady Annabelle's health, but she was so rarely refused when she came to call, she found it disquieting.

"No, no, milady," the elderly butler assured her. "It is just that Lady Annabelle is . . . er, very busy today."

Lady Margaret studied his lined old face, but she could read nothing there. Filbert had been in service for too many years to betray any emotion whatsoever when dealing with his betters.

Lady Margaret took her time searching through her reticule for a moment. She was in hopes that the duke might have heard her voice and would come out of his library to speak to her. But he did not appear in the hall, and after asking if the duchess was at home, and being told that she was not, there was nothing further she could do but leave her card and depart.

As she stepped back into her carriage, she told herself that at least that bold Miss Barton would also be unable to gain admittance. And then she frowned, and her eyes went up to the windows of Lady Annabelle's rooms. For all she knew, Miss Barton was there already, and she had begged the softhearted Lady Annabelle to refuse other callers, to pay her back for her lecture of the previous day. It was not a thought that did anything to commend itself to the lady. As her carriage took her on to her shopping at the Burlington Arcade, she told herself that she must write a note to the duke as soon as she returned home, asking him to call on her. For some reason, she was feeling increasingly uneasy about this whole situation, although she could not put her finger on why that should be so.

Rosemary had indeed been closeted with Lady Annabelle, and for several hours, although it had been the lady herself who made arrangements for them to be undisturbed. Both girls had lost track of the time as they discussed Belle's novel and the chapters she planned to write to conclude it. Rosemary was delighted when Belle asked her opinion of several possible synopses, and they had been deep in a discussion of whether the forbidding Mr. Stanwood should kidnap Miss Montclief so the hero could ride to her rescue, or whether Lady Guenivere should meddle in the affair in order to stir up all kinds of trouble.

At last Belle leaned back in her chair and sighed. Her eyes were shining, and for once her delighted smile was not a bit wistful. "Thank you, Rosemary," she said. "I am so glad you like the story, and, more to the point, do not find it terribly amateurish. I could hardly sleep last night, wondering if you would approve it."

Rosemary assured her again that she did, and added that she hoped Belle would write the ending very quickly, for she could hardly wait to read it.

Lady Annabelle laughed. "I cannot tell you how much fun this has all been! And you know, when I am involved in my scribbling, I can forget my crippled legs as if they did not even exist. I identify so with Marielle and all her problems! Isn't that strange?"

Rosemary did not think that strange at all; she thought it sad. For if you had no romantic life of your own, what better thing to do than pretend you were a lovely heroine who could ride and dance and trip lightly up and down the stairs, or run through the gardens. She was sorry that it must be so, however. Belle was so lovely, so kind and sweet. It did not seem at all fair that she could enjoy herself only vicariously.

She chanced to glance at the clock on the mantel as it struck three, and she gasped. "I had no idea it was so late, Belle," she said, rising quickly. Remembering Lady Margaret's lecture of the previous day, she added, "I hope I have not tired you, staying all this while."

Belle shook her head. "Indeed you have not. I have enjoyed myself immensely. Do say you will come soon again!"

As Rosemary hesitated, it seemed to both girls that the duke had entered the room and was standing between them. "Have you . . . have you told your brother of the novel, Belle?" she asked in some curiosity.

"No," Lady Annabelle said slowly as she straightened the pages on the desk before her, her eyes lowered. "I wanted your opinion on whether my work had any merit, first. But of course I must tell Mark, certainly before I show it to any publisher. You see, I would do nothing to embarrass him. He is such a proud man! If he feels the book would cause gossip, of course I shall never submit it."

Rosemary came to her chair to kneel beside her and take up her hand. "But that is most unfair, Belle!" she exclaimed. "Why, it would be terrible if you never published it, after all your work."

Lady Annabelle reached up to kiss her cheek. "Thank you, my dear," she said. "Since you feel so fervently, then if Mark does object, you would be willing to take it to a publisher for me, and pretend to be the author?" she asked.

"Me?" Rosemary asked, her blue eyes wide. "But I cannot pen more than a simple letter to my family! No one would ever believe I wrote it. Furthermore, I do not know society as you do, Belle. It would never be believed."

Lady Annabelle laughed at her. "But you would be anonymous, just as I planned to be." Seeing her friend still looked upset, she said lightly, "But I am teasing you, and we are borrowing trouble. There is no need to make any such plans until I have spoken to Mark. And he may very well applaud my efforts, and be proud of me, you know. By the way, he goes to our estate in Suffolk soon for a few days. I shall hope to see you more often then."

Rosemary agreed a little absently. She knew the duke was expected home at any time, for Belle had told her he was to take her driving that afternoon, and she wanted to be across the square and behind Lady Emily's doors before he arrived. Accordingly, her good-byes were hurried, and she fairly flew down the stairs.

She left a pensive Lady Annabelle behind her, one who wheeled her chair to the window so she could watch her friend make her way quickly home across the square. Lady Annabelle sighed. She still had no idea what had occurred between her friend and her brother the night of the dance, for neither one would discuss it, but she wished with all her heart that it had not caused such a rift. It hurt her to think that her dear brother and her dearest friend could not even like each other, when she loved them both so much.

Rosemary was going driving herself that afternoon. Mr. Edson had been most insistent, and finally she had been forced to agree, to stem the calls and notes that came with such distressing regularity. She was glad that it was a little cool today, however, for now she could wear her light pelisse without occasioning comment on her attire. The pelisse hid her figure from Mr. Edson's blue eyes and the intent, hot perusal she had come to expect from him.

She was ready when he came at four. Although she did not appear to have eyes for anyone but her companion, she did manage a quick inspection of the square, and she was delighted that there was no sign of the duke's landau, nor even the briefest glimpse of his tall, arrogant person.

Mr. Edson pressed her hand as he helped her to her seat, and Rosemary forgot the duke in her concern for present danger. She made her smile cool as she withdrew her hand from his.

"How very lovely you look, *Cousin* Rosemary," he

said as he took his seat and picked up the reins. His tiger bowed and stepped back, and Rosemary stiffened. It was evident that Mr. Edson had decided to dispense with his services this afternoon, and it made her very uneasy. Nor could she like the knowing grin the young tiger gave her as the phaeton drove away.

Before Mr. Edson could continue his compliments, she said, "You must instruct me, sir. Is it correct for us to drive without a groom in attendance? I am sure I have never heard of the custom."

Mr. Edson was too busy controlling his fresh team as they turned into Curzon Street and headed for the park, to take his eyes from the road. Rosemary thought that he looked more than a little pleased with himself, and she edged away from him on the seat.

As the team settled down, he laughed and replied at last, "But in an open carriage, where's the harm, dear cuz, especially when we are, to some extent, related?"

Rosemary did not care for his new name for her, and she was sure they could not possibly be kin, but she decided to ignore it.

"Besides, don't you want to be dashing?" Mr. Edson went on, avoiding an old-fashioned lozenge coach with ease. "I was sure that all young females wanted to be thought dashing," he added, his voice teasing.

"This one does not," Rosemary retorted a little bitterly, remembering the Duke of Rutland's assessment of her character.

Mr. Edson laughed. "You, my dear Rosemary, would be dashing, no matter what you do," he said, glancing sideways for a moment to admire her lovely profile. "Even incarcerated in a nunnery, you must still attract admiration and the most fervent attention."

"Mr. Edson, I must beg you to refrain from all these unseemly compliments," Rosemary told him earnestly. "They do not please me, and I know it is not at all the thing for you to be making them so blatantly. I do not think other ladies are subjected to such remarks."

"Of course they are not," he agreed cheerfully as they

entered the Curzon Gate. "But that is only because they cannot hold a candle to you. They are neither so beautiful nor so . . . so very desirable."

Rosemary felt his thigh pressing against hers, and she moved her legs further away.

"If you are not careful, you will tumble into the road, my dear cuz," he said, laughing down at her as the team settled into an obedient trot.

Rosemary took a deep breath. "And if you were not crowding me so much, there would be no danger of it!" she retorted. "I did not realize that you were such a large, bulky man."

Ronald Edson nodded, as if to acknowledge the hit, and then, to Rosemary's relief, he moved away to give her more room.

"How pretty the park looks today, does it not?" she asked, determined to change the subject. "It always reminds me of home, for once you are within the gates, you can almost pretend that you are not in London at all."

To her relief, Mr. Edson followed her lead, and there was no repetition of his earlier, objectionable remarks. She did not realize that he was afraid that such behavior would make her unwilling to spend any more time in his company, and he was on his guard to prevent that. Ronald Edson wanted Rosemary Barton more than he had ever wanted a woman before, and he was determined to get her, any way he could. If she insisted on a gentle courtship, he would oblige her. He could wait for her, for however long it took. Now he set himself to talking of any number of innocuous subjects, to allay her fears.

Knowing the Halstons' plans as she did, Rosemary was not at all surprised when she saw the Duke of Rutland's landau coming toward them. She told herself she was glad that the duke and Belle were in such deep conversation that neither of them noticed her beside the eager Mr. Edson. She could imagine the duke's reaction if he had seen them, unattended by any servant, his raised brows and that little curl of his lip that showed you so clearly his scorn. She knew he would not be at all surprised, for it would be just what he would expect of her.

Mr. Edson must have seen how she stiffened and turned her head away, for he said, "You are acquainted with the Halston family, cuz? But of course you are! I myself saw you sitting beside Lady Annabelle at the Kay dance, did I not? And I could not help but notice that you danced with the duke twice. My, you are traveling in exalted circles, are you not?"

"I am very fond of Lady Annabelle," Rosemary admitted, her soft lips tightening.

"Strange that you do not mention the lady's brother," her escort remarked. His blue eyes were narrowed now, but Rosemary did not notice. "I do so hope you are not *épris* there, cuz. He is not for you, and I would not like to have you hurt."

"You need not worry on that account, sir. I dislike the duke," Rosemary said stiffly.

Mr. Edson's brows rose. "Indeed? And yet you gave him those two dances, and during one of them, you allowed him to take you from the drawing room. It was greatly remarked," he added as she turned to stare at him.

"I cannot help what people say," Rosemary replied at last. "From what I have seen of the *ton*, they delight in gossip above all else. And where there is nothing to talk about, they have no qualms about making up a story to satisfy their need to denigrate others."

"That is only human nature, Rosemary," her companion said earnestly. "But I do beg you to watch what you are about there. The duke is arrogant, so arrogant, in fact, that I would not put it past him to make you an offer. And with your less-than-perfect antecedents, it would not be an offer that had anything to do with wedding bells."

Rosemary gasped. "Why do you say that, sir?" she asked, indignant now. "It is to insult me! I have told you I have no interest in the duke."

"I am delighted to hear you say so," Ronald Edson replied, nodding to her a little. "I tell you because I feel I stand in lieu of your aunt and uncle while you are in town, my dear. Lady Emily will not assist you; be assured you may have my counsel at any time."

Rosemary made herself thank him with as much courtesy as she could muster. Inwardly she was thinking it would be just like asking the devil to forgive her her sins, but she did not tell Mr. Edson that. Instead, she changed the subject yet again, asking him if he had seen the new play at the Drury Lane Theater.

Edson allowed her the diversion, and when the two carriages passed each other again a short time later, he made no further mention of the Halstons. But he saw Lady Annabelle raise her hand a little and then put it back in her lap and look away, and he wondered at her actions. It almost looked as if the lady did not care to acknowledge Miss Barton while she was with her brother. He did not understand it, and he told himself he must be sure to observe closely both the Halstons and the girl at his side at any future parties they all attended.

As they started back to Berkeley Square, he inquired for Lady Agatha. When he learned that she and her husband were to sail at week's end, his fair brows drew together in a frown.

"How unfortunate for you, cuz," he said. "I know you have depended on her escort to many parties. Does this mean you will be forced to give up your festive evenings?"

Rosemary shook her head. "Not entirely. Lady Agatha has been so good, introducing me to so many people, and explaining my plight, that I find several ladies have offered to serve as my chaperon anytime I care for it. For example, Mrs. Kay has kindly promised to take me up with her for the Throckmorton ball."

"At her son's instigation?" Mr. Edson asked, smiling down at her. "He is mad for you, as you must know, the infatuated young puppy!"

Rosemary shrugged as they turned into the square. "I do not know if you are right about that, sir," she said. "I am only grateful to the Kays for their concern. You, of all people, know what my life would be like, left alone with Lady Emily, if they did not help me."

As Mr. Edson halted his team, Rosemary was delighted to see the abandoned tiger lounging against the wrought-iron palings of Number 14. As he ran to the horses' heads, Mr. Edson leaned toward her and said softly, "How I wish it were possible to offer my escort instead. But perhaps there is a way I may do so . . ."

His face was close to hers now, those hot blue eyes devouring her face. Rosemary made herself remain very straight and still. "I do not think there is any way for a single gentleman who is not directly related to her to escort a young lady without causing even more gossip and ruining her reputation," she tried to say lightly as she turned away to step down.

"Wait, I will come around," he said, and she took a deep breath as soon as he left the carriage. When he reached up and lifted her down, without waiting for her permission, Rosemary could feel his hands tightening on her waist, and she stepped away from him as quickly as she could.

"Thank you for the delightful drive, Mr. Edson," she said as she curtsied.

"It would please me so much if you would call me 'cousin,' or better yet, Ronald," he told her, moving closer again.

Rosemary went up the steps to sound the knocker before she replied. "But you are not my cousin," she told him, feeling a bit safer now she was some little distance away from him.

His blue eyes shone. "You will never know how grateful I am that I really am not," he assured her. "The warmer relationship that I desire has nothing to do with kinship."

Rosemary was glad that the door was opened then by the surly Fallow, and she was quick to enter the house, leaving the eager Mr. Edson on the doorstep. As she went upstairs, she told herself she must take the greatest care where he was concerned. His offer of advice and counsel seemed ludicrous next to the barely veiled ardor to which he treated her. She knew very well what Mr. Edson wanted, and it was not at all to stand *in loco parentis* to her, no, indeed. Once again she blessed Lady Agatha for all her timely warnings.

The Duke of Rutland had seen Miss Barton and her escort in the park, but when Belle did not mention her friend, he refrained from doing so as well. He knew Edson vaguely, and he was not impressed with the man. Although of fairly good birth, he hung about the fringes of society, and he was not above boasting of the fortune that would someday be his when his reclusive aunt went to her last reward. The duke found himself hoping that Miss Barton would not be taken in by his charm, for there was no denying that he was a handsome man, well-built, and personable when he chose to be so. The duke was sure he was at his most impressive when in Miss Barton's company.

He frowned a little then, remembering the unpleasant half-hour he had spent discussing Miss Barton earlier that same afternoon when he had visited Lady Margaret at her invitation. He could not fault the lady for her concern for his sister—indeed, he had told her he admired her greatly for it—but he had felt uneasy as he did so. And when she had suggested perhaps there was something he could do to stop Miss Barton's visits, he had refused.

"But my dear duke, surely you can see how upsetting such a friendship is to Lady Annabelle?" she had asked in her gentle, well-modulated voice. "It tires her considerably, and she is not strong. I myself on one occasion practically had to tell the girl that she was staying too long, for she did not notice it herself." She sighed and lowered her eyes to smooth her gown. "She is heedless, of course, and, if I may dare to say it . . . ?"

She looked up anxiously, and waited for the duke's nod, before she continued, "I very much fear she has an ulterior motive. I cannot believe that she is so altruistic, or so fond of Lady Annabelle, that that is the sole reason for her caressing ways. Why, what could they possibly have in common, a cripple and a . . . a . . .? But I cannot say the word. Forgive me."

The duke stared at her, his expression enigmatic. He saw that a delicate color had come into her cheeks, and how she turned her head away modestly, as if afraid she had said too much.

"I myself have had the same thought, m'lady," he admitted when he saw she could not go on. "But fore-warned is forearmed, you know. Besides, Belle tells me how good Miss Barton is to her, and how very much she enjoys her visits. She has little enough to amuse her; I would not cut this tie. They are much of an age, and there was an instant rapport between them, even at first meeting."

"I have no doubt of *that*," Lady Margaret said, sounding a little ruffled now. "Surely Miss Barton would do her utmost to encourage such a rapport. And Lady Annabelle is such an innocent! She does not see the girl's true colors, as we do.

"And there is something about that young woman, something that does not seem truly 'ladylike,' is there not? In spite of all her careful pretensions to the title, she is so . . . so *obvious*."

Lady Margaret made a little *moue* of distaste as the duke tried not to picture Miss Barton's lovely face and shapely form. The lady sitting across from him in her mama's drawing room, with the door open so the proprieties could be observed, would never be called "obvious." Her charms were so refined, and so well concealed, that no one would ever be tempted to even a light flirtation with her. He forced his mind from these unworthy thoughts as she went on, "I do not believe Miss Barton's influence over your sister to be at all a good thing. Since they have become acquainted, Lady Annabelle has changed out of all recognition. She has become secretive and pert. Many times when I have called to see her, to relieve the tedium of her days, I have been denied admittance to her rooms. Surely this is cause for alarm, and must be a direct result of Miss Barton's machinations. I fear she has been using her un-healthy influence to try to separate Lady Annabelle and me. She must know from my deep concern for your crippled little sister that I see through her and perceive her motives. Because I do, she is determined to keep us apart. But forgive me. I did not mean to presume on our . . . friendship and cause you any distress. I only felt it my duty to point out these things of which, perhaps, you were not aware."

She paused and sighed a little. "If only your dear mother were a little more attentive, she could watch over Lady Annabelle better. My efforts are but a poor substitute, compared to a mother's or even a sister's concern."

As she raised her handkerchief to her lips, the duke came to his feet. Lady Margaret was going too fast, and for some reason, he was most reluctant to have his hand forced.

"I shall take my leave of you now, m'lady," he said easily as he came to help her from her seat. "I have remained too long, and I have an appointment in the City. But know that I am grateful for your solicitude and all your warnings."

Lady Margaret waved a thin, disparaging hand, and he made himself pick it up and kiss it. As he stood back and bowed, he added, "I know how painful it was for you to have to speak to me on a subject so distasteful to a lady of your quality. I shall not forget your kindness."

Lady Margaret assured him that no modesty of hers would ever stop her from coming to the assistance of her friends, and on this self-congratulatory note they parted.

Now, as he sat beside his sister in the landau, he remembered the things Lady Margaret had said, and he wondered again why hearing his own misgivings about Miss Barton repeated in that gentle voice had disturbed him so much. Why, it was only what he believed himself; he and Lady Margaret were in perfect accord, as always. Wondering why this pleasant state of affairs seemed so unsatisfactory, he made himself study his sister. He had to admit that he could see no sign of any change in her that was not for the better. Her eyes sparkled again, and she smiled and laughed often, things he had noticed had been in abeyance when Miss Barton had ceased to call. He had castigated himself then for being the cause of their estrangement, and he had felt only relief when the young lady began to come across the square again. Belle had told him of it that first evening at dinner, and her delight had been obvious. So now, in spite of Lady Margaret's warnings, he would do nothing more, for his sister's sake. But he promised himself that if Miss Barton hurt Belle, he would find a way to make her pay for it.

He had wondered, in the days that followed their reunion, why he never saw the girl. Surely if she were such a frequent caller, it was unusual that they had not encountered each other.

One evening, being so puzzled by it, he had asked Belle why it should be so. To his surprise, she had frowned as she said, "Rosemary will come only when you are not here, Mark. She will not tell me, any more than you would, what passed between you that evening you were testing her, but whatever it was, it has given her a sincere dislike of you. I am so sorry."

The duke had stiffened, his eyes turning an icy gray. *But how dare she snub me?* he wondered, his anger rising. And then he remembered that on the only occasion that he had seen her since that evening, she had turned away, refusing to acknowledge him. Belle had not attended that evening reception, so she had not seen it; now he recalled how furious he had been.

"Mark? What is it, my dear?" Lady Annabelle was saying now, reaching out to touch his hand.

When he saw her concerned face, he made himself smile. "I have no desire to see Miss Barton either, Belle. You might reassure her on that head. And she is not to worry that anything more than a few polite words will be exchanged if we should chance to meet on the stairs or in the hall. I am a gentleman, after all."

He fell silent then, remembering that he had said those same words to Rosemary Barton when he opened the door of the Kays' small back salon for her. And he remembered as well that once he had her inside with the door closed to give them the privacy he needed, he had not behaved as a gentleman.

His memories of the kiss he had forced on her returned, as vivid as if he had just raised his mouth from hers. How innocent and yet how ardent she had been! How wonderfully warm and shapely she had felt when clasped in his arms!

It was several more moments before Lady Annabelle was able to regain his attention.

12

The following morning, Mr. Ronald Edson was surprised to receive a most unusual note from Lady Emily Cranston, asking him to call on her that very afternoon, at three. As he sat over the remains of his breakfast in his rooms on Jermyn Street, he pondered her summons. He could not recall her ever asking him to come and see her before, and he wondered what unusual event had prompted this command. And as he rose from the table, he had no doubt it was a command. The footman had not even bothered to wait for a reply. Good old Aunt Em knew very well why he was so attentive to her, and why he would be sure to obey any summons of hers, no matter how many other appointments he had to cancel. She had a great fortune, and he was her only close living relative. True, there was her cousin, Mary Fleming, but she was far away in the country, and they never saw each other, or even corresponded. No, the fortune was his for the taking, and he most certainly intended to take it, just as soon as he could. Lady Emily was in her late sixties now; surely it would not be much longer before some opportune heart spell or fatal disease carried her off. He could wait.

Mr. Edson had inherited a tidy fortune of his own, but he had never considered it adequate for a gentleman of his scope. Besides his aunt's money, he also coveted the large mansion in Berkeley Square, the two extensive properties in the country, and her fortune in jewels. He had spent many an enjoyable hour musing over his rosy future.

When he arrived in Berkeley Square, prompt to the minute, he was admitted by Fallow, after a long wait on the doorstep. It was the footman's afternoon off, and the old butler was feeling aggrieved. He mumbled all the way up the stairs, and when Mr. Edson asked pleasantly if Miss Barton were at home, he returned a surly negative.

As Fallow opened the drawing-room doors, Ronald Edson brushed by him impatiently. It was very dim in the big room, and it took his eyes a moment to adjust to it after the bright sunlight outside. And then he saw his aunt, bent over her telescope at the far window, attended by the faithful Prinny.

As he watched, she straightened up and came toward him. She was dressed in her usual black, as thin as any scarecrow. The dog padded at her side.

"Behold me, dear auntie, at your service!" Edson said, bowing and giving her his most charming smile.

"Sit down," she ordered as she took a seat herself, and indicated the chair opposite. "No doubt you were surprised by my summons, Ronald? I can assure you it is not from any desire for your company, so do not take it as a sign I want you hanging about me from now on. I understand from Fallow that ever since Rosemary Barton has come, you are forever sounding the knocker."

"That should not surprise you, aunt," he said easily as he took his seat. "Miss Barton is a beauty, and I have ever been a connoisseur of beauty."

"So she is. Your interest in her does not surprise me in the least," Lady Emily agreed.

The huge mastiff, who was now sprawled at her feet, never took his dark eyes from her guest's face. The two had called truce long ago, but even so, Edson never turned his back on the dog. He was deciding that his first order when he came into his inheritance would be to have the animal shot, if he should outlive his mistress, when that mistress went on.

"I have summoned you here on a matter of business. Business that includes Rosemary Barton. But first, I wish to inquire how strong your interest in the girl really is."

Her nephew's fair brows soared. "It is fair to say it is very strong indeed, and becoming more so every day. Can it be that you do not approve, dear ma'am?"

He made his voice sound a little worried, but he was startled when she snorted in contempt and said, "And why should I care about her, or what happens to her? She is only a means to an end for me, and that is all she has ever been. Of course, I did dislike her coming here to live, at first, but I soon came to see how very opportune her visit has been."

She smiled a grim little smile that had nothing of amusement in it, and added, "Oh, yes, so very opportune."

Her guest crossed his well-breeched legs, feeling a little uneasy, although he did not know why. Perhaps it was because Lady Emily was unusually verbose this afternoon, or perhaps it was her puzzling words. She noticed his movement, and she leaned forward to say, "I will have some important things for you to do for me, nephew, and before much longer, too."

" Why, anything at all," he replied, eyeing the stern, resolute face under the white hair. "You have only to command me, ma'am. I do assure you I am at your service."

"I have no doubt of *that*!" she retorted. "I am well aware of your motives, sir. But I'll see you don't lose by it, Ronald, my word on it. No, neither one of us shall lose!"

Suddenly she threw back her head and gave a harsh, wild laugh. Her nephew stared at her in amazement, and not a little fear. He could not remember ever hearing her laugh before. She sounded almost mad, and he felt a shiver of apprehension.

At last the crazed sound died away, and she said, "Since you tell me you have such a great interest in Rosemary Barton, *she* shall be your reward for helping me. Your immediate reward, I should say. And if all goes as I plan, you may have her sooner than you think."

"But . . . but she does not care for me as yet, aunt," he told the tall old lady who sat peering at him.

She looked amazed. "What does that have to say to anything?" she asked him. "She will be in no position to refuse you. And no doubt she will soon grow accustomed to you, and your lovemaking. You can marry her or not; I don't care which."

She saw how shocked he looked, and she said sharply, "Here now, sir, you do wish to humor me in this matter, do you not? And you do want her, don't you?"

She held his eyes until he lowered them and nodded in submission, and then one hand came up to fondle the cloisonné locket she wore as usual at her throat. It was a familiar gesture that Edson had seen many times before, and he placed no special significance on it for he was leaning forward now to listen carefully to her words.

"Good!" his aunt said. "How very satisfying it will be for me, as well as for you Ronald."

She reached down to pat her dog. "Do you know the day of the Williamses' departure?" she asked, her voice milder now.

Confused by the abrupt change of subject, it was a moment before Edson told her their ship sailed at the end of the week.

"I see," she mused, nodding a little before she waved her hand toward the door. "Go away now. I shall send for you again when I am sure the time is right. There may be some slight delay, but I really do not expect it. Rosemary is such a beautiful girl, is she not? I am sure there is not a gentleman in London who has not remarked it."

He agreed, and then he bowed and went away as ordered. He did not think his aunt even heard his reassurances that he was hers to command, or his pleasant good-byes, for she seemed lost in some pleasant dream of her own.

After the door of the drawing room closed behind him, Lady Emily got up and went back to her telescope, to bend and peer through the lens. Her lips twisted in a grimace, and she whispered to herself, "'Ware hurry! Be very sure before you act, Emily, for there must be no mistakes to mar this wonderful plan of yours, nor any slips in its execution. All must be in tune, and thought out most carefully. It will be a masterpiece of precision, I vow!''

Across the square, the Duke of Rutland was taking tea with his sister in her rooms, and learning about her novel for the first time. Belle watched him carefully as she told him what she had been doing, but she could read nothing in his expressionless face. At last, she wheeled her chair to the desk to fetch her manuscript and take it to him.

"Here it is, Mark," she said a little nervously. "Please read it and tell me if you think it has any merit, Rosemary says it is very good . . ."

"Miss Barton?" he asked, his voice stern. "Did she put you up to this, Belle?"

His sister looked confused. "Of course she did not! I have been writing for some time now, why, weeks and weeks before I even met Rosemary. Whatever can you mean?"

The duke saw truth in her big green eyes, and he stared down at the sheaf of papers before him reluctantly. "You do understand that writing novels is not at all the thing for a Halston, don't you, Belle?" he asked.

"You are not to worry about that, Mark," she told him. "Of course I intend to publish anonymously."

The duke's lips twisted in a little grimace. "As if that would be any protection, my dear. How very young you are, to be sure! These things have a way of leaking out, no matter how many precautions you take. Don't you remember Caro Lamb and her book? And, more important, the scandal it made?"

His sister looked mutinous. "But I am not writing about my own notorious love affair, as you well know, Mark," she said. "My novel is merely invention, although I will admit I have used some people in society as models. They are well disguised, however, and there is nothing vicious about the story. And, Mark, I have enjoyed writing it so very much! Please, please, try to read it without prejudice, pretending you do not know the author!"

The duke was not able to resist her pleading eyes, and

he smiled as he rose and came to drop a kiss on her curls. "Very well, my little scribbler," he said. "I promise to read it at once, and you shall have my most careful critique. But I still do not think publishing is wise. Why, I know Father would have been horrified at the very idea. And since I am duke now, I suppose I am horrified too."

"Father was very old-fashioned in many ways, Mark," his sister told him earnestly. "And what happiness did it bring him? I can remember how formal and solemn he was, how seldom he laughed or seemed to enjoy his life. Well, I cannot enjoy life as an ordinary woman, so why should I not amuse myself as best I can? Writing makes me happy and content. I do not think either one of us should pattern ourselves on Father, nor take to heart all his strictures on behavior. And I must tell you, Mama thinks I have written a grand book! She actually missed a card party, she was so anxious to finish as much as I have written."

The duke chuckled a little, blowing her a kiss as he left the room. He was a little surprised at Belle's insight into their father's character. He had thought her too young to notice such deep matters.

Late that same evening, when he finished the last page of her manuscript, he was further surprised. She had another chapter or two to write in conclusion, but he thought the book excellent. Her characterizations were so well drawn, it was obvious that she had not wasted her time when out in company. She had seen all the strengths and weaknesses that men and women are prone to, and she had employed them well. There was greed here, and treachery and pettiness, but there was also laughter and love and kindness. The only fault he could find was that the plot was a little farfetched, but he knew that would not matter to the lady readers of the day. Some novels he had read were much more ridiculous, and they had attained great popularity.

He put the manuscript on his desk and went to pour himself a snifter of brandy. He was frowning now, for he still could not like the idea of his sister publishing a book.

If anyone in the *ton* found out she had penned it, she would be ridiculed and held up to scorn. And if Earl Norwell or Lady Jersey saw that they had been used, she might even be ostracized, if not sued, and he himself as well, for permitting it. And he was sure the *ton* would find out. His mother, who said whatever came into her head, would let it slip in a matter of days, even if he and Belle were circumspect.

And then, as he sipped his brandy, a thought occurred to him, and he turned over the pages, searching for Belle's description of a Lady Wanda Wardly. He read it again, but this time he did not chuckle as he had earlier. Lady Wanda, as quiet and well-bred as she was boring, was Lady Margaret Malden to the life. He had not noticed it before, because she was such a minor character, and so uninteresting. She entered the novel, mouthed a few pious platitudes, stirred up a minor storm by her inquisitiveness, and departed the scene. His lips tightened. No, Belle could . never publish this book, he decided, and that was final.

He fully intended to speak to her about the manuscript the first thing in the morning, until he remembered a previous appointment. His sister was still asleep when he left the house, but he promised himself he would see her as soon as he returned.

It was shortly after eleven when he came back to Berkeley Square. As he handed his hat, gloves, and clouded cane to his butler, he asked, "Has Lady Annabelle been dressed, Filbert? There is something I wish to discuss with her."

The butler bowed. "She has, your Grace. Miss Barton is with her at the moment."

The duke frowned before he went into his library to fetch Belle's book. He decided suddenly that he would go up to her now, for his avoiding Miss Barton just as assiduously as she avoided him was becoming ridiculous. And he would be polite and distant, he told himself, so the girl would see he meant her no harm, nor any further discourtesy. Since she was becoming such an intimate of the house, running in and out almost every day, they must meet sometime. He hesitated at Belle's door in spite of his good intentions, and he could hear his sister's young soprano clearly.

"But, my dear Rosemary, why do you say that about lovemaking?" she asked, sounding a little impatient. Mark Halston put his head close to the door panels.

"Because I don't think Marielle would like it at all, Belle," Miss Barton replied.

"Not like being in the hero's arms, and passionately kissed?" Belle asked. "Why ever wouldn't she?"

There was a little pause, and the duke found he was holding his breath.

"Because it is not at all the correct thing," Miss Barton explained at last. "And up to this point, he has not told her of his love, not in so many words. And now he just grabs her and subjects her to an embrace. No, no, Belle. Any girl would shrink from such an intimacy."

"Even if she loved him?" Belle persisted. "Wouldn't you like it, Rosemary?"

There was another, longer silence before Miss Barton spoke again. The duke had to put his ear to the door to hear her soft, hesitant reply. "I can't tell you how I would feel. If Marielle loved him, she would probably kiss him back. But if she were not sure, if it were only because it was her first real kiss, and she was attracted to him, she would still feel awful after it was over. Remember, Belle, she has been brought up as a proper young lady. She would know that such behavior might be misinterpreted by him, and she would be ashamed of herself."

The duke frowned as he heard his sister say, "I see. So I must either have Geoffrey declare himself before he embraces her, or do so immediately afterward. I rather like him telling her after the kiss, though, Rosemary. It adds to the suspense."

"And then Marielle will fall willingly into his arms, all breathless agreement?" Miss Barton asked.

Belle chuckled. "Of course! And live happily ever after!"

"The end!" her visitor said triumphantly, and they both broke into gay laughter.

Mark Halston went away quietly to his own rooms.
Miss Barton was a constant surprise to him. He put aside
her artless comments on Belle's hero's behavior, for he did
not want to think about that too closely. He was sure her
remarks had been prompted by his own actions the night of
the Kay dance, and her reaction to them. But he realized
now that all his dire predictions of why she had taken his
sister up were false. Far from trying to attach him via a
friendship with Belle, she avoided him like the plague.
And yet, she was so kind to Belle, so good! Even his
mother had remarked it, saying she had never met a young
lady she liked more.

They had been waiting for Belle to be carried down to
dinner the evening she mentioned Miss Barton, and he had
been astounded by her remarks.

"And besides *that*, dear Mark, she is such a *funny* little
thing," Lady Catherine had told him. "One moment, she
is all *playful* and *sparkling*, and *gay*, and the next, so
demure and *quiet*. She is such a bundle of *delightful*
contradictions, and so graceful and *lovely*. I have seen how
much she *cares* for Belle, how much she loves her. But
what pleases me the *most* about the young lady is that she
never *reminds* Belle of her crippled condition. She treats
her as an *equal*. Such consideration is *very rare* in one so
young."

Mark Halston remembered his mother's comments now,
and he pondered them.

When Miss Barton took her leave of his sister, he made
it a point to come out of his room and greet her. The
happy smile she wore faded at once, and she was careful
to lower her eyes as she curtsied.

"Good morning, Miss Barton," he said, his voice
noncommittal.

"Your Grace," she replied, as demure as anyone could
wish.

"May I say how delighted I am that you have resumed
your visits to my sister, Miss Barton?" he said next,
walking beside her to the top of the stairs. Rosemary
busied herself pulling on her gloves, and she made no

reply. "I hope you will call often. You may be sure you will always be treated with courtesy here."

"Thank you," Rosemary said, a bewildered expression on her face.

He stared down at her, drinking in those perfect features and glowing skin, that well-remembered mouth. "I wish you good-day, Miss Barton," he said at last, and then he turned and went back to his sister's rooms. A very puzzled Rosemary went down the stairs and out the door Filbert was holding for her, to make her way across the square.

Lady Annabelle was not at all pleased when he told her that although her book was excellent, he could not permit it to be published. "It is much too blatant, Belle," he said. "I recognized several of the *beau monde*, and if I did, you may be sure others will, as well."

She opened her mouth to protest, but he raised his hand and continued, "Calling yourself an anonymous lady will not suffice. Mama will let the cat out of the bag the first time someone mentions the novel to her, and you know it. I am very sorry, for I know how much it means to you, but I cannot permit it."

"But what if I were to change the characters, Mark?" Belle asked. "I could disguise them further, I know I could!"

"Including Lady Wanda Wardly, Belle?" he asked grimly. Wild rose flushed his sister's cheeks.

"So, you read Lady Margaret correctly, did you, Mark?" she asked with her wistful little smile. "But Lady Wanda could be any one of a number of society debutantes. She is in no way unique."

"I do not intend to discuss it, Belle, for I am adamant on this point," he told her. He leaned over her wheelchair to search deeply in her eyes. "I must have your promise that you will not have it delivered to any publisher. You see, I know it would be snapped up in a moment, it is so good—wise, and witty, and amusing."

"Do you really think so, Mark?" Belle asked eagerly as she grasped his hand.

"Yes, I do, but I do not intend to shower you with any

more compliments. Come now, Belle! Your promise on it!''

The two stared at each other for a long moment, and then Lady Annabelle sighed. "Very well, I promise, dear Mark. I would never do anything to embarrass you, you know.''

Surprised she had not fought harder for this new project that was so important to her, the duke rose.

"I shall finish this book, of course, but I shall consider it an exercise," Lady Annabelle continued. "And the next one I write shall have nothing to do with the *ton*, and then you will not be able to object!''

The duke threw up his hands in defeat, and she laughed at him. As he left the room, she called after him, "Do be a dear brother and procure me a great deal more paper, and a new supply of quills and ink, will you, Mark? I rather think I shall attempt a historical fantasy next. Set perhaps in Bohemia or a Turkish harem.''

"You, Belle, are becoming a saucy baggage!" he told her, and she nodded in complete agreement until he shut the door behind him.

13

The evening of the Williamses' farewell party, Lady Agatha sent the carriage for Rosemary, and Lord Williams himself was waiting for her in the lobby of Grillon's Hotel to escort her to the private dining room that had been engaged.

Rosemary was glad to see that the group of guests was small, for she was not feeling at all festive on losing her first London friend, one, moreover, who had been so kind and helpful to her.

For Lady Agatha's sake, however, she made herself smile as she conversed with the other guests, most of whom were connected in some way with the diplomatic world. Even in all her regret, she began to enjoy herself, listening to all the wonderful stories about strange places she would probably never have the chance to see.

After dinner was over, Lady Agatha took her apart to a small salon where they could be private for a few moments.

"We do not have much time, Rosemary," she said, as the two settled down on a sofa together. "The party will break up soon, for the carriage is called very early."

Rosemary's blue eyes filled with tears. "I shall miss you so much, m'lady," she mourned.

Lady Agatha gave her her own handkerchief, and her voice was not quite steady as she said, "And I shall miss you, my dear girl. I expect you to write to me, and tell me everything you are doing, for in some way, I feel you are the dear daughter I never had. Here now, wipe your eyes!

You must not be sad. You have a wonderful future ahead, I am sure of it.''

Rosemary did as she was bidden. "I promise to write often, ma'am," she said. "And I shall look for your letters so eagerly. Do be sure to tell me all about the jungles and the natives in that hot country. It is so far away!''

Lady Agatha grasped her hands. "I shall, Rosemary, but listen to me now," she said. As the girl nodded, she went on, "You remember the things I have told you about men? Remember them still, for now you will have to be responsible for yourself.''

She rose then and went to a small cabinet set against the wall. She opened a drawer and took out a small velvet box that she handed to her young friend.

"Open it, my dear," she said with a smile. "It is a little keepsake, to remember me by.''

Rosemary lifted the lid to disclose a pearl-and-gold brooch made in an open circlet. "How lovely it is, m'lady," she said. "Thank you so much!''

Lady Agatha fastened it to her gown, and then she kissed her cheek. As she led the way to the door, she said, "You see, it is a circle, and so has no end, as I wish the love you share with the good man you deserve to wed to have no end. But wear it to remind you, as well, of the caution you must use in all your dealings with men. Believe me when I tell you they are not all lustful animals, but only your own wits and wisdom can keep you safe from those who are.''

A short time later, all the guests took their leave, and after a pair of fervent hugs for Lord and Lady Williams, Rosemary once again found herself in a carriage being driven back to Berkeley Square.

The groom waited until Bert opened the door for her and she slipped inside. He wondered at the huge mansion Miss called home as the carriage started back to the hotel. It had seemed eerie to him, so dark and still. And he wondered that there had been no flambeaux lit for her, coming home alone.

For the next few days, Rosemary had very little interest in parties or amusements. She could not help feeling low, and when she mentioned it to Belle on one of her visits, that young lady decided they should have a drive to Richmond and a sumptuous picnic there, to cheer her up.

Rosemary saw the duke often now. He never remained in Lady Annabelle's rooms when she came to visit, but somehow Rosemary seemed to meet him more and more in the hall or on the stairs, much more than she cared for. But since he came no closer, and was so scrupulously polite, as if they were the merest acquaintances and had never shared a passionate embrace, she found herself relaxing. One afternoon, when she had come for tea, Lady Annabelle begged her brother to join them. Rosemary was much on her guard, and the gay, playful young lady the duchess had described was nowhere to be seen. Instead, a very demure young thing passed him his teacup. The duke was sure even Lady Margaret could not fault either her modesty or her demeanor.

Rosemary also continued to see her most fervent admirer, Mr. James Kay. She could tell by his mother's attitude that she was not best pleased with her son's infatuation, and sometimes she wished she might tell Mrs. Kay she had no interest in her son except as a pleasant escort. Sir Reginald Walllingford continued faithful as well, and Lord Greene was definitely smitten. Beside, Countess Norwell often volunteered to serve as her chaperone for dances and evening affairs, so she was not condemned to long, silent evenings in Lady Emily's library. Assured of a stream of partners and *beaux*, Rosemary began to enjoy the festive occasions once more.

One evening, about a week after the Williamses had sailed, she went with Countess Norwell to a ball given by Lord Greene's aunt, Lady Barrington. She was not at all happy to see the Duke of Rutland there, and without his sister as well, and she felt a little tremor of alarm when she saw his cool gray eyes studying her in her slim amber gown, from where he stood across the room. He was in a group that included Lady Margaret Malden and some others, but his deliberate gaze did not waver in his thorough inspection. Rosemary felt as if those icy eyes were hot probes reaching out to burn her, and she shivered again even as she told herself she was being ridiculous.

She turned away then, to answer a question put to her by Earl Norwell, and her lips curled in a little smile as she remembered the character in Belle's book that had been patterned after him. The earl was so stern, so unbending. But Rosemary had seen a completely different man when he looked at his tall chestnut-haired wife, and he did not intimidate her. She wondered if she would ever have a man look at her that way, with his heart in his eyes, as she agreed to dance with Mr. Kay.

Ronald Edson also came up and asked her to dance. There was something different about him lately, although Rosemary could not put her finger on what it was. Almost, he had an air of suppressed excitement about him, as if he knew a secret he did not choose to reveal. And she thought his gaze, when it rested on her, more than a little proprietary, and she did not like it one bit. However, since he had ceased saying anything that was the least objectionable anymore, she suffered his company, if not gladly, at least more easily.

Sometime later, she was sitting alone for a moment and fanning herself after a vigorous country dance, when the Duke of Rutland came to her side.

"Miss Barton," he said as he bowed.

Rosemary noticed he did not smile; in fact she could read no emotion at all in his stern, enigmatic face. As she rose to curtsy, she looked around for help, but there was no one nearby.

"I have come to beg a dance, ma'am," he said next, startling her considerably. "Will you honor me?"

The duke had been having a most fervent argument with himself all evening over the advisability of such a course of action. But not any of his cool reasoning that it would be most unwise had been enough to keep him from approaching her. He felt that now they were speaking again, they were on new footing, and she would dance with him, if not as a desirable partner, then as the brother of her best friend. Besides, she was so beautiful this evening in her clinging amber gown, he could not help himself. He admitted he was longing to hold her in his arms again, to feel that supple waist against his arm, to enjoy at close range her glowing cheeks and soft generous mouth, those lovely blue eyes. He was considerably taken aback when she hesitated, and then said in a rush, "You must excuse me, sir. I do not care to dance."

Her voice had been stiff as well as hurried, and one of his black brows rose.

"But how can this be, Miss Barton?" he asked, his own voice growing colder. "I have seen you dancing all evening."

Wishing she had Lady Agatha beside her, or Countess Norwell, Rosemary inclined her head in agreement, for she did not know what she could possible say in reply. She had danced every set, and of course he had noticed. Why, oh why, had she given him such a stupid excuse?

Mark Halston leaned closer, but he did not touch her, for which she was grateful. "Then I must assume that you only do not care to dance with me. Am I correct, Miss Barton?" he asked, his voice relentless.

Rosemary stole a glance at his stern face. She saw a muscle move in his cheek, and noticed that his lips had formed a thin, straight line above his firm-set jaw. His eyes seemed almost black with fury. Her heart fluttered in her bosom, and she swallowed before she nodded again. She knew she could not speak from such a dry throat, for if she attempted it, any words that emerged would be only a weak croak.

The duke raised his hands as if to grasp her arms, but before she could even attempt to step back and escape him, he lowered them to his sides.

"I see," he said bleakly.

He remained standing there for what seemed an age to Rosemary, and then he bowed, his lips white with his anger, before he turned away.

Helplessly Rosemary watched him stride across the room.

She did not see Lady Margaret Malden studying his face before she turned to stare at Rosemary, nor the way the lady folded her hands tightly in her lap as the duke left the ballroom. He did not return, and if Rosemary was grateful for his absence, Lady Margaret was most alarmed. Mark Halston had promised to take her in to supper, and he had forgotten it so completely after speaking to that bold Miss Barton that he had gone away without even a word to her. Inwardly seething, she sat quietly beside her mother, and it took all her self-control to accept with a semblance of smiling agreement, Mr. Nigel Delincourt's offer to escort her.

Lady Margaret was not a bit reassured by the flowers the duke sent her the morning after the Barrington ball, nor his note and later call of apology. He claimed a sudden indisposition, and begged her to forgive him his rudeness. Lady Margaret was not fooled. Something had happened between him and that Barton chit, and she could see it must have been serious. She decided that Miss Barton must be disposed of, and at once.

In the days that followed, she became very busy. She made a great many morning calls and attended a number of tea parties with her mother as well, and at every one of them she was quick to drop a little poison about Miss Barton in some receptive ears.

Surely Lady Wentworth would spread the news about Miss Barton's mother, who, Lady Margaret assured her listener, had been no better than a demimonde when Roger Barton married her. Why, Admiral Nelson's shocking liaison paled in comparison!

And surely Miss Boothby could be counted on to relay the information that Mrs. Barton had been an exotic dancer in all kinds of low establishments abroad that no decent woman would ever even enter.

Lady Margaret also called attention to the reclusive Lady Emily Cranston, and she was delighted when some of her older listeners shook their heads and pursed their lips. One elderly dowager duchess had even muttered darkly of bad blood, and how it would always tell.

Female London began first to whisper and then to exclaim. There were too many women both young and old who had envied Rosemary Barton's beauty, too many who had looked askance at her sensuality, not to believe the lies that were being spread. And like any flock of hens, they were quick to try to peck this unworthy member from their ranks. In only a few days, invitations stopped coming to Number 14 Berkeley Square.

The Kays were the first to withdraw, Mrs. Kay feeling she had been given a boon from heaven, for which she thanked the Lord most fervently in her nightly prayers. Countess Norwell would have continued kind, but she and the earl had left for their estate in Kent shortly after the ball, and she had no idea what was happening.

Rosemary tried to tell herself that her sudden seclusion was only because the Season was dwindling to a close, and people were leaving town, but in her heart she could not believe that. There had been a festive party only two houses away that she had not been invited to, although she had met the owners and chatted with them several times. But she only became positive that something was seriously amiss when Lady Greene gave her the cut direct in Burlington Arcade one morning, and whisked her son away, her face red with indignation.

She tried to ask Ronald Edson about it that afternoon when they were strolling in Hyde Park, but he would only make light of it.

"Just a bunch of old biddies intent on mischief, dear cuz," he said, pressing her hand where it lay on his arm. "Just ignore 'em. They cannot hurt you."

Rosemary was tempted to tell him how much it did hurt her, but he changed the subject smoothly then, asking her if she cared for an early-morning canter in the park some fine day soon.

When he took her home at last, she discovered something that drove all thoughts of her present treatment by the *ton* from her mind. There was a strange footman in the hall, a large burly man who looked as sullen as Fallow did, and a great deal more impertinent.

"Who are you?" she asked as she handed him her stole. "Where is Bert?"

The man leered down at her. "Been dismissed, missy, that's all I know. Him and that maid o' yours too. I'm Alvin Bobs, I am."

"Dismissed?" she asked in confusion. "But why?"

He shrugged. "Have to ask the old gentry mort that, missy. All I knows is that I wuz 'ired to take 'is place."

He walked away then, to drape her stole over the newel post. Somehow Rosemary did not like to reprimand him for his carelessness. Instead, she moved past him to pick it up and take it to her room. When she rang her bell, it was a very long time before Willa made an appearance. Rosemary thought her slight curtsy a travesty, and when she questioned her, the maid's answers were surly. She claimed she didn't know a thing about it. Bert was gone, and so was Maggie McGuire. Her main complaint was that no new maid had been hired to take Maggie's place.

"But mebbe Lady Emily don't feel you need a maid personal-like anymore, miss," she said, her little eyes keen with her dislike. "Seeing as how you ain't going out so much, I guess," she added with a smirk.

"That will be all, Willa," Rosemary told her. "Bring me some hot water, at once."

The maid shuffled slowly away, and Rosemary sank down into the chair by the window, hands to her face. She knew there was nothing she could do but wait until dinnertime, and hope Lady Emily would give her an explanation.

That evening, Lady Emily made no bones about her dismissal of two such excellent servants. "It came to my attention that the two of them were kissing and embracing and heaven knows what all in their attic rooms," she said after Fallow and the new footman had left the room. "I will not countenance such behavior in the lower classes that serve me. Let them carry on somewhere else. The new footman will suffice for my needs."

She would have risen then and left the room, except

Rosemary asked, "But where did you find him, ma'am? And on such short notice, too?"

Lady Emily stared at her, one hand absently stroking Prinny's rough fur. "Ronald found him for me, if you must know, Miss Inquisitive. My nephew has been invaluable to me lately."

Rosemary stared at her thin black-clad back as she left the room. It was true Mr. Edson seemed much more in evidence lately, and if she had not been so preoccupied with her own concerns, she would have wondered at it.

When she heard the footman coming back, she hurried to follow Lady Emily to the library. She did not like the man, not his looks or his behavior. He looked more like a thug than a servant, and she was uneasy in his company. And after the efficient, good-natured Bert and the sunny, friendly Maggie she could only deplore the change. She knew how much she would miss them both.

The next afternoon, she had a note from Lady Annabelle that asked her to call as soon as possible on a matter of great importance. She was only too glad to dress herself and set out across the square, for with Bert and Maggie gone, Number 14 was more dreary and depressing than ever. She only hoped the duke was not at home.

She found her friend waiting for her in her rooms, after she had safely negotiated the halls, and encountered no one but the duke's well-trained servants.

Lady Annabelle did not waste any time exchanging pleasantries. Rosemary had barely risen from her curtsy before she exclaimed, "The most terrible thing, my dear! I wrote to you as soon as Mama left me."

"What is wrong, Belle?" Rosemary asked, leaning forward in her concern for her friend. "Are you ill?"

Lady Annabelle waved her hands. "No, no, it is nothing to do with me! It is *you*, Rosemary. Mama says that the entire *ton* is buzzing about you. Somehow a story got started about your mother, and it has been given much credence."

Rosemary felt herself stiffening as her friend hesitated

and lowered her eyes to her lap. "What kind of story, Belle?" she asked quietly.

"It seems that someone has been telling the world that she was not a . . . a good woman. That when your father married her, she was nothing but a . . . a cantina dancer, and no better than she should be. I am so sorry, Rosemary!"

Rosemary began to pace the room, and Lady Annabelle watched her, concern in her eyes.

"So that is why I am not invited anywhere anymore," she said, as if to herself. "That is why people cut me when they see me, and why Mr. Kay, Sir Reginald . . . why, even Lord Greene, have all disappeared."

"Why didn't you tell me, Rosemary?" Belle asked, wheeling her chair closer to take up her friend's hand and press it. "Perhaps I could have discovered who started these dastardly tales, and we could have put a stop to them sooner."

Rosemary stared down into her wide green eyes, so full of loving concern, but she really did not see her. Instead, in her mind's eyes she was remembering the duke's face when she had refused to dance with him at the Barrington ball. He had looked like he might do anything, no matter how terrible, to pay her back for her discourtesy. Could it be possible that he had chosen to slander her for his revenge? At once both her heart and her mind refused to accept such a thing of him. She might not like him, might even be a little afraid of him, but such infamy was surely not part of his nature. And then she remembered that the only person in London, outside of Lady Agatha, that she had ever discussed her family with, even the slightest little bit, had been Lady Annabelle Halston. She knew that neither Lady Agatha nor Lady Annabelle had started the rumors, but might not Belle have, in her innocence, let some information slip to her brother?

Rosemary sighed. All signs pointed to the Duke of Rutland. Well, he had never liked her friendship with his sister; she supposed she should not be surprised at any methods he took to end that friendship.

"Rosemary, what is it?" Lady Annabelle wailed. "You

look so bleak! You must not take it to heart, my dear. We shall find a way to scotch these terrible stories. Why, Mama told me she would do her utmost to help. And even though Mama does not seem to be a very strong ally, I do assure you that once she is removed from a pack of cards, she can be very sharp.''

"Thank you, Belle," Rosemary said, trying to smile. It was good of her friend to offer, but she did not see how the crippled little Lady Annabelle or the absentminded, lighthearted duchess could be of any real assistance. And if it was the Duke of Rutland who had started the rumors, it would only bring them trouble and pain.

"Come and sit down, my dear," Lady Annabelle coaxed. "I have ordered tea. We must discuss this matter in greater depth, and try our hardest to find out how the rumors got started."

Just then a knock sounded on the door, and until the footmen under Filbert's direction had brought in the tea tray and arranged everything to that august butler's satisfaction, the two girls chatted of inconsequential things.

When the door closed behind them at last, Lady Annabelle frowned as she poured them both some tea. "What I don't understand, Rosemary, is how anyone knew anything at all about your mother," she said. "I know you have spoken of her to me, but I did not betray your confidence. Can you think of anyone else with whom you might have discussed her?"

Rosemary could not comment, not with her suspicions about Mark Halston in the forefront of her mind. Fortunately, Belle continued after a little pause to think, "Of course, it could have been Mrs. Kay or Lady Greene. I have often had to hide behind my handkerchief, watching their faces as their sons danced attendance on you. Too funny! Do you think they might have started the rumors about your mother as a way to wean their precious offspring from your side?"

"I don't know," Rosemary said slowly. "I do not know that much about either lady, or indeed, anyone in society."

She sounded so upset that Lady Annabelle put down her

cup to take her hands and hold them tightly. "Rosemary, my dear!" she said. "You are hurt, of course, for who would not be? But you must remember that people are people the world over. And there is nothing some of them like more than to gossip and stir up rumors and trouble. Surely you have found it so in Kent as well."

Rosemary nodded, remembering several past instances. If anything, people were more prone to gossip in the country, as a way of passing the time. And they saw everything. She remembered the vicar's daughter, who had had to be sent on a long visit to her aunt in Bath, simply because she had accepted a ride in a farm cart one afternoon when it came on to shower. It was true the farmer was young and good-looking, but the storm of talk that had arisen had been out of all proportion to the incident. To think that a simple act of kindness had led to a loss of reputation and banishment for one, and the amused jesting of his peers for the other! She knew neither of them would ever live it down.

Now she made herself smile and nod, although her heart was aching. She was discovering how different it was when the gossip was about you. Belle was not fooled.

"We will discover the culprit, Rosemary, never fear. And until we do, you may be sure the Halstons will stand your faithful friends. In fact, I have ordered the landau to take us driving in Hyde Park this very afternoon. Mama has said she will join us, so you see, we shall begin to show the *ton*, at once, our smiling unity."

Rosemary would have liked to refuse, but the duchess came bustling in then, declaring that both girls must make ready at once. Rosemary tried to thank her for her kindness, but her Grace would have none of it.

"Such a *stupid* thing, my dear," she said. "Pay no attention to it, *no* attention at all. *Everything* will work itself out, just you wait and *see*."

The *ton* was treated to a smiling trio that afternoon. Their way was of necessity slow, for Lady Catherine insisted on stopping the landau often, to greet her friends and draw Miss Barton into the conversation. Rosemary saw the eager stares she was subjected to, and heard the little sniffs of disapproval, but she was relieved when no one refused to speak to her or said anything blatant. She was a little surprised. She had not thought Belle's mother would be so respected, so deferred to, but it was obvious that where the Dowager Duchess of Rutland was pleased to smile could not be contradicted.

The duchess had just given her coachman the order to return to Berkeley Square, much to Rosemary's relief, when they saw the high-perched phaeton of the duke approaching. By his side sat Lady Margaret Malden, looking more prim than ever in such a dashing equipage.

"Pull *up*, Snell!" the duchess ordered, waving her parasol frantically. "I wish to *speak* to my son."

As the two carriages halted side by side, Rosemary forced herself to look up into the duke's dark, unsmiling face. She barely noticed the quiet Lady Margaret beside him, her eyes demurely lowered as she fiddled with the buttons on her gloves.

"Well met, Mark! As you *see*, Belle and Miss *Barton* and I are taking the air. Oh, give you good-*day*, Lady Margaret," the duchess added as an afterthought.

Lady Margaret inclined her head, first to the duchess and then to Lady Annabelle. She did not acknowledge Rosemary by even a flicker of an eyelash. As her gaze slid over her as if she were not even there, Rosemary cringed inwardly.

"Ladies, servant," the duke said, bowing a little.

Rosemary suddenly remembered that Belle had told her that her brother had gone out of town for a few days shortly after the Barrington ball. And now she remembered her comment about it, as well. "Just as well he has! Neither Mama nor I understand what is the matter with him lately. He has been so cross you would not believe it! Pray the country air will give him a better disposition."

Looking up into his stern, set face, Rosemary did not think it had made much of an improvement.

"My dear duchess, I am so delighted to have this opportunity to speak to you," Lady Margaret said suddenly. "Mama and I would be so pleased if you and Lady Annabelle—if she is feeling strong enough, of course—would join us on Tuesday evening next. Mama is giving a small reception. Just a select few, you understand." Her eyes studiously avoided any contact with Rosemary Barton's, as she went on, "The duke has already agreed to honor us. Do say you will come too."

The duchess would have returned a civil acceptance, but her daughter's hand pressed her arm. "I shall have to check my *engagements*, Lady Margaret," she said instead. "Do *thank* your mama, and say *everything* that is kind for me. *Assure* her she shall have my reply in the morning."

"Shall we drive on?" Lady Annabelle asked. Both her mother and Rosemary turned to look at her, surprised by her abruptness.

"*Certainly*, my dear," the duchess replied. "*So* nice to see you again, Lady Margaret. Mark, my *dear*. Drive on, Snell!"

As the two carriages pulled away, the duchess turned again to her daughter and said, "What *is* it, Belle? You are not feeling *ill*, are you, my dear?"

"No Mama, I am not," Lady Annabelle replied, her voice grim. "I just could not remain another moment and have to watch that odious Lady Margaret snub Rosemary. But stay! I wonder?" she mused, and then she fell silent.

Rosemary and the duchess were left to their own conversation, for Lady Annabelle remained deep in thought. When they reached the square again, she roused herself to insist Rosemary come up to her rooms for a little while longer.

The duchess excused herself. "I simply must *dash* away, dear girls!" she exclaimed. "Lady Mary is having a *teatime* loo party. So *unusual*, is it not?"

14

As Rosemary followed the footman who was carrying Lady Annabelle to her rooms, she noticed a lean, soberly dressed man seated in the hall. He was clutching his hat and looking very uncomfortable in these ducal surroundings. For a moment she wondered who he was, for he was not dressed as a gentleman. It was obvious that he was waiting for the duke to return, but recalling her own miserable problem made it easy for her to forget him. She would have liked to have gone home, even to that depressing mansion across the square. She wanted to be alone so she could think, but the pleading in Belle's eyes had been her undoing. For some unknown reason, her friend wanted her to remain, and so of course she must put her own feelings aside and do so.

As soon as the servants had left them, Lady Annabelle leaned forward in her wheelchair and whispered, "I have just had the most intriguing thought, Rosemary! Do you suppose it was Lady Margaret who started those rumors about you?"

"Lady Margaret?" Rosemary asked, a little bewildered. "But why on earth would she bother to do such a thing? You saw her this afternoon, Belle. She does not consider me of enough account to accord me common courtesy."

Lady Annabelle nodded. "Yes, that is so, but I have to ask myself why she dislikes you so much. She doesn't even know you!"

She paused for a moment, and then she smiled a little at

her friend, her eyes teasing. "And you know, Rosemary, I think I have discovered the reason. She has had four Seasons now, and she is still unwed. And my brother is such an excellent catch, is he not? I believe she has come to think of herself as his future duchess; she would not care to have such a beautiful girl as yourself on the scene, lest he become enamored of you and not ask her to marry him after all."

Rosemary felt herself flushing. "That is silly, Belle," she said quickly. "The duke and I do not care for each other. Besides, Lady Margaret told me herself they were as good as engaged."

"Did she now?" Belle asked, and then she chuckled. "But they are not engaged, or even 'as good as.' And Mark has hesitated for so long! I do not think it is any reluctance to enter the state of matrimony that stays his proposal. I think he is having second thoughts about the wisdom of taking such a prude to wife. Oh, I do hope I am right there! I could not bear to have Lady Margaret for a sister, always telling me I am not strong enough to do this or that, so I will keep to my rooms and not be a burden or an embarrassment to her."

Rosemary forgot to be uncomfortable in her compassion for her friend. Belle had sounded so unhappy at the thought of ever having to acknowledge the unsympathetic Lady Margaret as her brother's wife. And she had heard the way the lady spoke to Belle, too; how she was always reminding her of her infirmity and her helplessness. She hoped the duke would never propose to the lady either, for Belle's sake.

Trying to forget the depressing possibility that he might well do so, she said, "But surely Lady Margaret knows the duke does not like me, so why would she be so vile? And how could she ever find out anything about my family? Who could have told her?"

A little frown creased Lady Annabelle's thin brow. "I don't know," she said slowly. "And yet, there is her inquisitiveness to consider. She must always know everything; there is no way you can keep anything from her when she sets her mind to discovering a secret. Not, Rosemary, that your family background is a secret, of course, for surely many people in society knew your father and mother. I would not put it past Margaret to scurry around ferreting out information and then twisting it just enough to suit her needs."

Rosemary shook her head. "I do not think you can be right, Belle, even though I cannot think of anyone else who might have started the rumors."

Her voice died away as the duke's dark, stern face came to mind. The two sat in silence for a few minutes, and then Lady Annabelle said, "Let us forget her, Rosemary. She is too depressing to talk about for long. But you may be sure I shall do my utmost to discover if she is the guilty one. Mama will help me with that."

As she spoke, she wheeled her chair closer. "There is another mystery that we have to solve, my dear," she said. "I quite forgot it in the horror I felt when I learned of the gossip about you."

"Another mystery?" Rosemary asked, rising to tuck the light throw which had slipped a little, back around her friend's legs. "What mystery is that, Belle?"

"My manuscript has disappeared!" Lady Annabelle said.

"No!" Rosemary exclaimed. "But who could have taken it?"

Lady Annabelle shrugged. "I have no idea. After Mark said I must not publish, I only wrote the last two chapters rather hurriedly, and then put it aside. But yesterday I remembered wanting to change something I had written, and when I went to look for it, I could not find it where I had left it in my desk. I asked Patsy, but she had no idea where it might be."

"How unusual," Rosemary said. "Could one of the housemaids have moved it while they were cleaning your room, do you suppose?"

Lady Annabelle shook her head. "Patsy has questioned them all, and not a one of them has seen it."

She frowned then and looked down at her clasped hands.

Rosemary waited, sensing she was gathering her thoughts. "The only thing I can think of is that Mark took it away." She looked at Rosemary then, her big green eyes filled with her unhappiness. "It makes me so very sad, my dear, to think that he did not trust me, even though I promised I would not try to have the book published."

Rosemary realized she did not know the duke well enough to comment on any of his possible actions, although she found it difficult to believe he would do such a thing to the little sister she knew he loved so much. She knelt beside her friend, to take her hands and press them. "Have you asked him about it, Belle?" she inquired.

Lady Annabelle shook her head again. "No, not as yet. I kept hoping the manuscript would come to light, and I did not like to accuse him of such a thing until I was sure that it was missing. But I know I must do so now. He is dining in with me tonight. I shall ask him then."

The two sat quietly again, each busy with her own thoughts, and then Lady Annabelle sighed. "I am sorry to burden you with it, my dear. But I had to tell someone, and who better than my best friend?"

As the first dressing bell sounded, Rosemary rose to her feet. She could hear Patsy in the adjoining dressing room, and she knew the maid was waiting for her to leave so she could get her mistress ready for dinner.

"It is late, Belle," she said as she picked up her bonnet and stole. "I shall call on you tomorrow, if you like. Send word when it would be best for me to come."

Lady Annabelle agreed, and the two kissed good-bye. "Don't worry, Rosemary," she said as she hugged her. "Mama is right, you know. I have the strangest feeling that everything will work out for both of us in the end."

As Rosemary went down the stairs, she saw the unusual visitor leaving. He seemed to scurry out the door that Filbert held, and she wondered again who he was. And then, as she came further down, she saw the Duke of Rutland standing at his library door, and she checked for a moment before she put up her chin and continued to the bottom of the flight.

The duke came to meet her. "If I might have a moment of your time, Miss Barton," he said, indicating the library behind him.

Rosemary's heart was pounding now, for although she had seen him angry before, she was sure he had never been so angry as he appeared to be now.

"I am afraid that will not be possible . . ." she began, but he ignored her as he took her arm in a tight grip and almost marched her to the library. Filbert stared straight ahead, and the footmen were so still against the walls where they stood, they seemed to fade into the background and become invisible. Rosemary did not see how she could continue to refuse without making a dreadful scene, and so she allowed the duke his way.

Once inside the library, he released her to go and close the door with a decisive snap. Rosemary remained where he had left her, and she made herself stand just as still as the footmen when he came back to her.

"I have a few questions, Miss Barton," he said grimly. "They should not take long, but I must insist that you answer them—honestly."

"Certainly, your Grace," she said, more than a little confused.

He indicated a seat impatiently, but she shook her head. Whatever this was all about, somehow she preferred to face it standing up. She was unable to take her eyes from the duke's. Once again, they were almost opaque with fury, and his face was even sterner than usual. Irrelevantly, Rosemary realized how few times she had ever seen Mark Halston smile.

"Of course you know the identity of the man who just left me, do you not, Miss Barton?" he asked, leaning against his desk and crossing his arms over his chest. The casual pose did not hide the tight control with which he held himself, as if it were only with the greatest effort that he refrained from striking her or shaking her in his fury. Rosemary shivered.

"No, I do not," she made herself say. "I have never seen him before."

The duke raised a disbelieving brow. "I can assure you there is no sense in lying to me, Miss Barton," he said coldly. "I am well aware that you must be familiar with both the principals of Whittier and Rowe, Limited."

Rosemary took a deep breath, her blue eyes still steady on his angry face. "You are mistaken, Duke," she repeated. "I do not know the firm of which you speak. Why do you assume that I do?"

The duke straightened then and came toward her. "Because I know very well that you were the one who took Belle's manuscript to them. Mr. Rowe, the man who was just here, described the messenger as a heavily veiled female, who, he knew instinctively, was a lady. She told him she was acting as agent for the authoress, and she spoke in a whisper. How thrilling it must have been for you! Alas, that your costume and playacting were to no avail. My sister's name was on the title page, and that is how Mr. Rowe found me, to ask my wishes in the matter. I thank heaven he is an ethical man! There are many scurrilous publishers who would say nothing when presented with such a juicy plum."

He paused, as if awaiting her comments, but when Rosemary only stared at him, horrified, he went on, "Yes, Miss Barton, it was *you* who encouraged Belle from the beginning of your friendship in her writing folly, it was *you* who overrode my ultimatum that the novel should never be published, *you* who, in whatever misguided act of that friendship you considered it, decided you knew what was best for my sister."

"I did not!" Rosemary exclaimed, finding her voice at last. Suddenly she was as angry as the duke. How dare he assume such things about her? Even if he had never liked her, how dare he believe her capable of such treachery, and before he had even spoken to his sister?

He reached out then and grasped her arms, and shook her a little. Rosemary thought she would never stop feeling the firm pressure of his hands, even as she tried to free herself.

"Listen to me!" he commanded in a harsh, hurried

voice, shaking her again. "You have been a bad influence on my sister ever since the two of you met. Because of your friendship, Belle has abandoned other, worthier friends. I wish you had never come to London, moved in across the square, or met Belle. You have managed to make our lives a mockery, upsetting everyone and everybody. But there are steps I can take, Miss Barton, that will ensure that such treachery stops."

Rosemary could feel the blood draining from her face. She was sure now that it was the duke who had started the rumors about her mother, after all.

"I am none of the things you call me, and I have not upset anyone in this house but yourself!" she exclaimed, her voice quivering. "It is only you, so arrogant and unfeeling, who could never believe that I only wanted to be friends with your sister. Only you, who could not stand it when I did not fall under your spell. I have heard about men like you, your Grace. I knew what you were after all along.

"And you think I have made *your* lives a misery?" she asked sarcastically. Her voice was shaking now with emotion. "What do you think you have done to *my* life? How do you think I like being whispered about all over town, and snubbed, just because you decided to get rid of me by telling all those lies about my mother? How dare you even speak of her? You did not know her. She was not a wanton cantina dancer, and my father was not a fool to marry her. She was a wonderful, fine lady, happy and gay and good. Don't you dare point your finger at me, Duke, and tell me I have made your family unhappy. I have done nothing, nothing! But you, sir, you have been despicable!"

In his astonishment, Mark Halston had released her as she spoke. Now she reached up to dash away the tears that were sliding down her cheeks, before she said more quietly, "On my sacred honor, I did not take Belle's manuscript to that publisher. I do not care whether you believe me or not. I hope I never have to see you again. You are contemptible."

She flashed him one last look of scorn, and then she

hurried to the library door. The duke stood where she had left him, staring after her in complete disbelief. As the door slammed behind her, he started, and then he ran a shaking hand through his dark hair. It was true that he had lashed out at her without any real facts, but he had been so angry and frustrated after the way she had treated him at the ball, and so furious this afternoon when the publisher called to make sure he had given permission for his sister's book to be published, that when he had seen her coming down the stairs, so lovely and innocent-looking in spite of her duplicity, he had lost control of his temper. He had been determined to force her to a confession, and he had been looking forward to telling her exactly what he thought of her. Instead, she had rounded on him like a spitting wildcat, snarling and scratching.

Now he was ashamed of himself. Her angry, sarcastic words had seared deep. He took an uncertain step or two as he recalled her tears, and the anguish in her voice when she had accused him of maligning her mother. But I didn't do that, he told himself, and then he realized that he had been so stunned by her bitter accusations that he had never denied it.

Startled, he ran to the hall. In his rush, he reached the front door before his butler, and he threw it open impatiently and ran down the steps. It took him only a moment to spot her. She was hurrying through the park, her head bent, and as he watched she reached up and wiped her eyes with her gloved hands.

Not hesitating, he ran after her, dodging two hackney cabs and pushing past the elderly Bell sisters who were even then leaving the park.

''Miss Barton!'' he called. ''Wait for me!''

The elderly sisters looked at each other in horror. They knew the Duke of Rutland, of course, for they had lived on the square even before he was born, but never had they seen him in such disarray. Why, he had no hat, no cane, no gloves! And he was running! Whatever could the world be coming to? they whispered to each other as they hurried home.

Mark Halston saw Rosemary glance over her shoulder, and then quicken her pace, and he increased his own. She tried to run, but her narrow skirts would not permit it. He caught up with her just as she reached the gate on her side of the square.

"Miss Barton . . . Rosemary!" he panted, grasping her arm and turning her to face him.

"Let me go!" she demanded, writhing in her efforts to free herself.

"No, you must listen to me," he said. "Listen! I am sorry. I did not mean to upset you so—my wretched temper!—but you must believe me when I tell you I did not start any rumors about your mother. Why, such a course of action would be repugnant to me. I would never do so, never!"

Rosemary was still struggling to escape him, and sobbing a little in her distress, and he pulled her into one arm, holding her close to his side and raising her chin with his free hand. His hands and arms were like iron; there was nothing she could do but stand helplessly looking up at him until such time as he let her go. She caught her breath at the wild light that gleamed in his eyes, and for moment she wondered if he had lost his sanity.

Now that she could not struggle anymore, he made an effort to speak more evenly. "I see clearly why I lashed out at you a moment ago. I wonder that it has taken me so long to discover that my feelings for you had nothing to do with dislike, or hatred. No. I have behaved as I did because I was trying to fight my great attraction for you. I did not want to fall in love with you, Rosemary, and so I tried to pretend that I did not like you. But it was no use, my dear, no use at all. You are so very beautiful, how could I not want you?"

Rosemary stared at him, speechless. He groaned a little then, and added, "Forgive me, for I will never be able to forgive myself for causing you pain, for making you cry."

He let her go, but before she could even think of escape, he swept her into his arms again, this time to gently hold her close to him.

"Rosemary? Love?" he whispered against her hair.

He was cradling her head against his chest, but she looked up, her eyes full of shock. They stared into each other's eyes for only a moment, and then he bent his head and kissed her.

His mouth was just as she remembered, warm and firm. And then she realized that is some inexplicable way it was different. There were none of the passionate demands that she remembered. No, this time there was only a loving tenderness that made her ache with longing. But even as her senses spun, she realized she should not trust him, nor believe him, and she put her hands up on his broad chest to push him away.

He let her go at once, and she stepped back. She noticed that his hair was disarranged from his mad dash across the park, and one black lock fell over his broad forehead, and she wondered why she longed to smooth it back. She looked again into his eyes, but even the warm glow she saw there that had melted the icy gray completely, and the eagerness of his expression that was mixed with pleading that she believe him, could not make her change her mind. Lady Agatha's warnings rang in her mind, and she shook her head.

"It is no use?" he asked, his voice quiet. "You do not want me as I want you?"

She shook her head again, her throat aching with her tears.

"Perhaps you will come to do so someday, when I show you the kind of man I really am," he persisted.

For a moment Rosemary stared at him, and then, without saying a word, she turned her back on him and walked away. He raised one hand, as if to beg her to reconsider, before he dropped it to his side. He continued to watch her until the front door of Number 14 closed behind her, and only then did he turn and make his way slowly back to his own house.

The lamplighter was just starting his rounds, and the square was quiet. Mark Halston felt as miserable as he had made Rosemary feel, and he wondered what on earth he was to do about it. But even though she had said she did not love him, he would not give up. He would write to her, call on her, even beg his sister to help him, if he had to. Somehow, he would make Rosemary Barton see how truly and deeply he loved her.

Lady Emily Cranston straightened up from her telescope as the door of the duke's town house closed behind him. Even as she stretched her tired back, her eyes were shining, and a most uncharacteristic smile curved her thin lips. Both hands reached up to fondle the cloisonné locket.

At her feet, Prinny pricked up his ears, whining a little as he lumbered to his feet.

His mistress reached down to pat him absently. "*Now*, Prinny, *now* I move,' she whispered. Her hands tightened in the mastiff's rough fur, and he whined again, but she did not notice.

"After all these long, lonely years, the time is right," she muttered, as if to herself. "And now the mighty Duke of Rutland is delivered into my hands at last!"

She put back her head and laughed out loud then, a harsh, keening laugh of complete triumph.

Rosemary, on her way up the stairs, shuddered at the sound, and in the hall below, the burly footman shuffled his feet and looked almost nervously at Fallow. The old butler ignored him.

15

Lady Annabelle had no chance to speak to her brother about her missing manuscript before dinner, for he made his appearance in the drawing room only moments before Filbert announced that dinner was served. As the duke carried her to her seat in the dining room, she thought he looked strange somehow, and she wondered at it. Besides an uncharacteristic pallor and a little frown, he seemed abstracted, and his butler stood patiently for several moments, extending the first bottle of wine, until Lady Annabelle herself called him to attention.

Mark Halston seemed to make an effort to shake off his reverie then. "I beg your pardon; I was not attending," he said, and then he nodded at his butler's choice, and turned his attention to his sister.

"Mama does not join us tonight, Belle?" he asked.

Lady Annabelle thought he sounded most unlike himself, almost wooden. "How could you forget, Mark?" she tried to say lightly. "She is to dine with the Cowpers before going on to play whist at Lady Talbot's. It is the usual Thursday-night game that she has been going to this age. How could you forget?"

The duke nodded again at the platter of pheasant breasts his butler was presenting, before he spoke. "As you say, Belle. I find myself somewhat distracted this evening. Your pardon."

Lady Annabelle searched his face, her green eyes full of

concern. "I do hope you have not had bad news, Mark," she said.

The duke waited until she had been served from the various platters, and then he dismissed the servants.

Lady Annabelle put down her fork. "What is it, Mark?" she asked. She could not hide her uneasiness now, for it was most unusual for her brother to dismiss the servants in the middle of the meal. Whatever could have happened that it could not wait until they would be alone in the drawing room after dinner?

Before the duke could explain, the dining-room doors were thrown open and the duchess surged inside. "I have come to say good *night*, my dears," she said as she came up to the table. "*And* to join you, if I may, until the carriage is at the door. Some *stupid* delay. Pray the Cowpers will not have my *head* for it!"

She took a seat, beaming impartially at them, and then her smile faded. "What *is* the matter?" she demanded. "And *where* are the servants?"

"I dismissed them," the duke told her, making no further effort to eat his dinner. As he pushed his plate aside, his mother and sister exchanged glances.

"You see, I had a most distressing caller just a while ago," he continued. "A Mr. Rowe from Whittier and Rowe, Limited. The publishers."

He paused then to stare at his sister, but her concerned expression did not change. "Someone took your manuscript to them, Belle," he explained. "Would you know anything about it?"

Lady Annabelle shook her head, and he closed his eyes for a moment before he continued, "Unfortunately, I accused Miss Barton of doing so. She told me she knew nothing about it, but at the time, I did not believe her. You see, I—"

"But of *course* she knew nothing about it!" the duchess interrupted. "How *could* she, when it was I *myself*, who delivered the novel?"

The duke's startled glance spoke volumes.

Lady Annabelle's eyes were dancing now. "How could

you, Mama?'' she asked. "Why, even if Mark had agreed it was to be published, it had to be done anonymously.''

"Of course I was *disguised*, and *heavily* veiled," her mother said with dignity. "I am not a *complete* niddicock, Belle!''

The duke groaned a little, and smote his forehead with one big hand as he eyed his mother's massive figure. Why, oh why, hadn't he asked Mr. Rowe about the size of the lady messenger? he wondered. And now that he thought of it, it was typical of his mother not to check the name on the title page.

"But why did you do such a thing, Mama?'' he asked when he trusted himself to speak again.

For the first time, the duchess looked a little uncomfortable. "I knew that *you* did not want the novel *published*, Mark, but I thought you much too *stuffy*,'' she said. "There is nothing *slanderous* in the work, and it is an excellent, *rousing* adventure, I considered it a *pity* that it was not to be printed, after all Belle's *hard* work. And it would be such a *plum* for her!''

"Why didn't you discuss this with me, then, before you took such a drastic step?'' the duke asked, his mouth set in disapproving lines.

The duchess straightened her shoulders and gave him a stern look. "Because, my son, I knew you would *not* give your approval, even to *me*. *You* have become almost as proud and formal as *ever* your father was. And since we are speaking *frankly* here, I must tell you I know very well who has made you so. The Lady *Margaret*, of course. You have embraced all her prim and prudish ways, and it is so very *unfortunate*. You never used to be such an insensitive, *humorless* clod.''

The duke sat stunned as she pointed an accusing finger at him. "And let me tell you something else, son, since we are finishing this bout with the gloves off. If you *marry* that woman, you will be miserable *all* your life. And *I*, of all people, can tell you that a marriage of convenience is a *wretched* thing!''

Her color was slightly heightened, but before the duke

could reply to her amazing speech, there was a discreet knock, and Filbert entered to announce that the carriage was at the door at last.

Lady Annabelle thought her mother seemed almost relieved as she gathered up her gloves and stole. "I *must* not tarry, positively I must *not*. The Cowpers keep a French chef, and he has such a *fiery* temper. I shall run along now, but perhaps we can speak of this some other time, Mark?"

She bent to kiss Lady Annabelle, and then she turned to her son. "*Do* eat your pheasant, my dear," she said, at her most motherly. "It will be *quite* cold if you delay longer."

Both her children stared at her back as she sailed to the door.

"Well!" Lady Annabelle said as it closed behind her. "Did you ever?"

"You heard what Mama said, Belle. Eat your dinner," the duke ordered, before he sipped his wine and picked up his fork again. "We will discuss this later."

Dinner seemed to take forever to his impatient sister, but at least Mark did not linger over his port, as many gentlemen did. Instead, when he carried her back to the drawing room, he had his port in her company, as was his custom.

Lady Annabelle was almost bouncing up and down with impatience by the time the butler left them and slowly closed the doors behind him.

"Tell me what Mr. Rowe had to say about my novel, Mark!" she began without preamble.

The duke had to smile. She was so alive in her eagerness. For a moment he wondered if perhaps his mother was right, and he should allow publication. Pushing this unworthy thought from his mind, and his mother's assessment of his character and Lady Margaret's influence as well, he said, "He thought it was excellent, and far above the usual quality of first manuscripts he sees. He said he would be glad to publish it, but, Belle, I still cannot like it, no matter what Mama says."

He paused and looked at her sharply, as if to gauge the degree of her disappointment. To his complete surprise, her thin little face wore a rapturous grin, and she was holding her hands tightly to her breast.

"I know, I know!" she said. "You do not think it suitable, but publishing it doesn't matter to me anymore, Mark!"

His brows soared, as she took a deep breath to steady herself, and then she whispered, "He liked it! He said it was good! I have never been so happy!"

He went to her then, to raise both her hands in his and kiss them. "What a funny child you are, Belle," he said. "Here I thought you would dissolve in tears because I refused permission, and now you say it doesn't matter."

"But of course it does not," she said earnestly. "Now I know I can write, I can make the next one unexceptionable, and so much better. You'll see, Mark, you'll see!"

Her nod was decisive, and he smiled again as he took a seat nearby. They both fell silent, Lady Annabelle to dream of her new, exciting future as an authoress, and her brother to brood into the fire. Not that he saw the bright flames or heard the crackling of the wood. Instead, Rosemary Barton's lovely, glowing face with its speaking eyes and soft, generous lips hovered there. Around that face, beginning at the distinctive widow's peak, clouds of black hair swirled in the flames.

It was several moments before he recalled himself as his sister said in quite a different voice, "Mark? May I speak to you about something else? Something serious that is troubling me?"

He shook his head to banish the vision in the flames, and when he looked at his sister, it was to see a sad expression on her face.

"What is it, Belle?" he asked, concerned for her now. "You know you may speak to me of anything."

"It is Rosemary Barton, Mark," she said. "I have discovered that someone is spreading lies about her in the *ton*. Oh, not about her directly, but about her mother. Mama told me today. I sent for Rosemary and told her the whole. She had no idea, although she had wondered why she was never invited anywhere anymore, and why some people snubbed her. She is so unhappy, Mark! I do think I should do all I can to help her, don't you? Besides being my good friend, she is such a wonderful, kind girl. It is not fair that she should be maligned like this.''

Mark Halston felt his throat constricting with emotion. He wondered if he should confess everything that had happened between him and Rosemary this evening, but he could not bring himself to do so. The pain of it was too raw, her accusations and rejection too searing still for him to bare his soul.

Instead, he said, ''Yes, I think you should help her. I have heard the story, and I cannot imagine who would do such a thing, unless it is some ugly debutante, consumed with jealousy.''

''I have a pet theory about the perpetrator, Mark, and although I would not call her a complete antidote, she is nowhere near as beautiful as Rosemary is. I think she has a different motive.''

''And whom do you suspect, dear Belle?'' he asked lightly, as he went to pour himself another glass of port.

To his surprise, his sister did not reply at once. He wondered why she looked away and hesitated before she said, ''I am sure it must be Lady Margaret Malden.''

''What?'' he cried. ''You cannot be serious, Belle! Margaret is too much a lady to indulge in malicious gossip!''

''You would certainly think so from her demeanor, would you not?'' his sister agreed. ''But I know she expects you to ask her to marry you, Mark, and she might well be nervous that now Rosemary is my friend, her grace and beauty might cause you to change your mind. And she has been horrid to Rosemary, just horrid!''

The duke's mouth tightened in a little grimace when he remembered how horrid he himself had been to Miss Barton.

''I had a word with Mama this evening while I was being dressed,'' Lady Annabelle went on. ''She promised to begin tonight, at dinner and the whist party, to try to discover how the rumors got started. And then we shall see.''

Mark Halston shook his head. "I think your dislike of Lady Margaret has led you to suspect her needlessly, Belle," he said. "But, as you say, we shall see. I will do all I can to discover the culprit, myself."

He changed the subject then, to ask her what she planned for her new book, and he was glad that his sister was so easily diverted. He found himself in the unusual position of desperately wanting to talk about Rosemary Barton, and afraid that if he did so, he would make a confession he would so much rather his sister did not hear. He knew how she adored him, and he could not bear to topple off the pedestal she had placed him on.

Lady Annabelle sent a note to Rosemary early the following morning. She was a little surprised when she did not receive an immediate reply. When it was finally delivered, she studied the strange, crabbed hand that had inscribed her name, before she broke the seal. To her surprise, her note tumbled out, unopened. Frowning now, she spread the sheet wide and bent to read this unknown person's reply.

"To Lady Annabelle Halston," it began abruptly. "My relative, Rosemary Barton, has asked me to write to you to say that she wishes to terminate the friendship you have enjoyed. In fact, she does not intend to see you, or speak to you, again. Lady Emily Cranston."

Lady Annabelle's eyes grew wide. What could the woman mean? She would never believe that Rosemary would do such a thing, never!

She wheeled her chair to the window and stared intently at the dark, gloomy gray stone mansion across the square, almost as if she wished her eyes could pierce the shuttered front and reveal the secrets inside.

She knew something was wrong, very wrong indeed. Rosemary would not treat her this way. Rosemary could never have asked Lady Emily to write such a callous dismissal.

Impatiently, Lady Annabelle called for her maid. After Patsy inquired, she discovered that both her mother and the duke had left the house and were not expected back for some time. There was nothing she could do but wait for their return, and for the first time in a long while she cried a little over her crippled legs. If only she had been sound, she would have run around the square at once and demanded to see her friend! Instead, she was tied to this chair, impotent and useless.

The duke returned home first. He had passed a restless night after spending an hour in his library writing the most fervent letter he could pen to Rosemary. He had sent it to her in a bouquet of dark red roses before going for a canter in the park. As he entered the house, the first thing he saw were his flowers, lying neglected on the hall table. Then he noticed the note Filbert was presenting, and he almost snatched it from the tray.

"Your pardon, your Grace," his butler said. "Lady Annabelle is most desirous of seeing you as soon as possible."

"Thank you, Filbert," the duke said, frowning down at the note he held. "I shall go up to her presently," he added over his shoulder as he strode to the library. He did not bother to sit down at his desk before he slit the seal and stared in amazement at the contents. There, ripped in half, was his fervent letter. Since the seal was broken, it had obviously been read, and here he had his reply. She had not bothered to write even a word, and he felt such profound disappointment that his lips tightened and his gray eyes grew bleak.

It was some time before he remembered his sister's summons and went up to her rooms.

Lady Annabelle was quick to tell him about her own disturbing communication from Number 14 Berkeley Square. She gave him Lady Emily's note, and she wondered why his face seemed to turn to stone as he read it.

"Rosemary would never do this, Mark, never!" she said passionately. "There is something wrong, something terribly wrong!"

To her surprise, he not only did not reply, he turned his back on her and walked to the other side of the room. She stared at his broad shoulders, and watched them slump a little with whatever emotion held him in its grip. At last he turned, and she almost cried out at the pain she saw in his face.

"I see I must confess to you after all, Belle," he said. A faint color tinged his cheekbones as he continued, "I am the cause of this letter you have received. You see, yesterday, besides accusing Miss Barton of taking your manuscript to the publishers, I told her what a disruptive influence she had been in this house, and how I wished she had never met you or become your friend."

"Mark, how could you do such a thing?" Lady Annabelle wailed. "You, who say you love me?"

He knelt beside her chair. "I did it because I did not realize how much Rosemary Barton was disrupting *my* life, not yours, dear Belle. And when she flared up at me and accused me of spreading those rumors about her mother, I was so stunned I could not bring myself to deny it. But after she left, I ran across the park to do so. I caught up with her at the gate, and I made her listen to me. And then I told her I loved her, and I kissed her."

He fell silent, and his sister looked at him in wonder. "What was her reply, Mark?" she asked quietly.

"She left me without a word," he said. Then he rose to pace the room again. Lady Annabelle never took her eyes from his tall, well-built figure. "I have had a communication from Rosemary too," he went on at last. "I sent her flowers this morning, and a letter. Both have been returned, the letter ripped in half. I pray you will not hate me, Belle, for being the cause of your estrangement from your friend."

His voice was so full of pain, Lady Annabelle's heart was breaking for him. "Of course I shall not," she told him. "But, Mark, Rosemary never asked Lady Emily to write that note to me, no matter what passed between the two of you. I know her, she is as close and dear to me as any sister could ever be. No, I am sure there is something wrong over there, and I am frightened.''

She seemed to see some disbelief in his face, for she leaned forward and cried, ''After all, we know nothing of this Lady Emily, just that she is a recluse. Rosemary rarely discussed her, although she did say once she never saw her until dinnertime, and then the woman read a book throughout. Even after dinner, she spent the evening in the library reading, that ugly mastiff at her feet. Some nights, she never said one single word to Rosemary. Could not such a woman be deranged? Perhaps Rosemary is in danger, Mark!''

The duke's face grew bleaker until he remembered how fertile Belle's imagination had become, ever since she had begun her scribbling. ''She could hardly hold Rosemary prisoner against her will, Belle,'' he said. ''She is an old lady! Come, you are imagining things! But to make you feel better, I shall call on Lady Emily this very day, and I shall insist on seeing her.''

He saw the relief that spread over his sister's thin face, but he was glad that she was not beside him that afternoon when he presented himself at Number 14. The elderly butler, who had opened the door only a crack, found himself staggering back as the duke pushed it wide and strode into the dark hall.

'' 'ere now, wot do you think you're about?'' Fallow demanded, peering up at this intruder.

The duke looked around before he spoke. The hall he stood in was not only dark, it was close, almost airless. And there was something else as well, a brooding atmosphere that seemed to hang over the place like a thick, dank fog. It was all he could do not to shiver. He realized it was silent as well. Although he strained his ears, he could not hear a single sound.

Shaking off his apprehension, he handed the elderly butler his card. ''Be so good as to tell Lady Emily that the Duke of Rutland has called and wishes speech with her,'' he said. His brows rose as the elderly retainer suddenly cackled and slapped his knee.

"Won't see you, wouldn't see you if you wuz the King o' Spain," the butler told him.

"Indeed?" the duke asked. "Then ask Miss Barton to receive me. Tell her it is on a matter of grave importance that concerns my sister, Lady Annabelle Halston."

Fallow sniffed. "That one's gone away," he said.

"Where has she gone? Quick, man, tell me!" the duke demanded, reinforcing the request by handing the butler a shining guinea.

Fallow took it and tucked it in his waistcoat pocket before he said, "Can't say. Left 'ere early this morning, she did, and Lady Em told me we wouldn't be seein' *'er* again."

He shuffled back to the door and held it open. Mark Halston knew he must leave. He could hardly force his way upstairs and search every room. Still, he hesitated, and as he did so, a muscular footman came from the gloom at the back of the hall and stood glaring at him for a moment before he went up the stairs.

The duke was frowning as the butler shut the door behind him. He was afraid Rosemary really had left town. Surely, even putting aside his distressing behavior, she could hardly care to remain in such an unpleasant house.

In the days that followed, Mark Halston thought of and rejected several things he might do to discover where Rosemary had gone. Unlike his sister, he was sure she had left London, and at last he wrote to Lady Emily herself and demanded an answer.

Her reply did nothing to reassure him, although after several readings he could only admit that although she sounded most strange, she did not seem the insane creature Belle feared she was.

She did not begin her letter with any salutation; instead, she wrote abruptly, "My young relative has left my home, and I am not at liberty to reveal her current address. I can tell you, however, that she did not leave alone. She has chosen another man. Perhaps she is in his arms even now. Think on that, Duke, and may it cause you many a sleepless night! You will never see Rosemary Barton again. No, for once, one of the arrogant Dukes of Rutland, so proud and so omnipotent, will learn how painful it is to be denied the one he loves. She is lost to you—you will never have her, never!''

He crumpled the letter in his hand, feeling a misery that he had never known. He had driven her away, upset her to the point that she had fled into another man's arms to escape him.

When he finally went upstairs to give his sister an expurgated version of Lady Emily's letter, he found the duchess with her, their heads close together.

The duchess rose as he entered, and came to lead him to the sofa where the ladies had been having tea. ''Well, it was *just* as Belle suspected, Mark,'' she said in her breathless way. ''I have had it from several *impeccable* sources, that it *was* Lady Margaret Malden who began the rumors about Miss Barton's mother. *Imagine*, ruining a young girl's reputation, and all for *jealousy* and *spite!*''

''Are you positive, Mama?'' he asked, his face grim.

When she nodded emphatically, he strode from the room without another word. The duchess went to the window and waited, and she nodded in satisfaction when she saw him leave the house in a rush.

''If I am not *mistaken*—and I really do not *think* I am, dear Belle—your brother is on his way to *chastise* the nasty Lady Margaret right now. I daresay we can *all* be more comfortable from now on, for I doubt very much that *any* of the Halstons will have to be *bothered* with her again.''

She looked so satisfied that Lady Annabelle was forced to smile a little.

''Begging your pardon, milady,'' Patsy said from the doorway. Both ladies turned, and she added, ''I didn't like to bother you, but that maid of Miss Rosemary's, Maggie McGuire's her name, has come to see me. From what she has told me, I think you'd better see her too, milady, and at once.''

16

Rosemary had been in a state of complete shock when she left the duke at the park gate. Later, she could not even remember crossing the street, sounding the knocker, or being admitted by Fallow to the house. The only thing that registered in her mind, besides the terrible need to get to her room and complete privacy, was Lady Emily's maniacal laughter. That had been so unusual, so wild and frightening, that even in all her distress, she had paused, frozen there halfway up the flight of stairs, until the last echoes of it died away.

She closed the door of her room behind her with a sigh of utter relief, feeling as if she had reached sanctuary at last. And then without even removing her bonnet or her gloves, she sank down before the cold hearth and began to sob.

It was all too much. First, learning about the gossip that was denigrating her mother. The little she could remember about her mother was the comfortable warmth of her, her constant love, and how gay and happy she had been. And she remembered, too, her father's face whenever he looked at his wife, the devotion there, the caring. Rosemary's sobs grew in abandon, but after awhile she sat up and wiped her eyes. It was no use repining, for they had been gone for a long time, no matter how much she wanted and needed them now. But today she had discovered that the way the *ton* was reviling her mother could not be borne with the same fortitude she would have brought to bear if they had been reviling her. And then, as if learning of this horrible state of affairs were not bad enough, she had had to listen to the duke accusing her of duplicity in taking Belle's manuscript to the publisher behind his back, and being called a disruptive influence in his house as well. She had run away from him in utter despair. True, she had lashed out at him before she left, and she had felt a wild exultation as she did so, but even as she reveled in his white, shocked face, she had felt an anguish inside that destroyed any satisfaction she might have felt that she was putting the mighty Duke of Rutland in his place at last.

And when she had finally escaped him, what had he done but come after her, to completely confuse her with his apology and claims of love, that tender embrace. What was she to believe? Whom?

The knock that came at the door startled her, and she jumped to her feet. Silently she watched Willa come in and put a pitcher of hot water on her washstand. As she slouched back to the door, the maid said in her insolent way, "Dinner's been put back. It's not till eight tonight, for Mr. Ronald is expected."

Before Rosemary could question her about this unusual arrangement, she disappeared.

Wearily Rosemary undressed and washed. She was glad for the delay, for she needed the extra time to compose herself and to make sure not a trace of tears remained in her eyes.

When she came down to the drawing room just before eight, she found Lady Emily and Mr. Edson sitting close together on a sofa, whispering together. A little frown creased her brow as she walked toward them. What was going on? Why was he even here? Lady Emily never had dinner guests, indeed, no guests at all. Even the doctor she claimed took care of her heart condition had never made an appearance since Rosemary had come to live here.

Mr. Edson gave her a reverent bow, his blue eyes gleaming as he openly admired her soft shoulders and tempting mouth. Rosemary took a seat near Lady Emily and set herself to an unpleasant evening, parrying his effusive compliments and trying to ignore his hot, eager glance.

As had become his custom now, he acted in a proprietary way toward her. Rosemary was sure that if any strangers had been in the room with them, they would have been sure she was engaged to Mr. Edson. She grew colder and quieter in her displeasure at his possessive ways, and she wondered why Lady Emily seemed amused.

When they had been seated in the dining room, Prinny at Lady Emily's feet as usual, Rosemary saw that even though they had a guest, boiled mutton was to be featured on the menu once again.

It was halfway through the unappetizing meal that she began to feel ill. She put her hand to her forehead in confusion, and then she looked up to see Lady Emily leaning toward her, her eyes intent.

"There is something wrong, girl?" she asked in her harsh voice. "Drink your wine. No doubt it is a temporary weakness that will soon pass."

Obediently Rosemary sipped what was left of her wine, as her hostess turned to Mr. Edson and instructed him on the indifferent stamina of the modern young woman.

"Although, I must say she has shown none of these distressing symptoms before this evening," she was saying, when suddenly the room began to spin. Rosemary closed her eyes, her hands clutching the edge of the table. When she opened them, she saw several Lady Emilys and Mr. Edsons staring at her, and her last conscious thought was to wonder why they all looked so very pleased.

When she woke, it was daylight. For a moment she lay very still, a little frown on her face as she inspected the rough, stained ceiling so close above her head. Her hands were clutching an unfamiliar blanket and coarse sheets. She was fully dressed, only her sandals had been removed.

But how strange! she thought to herself. I do not think I have ever gone to bed in my clothes before. Why, what would Aunt Mary think of such slovenliness?

She swung her legs out from under the blanket and sat up, and then she put her hand to her head as a wave of dizziness swept over her. Now she remembered! She had been feeling ill at the dinner table, but that was the last she could recall.

She looked around her in some amazement. She had never been in this room before, and she had no idea where she was. It was most certainly not the large, comfortable front bedroom that had been hers ever since she came to Lady Emily's house.

She inspected it carefully. There was only one small window to admit light, and the low, sloping ceiling told her she must be in an attic. Besides the narrow, lumpy bed and the nightstand beside it, there were a straight wooden chair, a small chest of drawers, and in one corner a screen that partially hid a washstand and chamber pot.

The rough, unfinished floor was bare, but she was not cold, even without her sandals, for the room, being directly under the roof, was almost too warm from the June sunlight beating down on it. Rosemary tried to swallow. He throat and lips were dry, and she was glad to see a chipped cup and a pitcher of water on the stand near the bed.

After she had drunk a cupful, she felt better, and she got up cautiously, ducking until she could stand upright in the center of the floor.

She went to the window and looked out. London was stretched out before her, but she did not waste any time inspecting it. Instead, she looked down into a narrow mews. As she watched, a liveried groom brought a saddled horse from a stable three houses away and led him out of sight. Directly below her she could see the unused stables of Lady Emily Cranston.

She continued to feel a little dizzy, and she clung to the bedpost for support. She must still be at Number 14, but for some inexplicable reason, when she had become ill last night, she had not been taken to her room, but brought up to this attic. She did not understand it at all, but she looked around for her sandals, determined to put them on and quit this place. When she could not find them anywhere, she shrugged and went to open the door.

As she turned the knob, she discovered she had been locked in. She could hear somebody stirring outside, and she called out, asking to be released. At the sound of her voice, Lady Emily's dog began to growl, and then to yelp. When she continued to call, he threw himself against the thin panels, and the whole door shook.

Rosemary backed away from it, her hands to her mouth. The dog had stopped barking now that all was quiet again, but she could hear him settling down before the door, very much on guard.

Rosemary dropped down on the straight chair, feeling as if she were in the middle of a nightmare. Who had put her here? And more important, for what reason? And why had she been locked in, with Prinny set to guard her?

It was a very long time before she heard footsteps approaching, and then Willa's voice.

"Get that 'urly-burly animal out of the way, Mr. Bobs," she said. "You'll 'ave to 'old 'im when I open the door."

Rosemary heard the footman's mumbled assent, and a moment later a key turned in the lock and the door swung open. The large, surly maid stepped inside, carrying a tray. The footman had his hands full, for Prinny suddenly decided his job demanded closer attention, and he tried to get inside too.

Willa kicked the door shut on his ugly muzzle with her foot. She put the tray down on the nightstand beside the bed, and then she turned to Rosemary and grinned, her hands on her hips.

"Not quite wot you're used to, is it?" she asked insolently.

"What is going on here, Willa?" Rosemary asked, trying to keep her voice even. "Why am I here? And why am I locked in?"

"You'll 'ave to ask Lady Em about that—if you see 'er," the maid told her as she moved back to the door.

"Wait!" Rosemary cried. "I demand an answer!"

Willa stopped and swung around, her beefy arm upraised. For a moment Rosemary was sure she was going to be struck, but the maid controlled herself with a great effort. "You demand, do you? And 'oo do you think you are, anyway?" she asked with a sneer. "No better than me, not now, you ain't! You won't give no more orders in this 'ouse, no, not never again. Eat your dinner and be quiet, if you know what's good for you!"

Before Rosemary could protest further, Willa had opened the door and slipped outside. Prinny growled, held tight in Alvin Bobs's grasp. Rosemary saw the cheeky grin the footman gave her before the door closed and the key was turned in the lock. As the pair moved away, she could hear them laughing, and then she heard the footman say, "Come along then, Prinny, you ugly brute. Time for your walk."

She sank down onto the bed, the meal Willa had brought her forgotten. For some unknown reason, she was a prisoner, and one who had no way to escape.

She jumped up then, hitting her head on the low ceiling, and for a moment she almost burst into tears from the pain. More cautiously now, she went back to the small window, to see if she could open it. Perhaps if she were to call for help, someone would come and rescue her, she thought, but when she tried to open the window, her heart sank. Besides being set deep between two ornamental pillars, and barred, it had been nailed shut. It had obviously been done recently, for she could see six shiny new nails, much in contrast to the ones that had been used to put the window together originally.

As she turned in despair, she noticed the room was growing darker, and when she looked out the window again, it was to see that it was almost dusk. She looked around, but there was no candle for her use. In a very short while she would be here alone in the dark, and she whimpered. And then she put her chin up. No, she would not give in to weakness, she told herself. She reached up to touch Lady Agatha's brooch at the neckline of her gown, as if this talisman from her friend would give her courage. She knew that if she were ever to escape from this room, she would need all her wits about her, and all her strength.

With this new resolve, she made herself lift the napkin

from the tray. She had no appetite for the watery stew, but she made herself eat two slices of bread and butter, and the apple, and drink the tepid tea. As she was stirring the tea, an idea came to her, and she took the metal spoon back to the window.

It was almost full dark before she stopped, and Prinny was once again on guard at the door, but by then she had loosened one of the nails a little. Even if she could not escape through the window, if she could open it, she could call for help. It was all she could think of to do.

In the dark, she washed her face and removed her creased dress before she got under the covers again. She was glad she was so tired, for she knew it would be a long time before the sun came up again.

In the days that followed, Rosemary came to know fully what prison is like, all those endless solitary hours, the stultifying effect of confinement. It began to seem as if she had spent all her life in this small steep-ceilinged cell. She saw no one but the footman and the two maids. She had been glad the first time it was Mabel who brought up her tray and went to fetch her chamber pot, for she knew she was much the weaker of the two. But all her eager pleading could not induce Mabel to help her. The most she would promise to do was bring Rosemary some of her clothes and a few books to read. The evening gown she was still wearing was dirty and stained now, and she had no change of linen.

Rosemary soon lost track of time. She did not know what day it was, or how long she had been imprisoned, and her hopes that Lady Emily would come and see her and explain this madness faded. Because it is madness, she told herself. Remembering the screeching, insane laughter she had heard right after she left the Duke of Rutland, she shuddered. Perhaps it was just as well the lady stayed aloof.

But still she could not help but wonder why Mr. Edson did not come to her rescue. He had been there when she had lost consciousness. Was he in this too?

She spent many hours thinking of Lady Annabelle, so

near, and yet as far away as if she had been across the wide ocean on the other side of the world. And she thought even more of the Duke of Rutland, reliving his kisses and trying to recall the exact words he had used that last evening she had been free. Was her memory betraying her? she wondered. Surely he had said he loved her! Hadn't he?

Perhaps he would try to find her. And even if he doesn't, she told herself stoutly, Belle will be worried, wondering where I am. These thoughts were the only things that cheered her through the long, lonesome days and endless dark nights.

Since the only time she dared to work on loosening the nails that held the window shut was when Prinny was taken for his walks, her progress was slow. She had four nails loose now, however, and she knew it was only a matter of time before she had freed the other two. And when she had the window open, she would wait until there were people in the mews. Surely someone would hear her and look up, before Prinny's barks brought the footman or Willa up to investigate.

Late that afternoon, she was surprised when Willa arrived without the usual tray of dinner. She stood just inside the door, arms akimbo, while Alvin Bobs held Prinny's collar in a tight grip.

"Well, come along then, do," the maid muttered, jerking her head toward the hall. "I don't 'ave all day, you know."

"I am to leave here?" Rosemary asked, her voice full of hope. Both servants burst out laughing.

"Don't know about that, missy," Bobs said when he could speak again. "But Lady Em wants to see you downstairs."

"I have no shoes," Rosemary said with dignity. "Please bring me a pair before I join Lady Emily."

Willa seemed to relish shaking her head. "You'll come as you are, and that's Lady Em's orders," she growled.

Afraid she might be locked up again if she protested any more, Rosemary put up her chin and walked with as much dignity as she could in stocking feet out the door. Willa grasped her arm so tightly she almost cried out. Close behind her was the footman, and the dog padded at her heels.

Rosemary felt her spirits lift to be even this free, and she tried to ignore the maid's painful grip as they went down two flights of back stairs. When Bobs opened the drawing-room door, Prinny bounded past her to greet his mistress. Lady Emily was at her telescope, but she straightened up and made much of him as Willa thrust Rosemary into the room.

"Shall I stay, ma'am?" the maid asked. "Just in case, I mean?"

Lady Emily looked up and saw Rosemary rubbing the ugly red marks on her arm. "I told you the girl was not to be touched or hurt, Willa," she said in her harsh voice. "I am much displeased with you. Go! Besides, Prinny will be all the protection I need, and Bobs will be right outside the door."

The maid curtsied and left, closing the door behind her.

Lady Emily came to the sofa, and indicated a chair opposite. "No doubt you are wondering why I had you brought down, girl," she said as she sat down. Prinny lay at her feet. Rosemary saw how tense he was, and how he never took his eyes from her face.

"No," Rosemary said, staring just as hard at Lady Emily. "I am wondering why I was imprisoned in the attic in the first place, and why you have taken my sandals away."

As Lady Emily frowned, she hurried on, "I do not know of anything I have done to merit such punishment! But if there was something, I pray you will tell me what it is, so I might beg your pardon."

Lady Emily waved an impatient hand. "Be quiet!" she ordered. "Of course you have done nothing wrong. You have been nothing but a pawn to me. It occurred to me, however, that it was only fair that I explain the situation to you, for you have been so very helpful. As for your shoes, removing them was only a final precaution, for even if you should be able to escape from a locked room and Prinny's vigilance, you would not get far in stocking feet. Besides, it would make it that much easier for him too track you."

She paused for a moment, as if gathering her thoughts, and Rosemary waited, stunned at the very thought of being chased by the big, ugly mastiff.

"How much do you know of my history, girl?" Lady Emily asked abruptly.

"Why . . . why, I do not know anything, " Rosemary said in confusion.

"You mean Mary Fleming told you nothing about me when she sent you to me?" Lady Emily asked sharply.

Rosemary shook her head.

"Perhaps she did not know herself," the older woman said, shrugging her bony black-clad shoulders. "No matter, I shall tell you the story, and when I am through, you will understand why I have done what I did. You see, many years ago, while I was married to Lord Cranston and living here at Number Fourteen, I met the Duke of Rutland."

As Rosemary's eyes widened, her jailer gave a bitter laugh. "Not the current Duke of Rutland, girl. His father, Everet Halston. He was unmarried then. We fell in love at first meeting."

Suddenly Lady Emily rose to pace the room while Rosemary watched her with puzzled, apprehensive eyes. 'It was a great love affair," Lady Emily continued. "I would have moved the stars for him, brought him the moon on a silver salver, if I could. He was my food, my drink, the very air I breathed. There was nothing I would not have done for him, up to and including murder, if he had asked it of me."

Rosemary felt the hair on the back of her neck stir at these impassioned words that were all the more incongruous when spoken in that harsh old voice.

"My husband, Lord Cranston, had little interest in women, any women. He preferred his cronies, his sports and gambling. Our marriage had been arranged between the families, so you need not think I was cheating him by giving the duke what was rightfully his. Not that that would have stopped me, even if he had cared.''

She paused then, and went to pour herself a glass of wine, to sip it. Rosemary waited, wondering why Lady Emily was baring her soul this way, and to her, of all people.

''The duke and I met as often as we could,'' Lady Emily went on. ''He took rooms in another, unfashionable part of town. We spent many happy hours there, lost in our lovemaking.''

The storyteller's reminiscent smile was grim. ''And later I would come back here to Berkeley Square and have my maid dress me for a party or a ball. When we met that evening, we would dance, or perhaps just exchange a few words, as if we were only the most casual of acquaintances. How we would laugh at our behavior the next day when we met secretly again and we were naked in each other's arms. Oh, yes, it was a great love affair. He was my only happiness. I told him I would surely die if he ever left me.''

Suddenly the old woman came back to the sofa and sat down, clasping her hands tightly together in her lap. She looked past Rosemary's shoulder as if staring into a great distance.

''My husband died a year later,'' she went on. ''A sudden chill rain on the hunting field brought on a fever from which he never recovered. I went down to the country to bury him, but I was back here in a week. I knew I should have waited for a decent period of mourning, but I could not bear the separation from my lover. And since we had defied all the conventions while he was alive, why should I play the hypocrite now?

''For the first time, I sent for him openly. The footman ran across to his house, the same one you have visited so frequently, girl. But when he came back, I discovered the duke would meet me only secretly, as we had before. I did not understand it, but I bowed to his wishes. How endless those hours seemed!

''I went to our familiar rooms the next afternoon at the

time he specified. When he joined me, I threw myself into his arms, reveling in our freedom to marry at last.''

Lady Emily sipped her wine again. Rosemary thought she looked more bitter and distraught than she had ever appeared before, almost as if the retelling of her story had made it live for her again, and brought back all her painful memories.

When she spoke again, her voice was even deader and harsher. ''But I was foolish to believe that heaven was to be mine at last. You see, the mighty Duke of Rutland refused to marry me. He put me away from him, and told me quite kindly, in an even, reasonable voice, that we would never meet again. He said he was determined to marry a good virginal woman for the sake of his name. And since I had been so abandoned as to take him for my lover while I was married myself, I was not a suitable candidate for the exalted role of his duchess. I am ashamed to admit that not only did I plead with him to reconsider, I threw myself on his mercy. That is when he told me the other reason he would never marry me. He pointed out that in all the years of my marriage, I had never conceived, and he told me he would never take a barren woman to wife. The direct line was all. He even mentioned the lady he had in his eye. She was several years younger than I, and her mother had produced thirteen children.

''I was stunned, so stunned I could only stand there and stare at him. He left me shortly thereafter, but not until he had given me a farewell present to thank me for all the joy I had brought to his life. And what do think that present was, my girl?'' Lady Emily demanded, leaning forward to glare at Rosemary. At her feet, Prinny growled at her high, disturbed tones.

Rosemary shook her head, not daring to speak. Lady Emily snatched up the cloisonné locket from a table nearby and waved it in Rosemary's face. ''This is what he gave me! This! It holds his miniature so I might always remember our great love. Surely you must have wondered why I always wore it?''

Lady Emily rose then, and hurled the locket as hard as

she could against the wall. Rosemary cringed back in her seat as she rounded on her and said in a quick, breathless voice, "But I did not wear it always out of fond memory, girl, oh, no! I wore it constantly to remind me of his cruelty and perfidy, and on it I swore my revenge!"

She was panting now, and for a moment there was silence in the drawing room as she stared at Rosemary. "You see, I have removed it at last, after all these years, because now I have *had* my revenge. And you, girl, were the instrument I used to get it."

"I . . . I do not understand," Rosemary whispered.

Lady Emily went on as if she had not spoken. "Unfortunately, all the books are wrong. You do not die of a broken heart, no matter how much you want to. But perhaps it was my thirst for revenge that fed the fires of my life. No matter. I never went out again after that day. Instead, I watched his house, day after day, month after month, year after year. I saw the proper bride he chose come home from her honeymoon on his arm. I saw his children carried out to be christened at church, and I watched them grow up. I even saw the carriage that crushed Lady Annabelle's legs. When that happened, I was glad, glad because I knew it would give *him* pain. I only regretted that it was not his heir. And over all the years, I watched the duke's comings and goings, his life completely unaffected, while mine lay in ruins around me. And I waited, making and discarding plans for the revenge I sought, because I wanted it to be perfect."

She sighed, as if in regret, and then she said, "Unfortunately, he died before the perfect plan appeared to me. How distraught I was then! He had escaped me forever. My life became meaningless, empty . . . and then you came."

"Me?" Rosemary asked, one hand to her throat.

Lady Emily nodded. "Yes, you, my girl. When I saw you, I knew the gods were still good, for they had sent me the ideal weapon. Here you were, so seductive and beautiful. And there, right across the square, was *his* son. His *only* son. All I had to do was get you together somehow, and I knew Mark Halston would be lost. And I waited for the perfect moment, lusting after it as much as I ever lusted after Everet Halston. It was so appropriate, so ideal, for I knew that hurting his son would be just as satisfying as if I had been able to hurt him. Perhaps more. And when Mark Halston embraced you in the park, when I saw the expression on his face as he pleaded with you, I was ready to act!''

Rosemary's eyes were wide with foreboding as her hostess pointed a bony finger at her. ''Oh, yes,'' she crooned. ''He loves you, and he wants you, but now he will know the pain I have suffered all these years. He will never hold you in his arms, never even see you again. When he came and inquired for you, as arrogant as ever his father was, I told him you had run away with another man.''

She put back her head then and laughed, that same crazed, wild sound that still troubled Rosemary's dreams.

Rosemary shivered. Although for the most part Lady Emily's recital had been made in her normal tones, the words she spoke told clearly of her madness. To think she had lived here all these years, obsessed with thoughts of revenge! To think the only thing she regretted about Belle's accident was that it had not been Mark Halston who had been crippled! To think she had made her careful plans, using an innocent person as coldly as she would bait a hook with a worm to catch a fish! She was more than mad, she was evil.

And then, as the demented laughter died away at last, Rosemary wondered what else the lady had in store for her, and she felt a quiver of alarm. Surely knowing the truth placed her in even greater jeopardy than she had been in before. Lady Emily would make very certain that she never had the chance to tell another living soul what she had learned.

17

In the silence that followed Lady Emily's laughter, Rosemary stared at her in horror. She knew that not only would the elderly recluse make sure she never told anyone the story she had just heard, she would take care that Rosemary was never seen again. If she did not, if her prisoner escaped, all her revenge would count for nothing. For a moment the sum of the long years she might be kept in that attic cell invaded Rosemary's mind. She clenched her fists. She would do anything to escape such a fate, anything! She did not care to contemplate another, simpler solution to Lady Emily's problem, that of bringing about her now unwelcome prisoner's death.

Rosemary's first desperate thought that she might take the older lady by surprise and escape right now was quickly discarded. A glance down at the ever-watchful Prinny, and Alvin Bobs's muted cough outside the door, told her it would be useless. She would have to find some other way.

She looked up to find Lady Emily staring at her, and she tried not to shudder. There was no regret for what she had done on her white, wrinkled face, not even the tiniest hint of remorse.

"What will happen to me now, m'lady?" Rosemary forced herself to ask in an even voice. "I would know my fate, if you please."

"You are a brave girl, and so I shall tell you." Lady Emily said almost grudgingly. "You are not to be imprisoned in the attic room for much longer. As soon as I feel it is safe, you will be released.''

Rosemary must have looked skeptical, because Lady Emily added, ''Released, but not entirely free. You see, I have promised you to my nephew in return for the help he has given me.''

Rosemary stared. ''Promised me to Mr. Edson?'' she asked as if she could not believe her ears.

''Yes. He wants you too, and since I do not care to have you here, so close to Rutland, I have told him he might take you away. He is so besotted, I daresay he might even marry you, if you play your cards right.''

''But I don't want to marry him!'' Rosemary exclaimed.

''And what has that to say to anything?'' Lady Emily demanded. ''You will do as you are told, of course. You have no choice.''

''But my aunt, my uncle! They will wonder what has become of me and make inquiries,'' Rosemary reminded her.

Lady Emily sniffed. ''I doubt that very much, after the letter I intend to write to them. You see, I shall tell them that you have run off with my nephew, without benefit of matrimony, that you turned out to be nothing but a brazen wanton.'' She chuckled. ''Mary Fleming will be delighted to believe me. How can you doubt it?''

Before Rosemary could reply, there was a knock on the door, and both ladies turned toward the sound. Only when Lady Emily learned that it was Mr. Edson who waited outside did she give permission for the footman to open the door.

As Ronald Edson stepped inside, he checked for a moment when he saw Rosemary there, and then he came forward and bowed. His eager blue eyes slid over her, assessing her charms as she stared at him. What kind of a man was he, she wondered, who would help a madwoman do such terrible things?

Lady Emily rose. ''I shall leave the two of you alone now,'' she said as she walked to the door. ''No doubt you have a great deal to say to each other, and I am tired of talking." She paused, and added without bothering to turn around, "I have told her the whole, Ronald. She is calm; therefore, I can see no reason why she should not remain belowstairs for dinner, do you?"

"No reason at all. It would be such a pleasure, my dear Rosemary, if you would join us," he told her as he took a seat nearby.

"I do not care to dine with you," Rosemary said. In her mind's eye she could see the spoon she had hidden under her lumpy mattress. Besides recoiling from any more contact with either of them than she was forced to endure, she was anxious to get back to work on the nailed-shut window in her room.

Lady Emily waved a dismissive hand. "Just as you prefer, girl," she said. "I suggest you resign yourself, however, to spending a great deal of time in my nephew's company in the very near future."

The door closed behind her and her dog, and Rosemary turned to Mr. Edson. Her still, accusatory face made him flush under his dark blond hair. "You must believe that this was not my doing, Rosemary," he began earnestly. "It was all Aunt Em's idea."

Rosemary swallowed a sharp retort that he did not appear to have protested overmuch before he agreed to the scheme. She knew she would have to be cleverer than that.

"Please help me, Mr. Edson!" she said breathlessly, trying to make her eyes as imploring as possible. "Lady Emily is mad! Surely *you* can help me escape her, and I would be so grateful!"

He rose then, chuckling as he came to draw her to her feet. Rosemary tried not to cringe as he pressed her hands. As his fingers wandered up the soft skin of her inner arms in a lingering caress, he said, "But I do not think your gratitude would be expressed in the way I so fervently desire. No, no. You have a lovely, warm smile, my dear, but I am looking forward to so much more. Besides, you are not thinking clearly. For even though I did not conceive this plan, you must see how invaluable it has been to me. I have made no secret of the fact that I want you.

Perhaps I even love you. But you have shown me no signs that you might ever return that love. You do see why I cannot like risking the chance of a turn-down.''

''I will never love you if you persist in this insanity!'' Rosemary exclaimed, abandoning her plan to cajole him into helping her. ''How could any woman love a man who would treat her this way?''

Mr. Edson put his arms around her to draw her close. Rosemary tried to push him away, but he was too strong.

''Whether you love me or not, I shall have you, Rosemary,'' he told her, his eyes gleaming as they admired her lovely face, the column of her neck. Rosemary was glad she was wearing a high-necked gown.

''And besides your very desirable self, my poppet, there is all Aunt Em's money to consider,'' he went on, as if anxious that she understand his position. ''If I had not helped her, she might have cut me out of her will without so much as a ha'penny. You do see I could never support that, after putting in so many years being charming and supportive! But now, in return for my assistance, she has promised to leave her entire fortune to me. How very wealthy we shall be! I am sure you will soon grow accustomed, my dear. To wealth—and to me.''

Rosemary felt his fingers on the buttons at her neckline, and she wrenched away from him. As she retreated, he watched her with a possessive little smile. ''I should like to go back to my room now, sir,'' she said.

When he moved toward her, she stepped back, horror in her eyes. Her face was pale now, and there was scorn and defiance written there as well, and he checked. Perhaps when Miss Barton had had a chance to think it over, she would come to see that their liaison would not be the disaster she predicted. After all, he told himself smugly, she had no choice and must accept the inevitable.

''Very well, my dear,'' he said. ''I would not force you . . . not yet. Go back to your attic prison, and think on what you have learned this afternoon. I am sure you will be—shall we say?—more amenable in a little while.''

Rosemary walked to the door, trying not to hurry as she

prayed he would not change his mind. When she stepped outside, Alvin Bobs was there, his hand on Prinny's collar. Putting up her chin, Rosemary moved to the stairs, escorted once again by the footman and her eager canine jailer.

She did not sleep very well that night. Over and over in her mind and her fitful dreams, she kept hearing Lady Emily telling her story of revenge, and her mad laughter at the end. And over and over she saw Ronald Edson's searing glance, and felt his lustful hands touching her, so eager to possess her.

She was at work on the last two nails in the morning as soon as she heard the servants leave their adjacent attic rooms. Somehow she knew she must not delay, that time was growing short. She did not even care if Prinny heard her now, although fortunately he made no sound outside the door as she pulled and pried as hard as she could.

In the early afternoon there was a commotion in the mews, and she glanced down. She did not watch the coachman fighting the fresh team that was the cause of the clamor for long. Instead, her eyes were drawn to Maggie McGuire, standing near the back gate. Maggie was looking idly toward the restless team, and Rosemary put her face as close to the window as she could, and began to wave her hands. "Look up, Maggie, oh, please look up!" she prayed.

For a long moment she thought she had failed, for the maid only settled her shawl more closely about her shoulders before she began to walk away.

Oh, why didn't I have all the nails loose? Rosemary thought wildly as she struggled with the window. In a moment she will be gone, and with her, perhaps my only chance of escape.

She was sobbing now in frustration, when Maggie paused and turned back. Curiously, her eyes lifted to the attic room that had once been hers, and Rosemary's heart soared when she saw how the maid's eyes widened. She waved again, and then she put her hands together as if she were praying. For a long moment the two girls stared at each other, and then Maggie nodded before she waved in return and hurried away.

Rosemary collapsed on the floor, her hands clutching the sill. Hot tears of relief poured down her cheeks. Maggie had seen her, and surely she would go for help!

But although she listened carefully, there were no sounds in the house that showed help had arrived. Rosemary paced up and down, the nailed window forgotten except when she paused every now and then to stare down into the mews. Even with all her eager anticipation, she missed Bert when he hurried down the alley and slipped into the back gate of Number 14. She was considerably startled when she heard his voice outside the door, speaking to the dog in his normal tones. Rosemary ran to the door, but she did not dare to call out, lest the dog bark. She could hear him snuffling, probably as he inspected Bert's boots.

"Are you there, Miss Rosemary?" the footman asked.

"Yes, I am!" she cried. "Oh, thank God you have come, Bert!"

Prinny began to growl as soon as he heard her voice.

"Don't say any more, Miss Rosemary," Bert warned her. "There's no way I can keep this 'ound of Satan quiet otherwise. And no one suspects I'm in the 'ouse. I waited till they were all at their tea. I 'ave the extra key to this door, and I'm going to slip it underneath. You'll 'ave to let yourself out when the dog's not at his post."

Rosemary waited breathlessly until the key to her deliverance appeared. She snatched it up and held it close to her heart.

"Thank you, Bert," she said, *sotto voce*. "You must go now! I shall find a way to escape myself, for I would not bring trouble to you or to Maggie for helping me. Leave the house before you are discovered . . . and, Bert, thank you, thank you, from the bottom of my heart!"

Bert told her in a low voice that he and Maggie were putting up in rooms near St. Paul's and that they would be glad to give her refuge as soon as she managed to free herself.

Rosemary was relieved when she heard his footsteps

going away at last. All through his directions on how to reach them in Bread Street, she had been on pins and needles, afraid they would be discovered and her hopes of escape destroyed. Now she crept back to the window, and she did not draw a deep breath until she saw the big footman safely back in the mews, and with no hue and cry after him. She watched him out of sight before she went back to rest on the bed and make some plans.

She knew it would be difficult to wait, now that she had the key, but she also knew she had no chance of escape until Alvin Bobs took Prinny for his evening run. Then, she told herself, she must be quick to act. She decided to creep down the first flight of back stairs and then let herself into the house proper. Lady Emily would no doubt be in her rooms, or in the drawing room at her telescope, and the maids would all be busy in the kitchen. The only person who might stand between her and freedom was old Fallow, the butler. If he should be in the front hall . . . But she refused to dwell on it. Somehow, some way, she would escape—and tonight.

When Maggie had left the mews, she had started to hurry back to Bread Street so she could tell Bert she had seen Miss Rosemary in the attic. She was more than amazed, she was stunned. And it was only by chance that she had returned to Berkeley Square at all. If she had not still been feeling guilty that she had not even had time to say good-bye to Miss Rosemary the day she and Bert were turned off, she would never have come back. As it was, she had decided just that morning to see if she could speak to her. But Willa would not even let her come into the kitchen, and she had been very definite that Miss Rosemary had left London. There was nothing Maggie could do but go away. And then something—she did not know what it was—had made her look up to her old room. To say that she had been shocked to see Miss Rosemary there, waving and imploring, was an understatement.

As she came out into the square, Maggie stopped short. What was the use of her going and telling Bert? What could he do? If she had been unable to get into Number 14, they would not admit him either, especially now with all they had to hide. Maggie did not understand what this was all about, but she was shrewd enough to realize that she must have stronger allies. She and Bert were servants. If they made trouble by themselves, Lady Emily might well have them taken up and jailed. But whom can I go to? she wondered. Miss Rosemary's friend, that Lady Agatha, was on the high seas, more's the pity.

Maggie looked around the square, despairing. Suddenly she saw the Duke of Rutland come down his front steps, to mount the horse his groom held ready, and her puzzled expression brightened. Of course! She would speak to Miss Rosemary's friend, Lady Annabelle. As she hurried toward her house, she realized that she could be seen from the drawing-room windows of Number 14, and she changed direction, determined to seek admittance at the tradesmen's entrance.

The duke's butler looked her over with hauteur when she asked to speak to Lady Annabelle, and he would have turned her away if she had not added quickly, "Please, sir! 'Tis most important! It's about Lady Annabelle's friend Miss Barton."

Filbert relented then, but he insisted Lady Annabelle's maid interview the young woman first.

And now Maggie stood before the duchess and her daughter, who was leaning forward in her wheelchair, her big green eyes intent.

"And that's all I know, your Grace, milady," she concluded, twisting her shawl in nervous hands.

"You say you saw Miss Barton at an *attic* window, girl?" the duchess asked in her breathless fashion.

Maggie nodded. Her face was white with strain, and every golden freckle showed clearly. "Yes, your Grace, that I did," she said. "She waved to me, and then she put her hands together like this—and she looked so pleading, like. She must be being held prisoner there, but why that should be, I 'ave no idea, ma'am."

"And the other maid told you she was not there anymore? That she had left London?'' Lady Annabelle asked. Maggie nodded again.

"Can this be *possible*?'' the duchess asked no one in particular. "It seems *insane* to me!''

"Mama, we must do something! Where is Mark? He must go there and secure Rosemary's release at once!'' Lady Annabelle said quickly.

"I *quite* agree, my dear, but he had just *left* the house. You know his custom *lately*, how he rides out alone for *most* of the day. I doubt we will see him before *evening*,'' her mother told her. Lady Annabelle's face fell.

Maggie stood very still, holding her breath as the two ladies pondered the problem. The duchess recalled her presence finally.

"You are a *good* girl, Maggie McGuire,'' she said. "Thank you for coming and *telling* us. You may be sure we will see to Miss Barton's *escape*, as soon as ever the *duke* returns.''

Maggie curtsied and took her leave, and as she walked to Bread Street behind St. Paul's, she thought about the situation. She was glad Bert was at their lodgings, and somewhat breathlessly she told him the story. It was then that they contrived their own plan. Bert was sure, knowing the routine as he did, that he could get into the house unseen and make his way up to the attics to speak to Miss Rosemary, without anyone knowing he was even in the house. And, he told an uneasy Maggie, he knew where all the spare keys to the rooms were kept. Why, he boasted, he might be bringing Miss Rosemary back to Maggie within the hour!

As he rose to leave, Maggie threw her arms around him and begged him to take care. They might not have been carrying on quite as Lady Emily claimed, but since then they had posted the banns for their coming marriage, and they were busy looking for a situation that required a couple. Bert told her not to be so foolish, but he kissed her soundly before he hurried away.

Back at the duke's town house, Lady Annabelle and the duchess were discussing what they had just heard.

"I knew Rosemary would never dismiss me that way, or run away from London with some other man," Lady Annabelle told her mother.

"Of course *not*, my dear. *Quite* unlike her," the duchess agreed, taking out a pack of cards and laying out a game of patience on her daughter's desk.

"But, Mama, do you think it will be all right to wait until Mark returns?" Lady Annabelle asked next. "I am so worried about Rosemary!"

The duchess put a red queen on the king of spades before she answered. "He will know best what should be done, my dear," she answered. "As well as what authorities should be called in, and whom to contact first." She turned over a card, and discarded it.

Lady Annabelle wheeled her chair to the window. "If only I did not feel so distraught, so uneasy," she said.

The duchess looked up, and then she swept her cards into a neat pile. "*Very* well, dear Belle, if it would make you *feel* better, I shall go and call at Number Fourteen, and *insist* on seeing this Lady Emily. I will do nothing to give the game *away*, but I will take her measure. To tell the *truth*, I have been dying to see the woman this age! And perhaps my unusual call will distract her from whatever *plans* she may be making for Miss Barton."

Once again, Lady Annabelle cursed her useless legs. She would have to remain here waiting and wondering until her mother returned. It did not seem fair, not when she wanted to help free Rosemary so very badly.

As her mother left the house, taking a footman with her, Lady Annabelle told herself she must be patient. Since it was all she could do, she made herself pray for Rosemary's release as fervently as she could.

Fallow would have liked to shut the door on the duchess when she knocked, but he was no match for her superior look of authority, nor the way she took it for granted that he would bow her inside.

She looked around the hall, much as her son had done, and she made a little *moue* of distaste before she turned and said, "You will inform Lady Emily Cranston that the

Duchess of Rutland is here, and you will do so at once.
Here is my card. Tell her that if she refuses to see me, it
might be very unpleasant for her.''

Without waiting for his reply, she turned to her footman. "Wait over *there*, Harris. I shall call if I need you.''

As the footman retreated to a position against the wall,
Fallow went up the stairs, mumbling under his breath as he
did so. Lady Em wasn't going to like this intrusion, he
knew, but there was no way he could have refused such an
imposing lady. And perhaps it was for the best. Fallow
had always thought it a mad do, locking that Miss Rosemary in the attic, although he had obeyed Lady Em, as
always.

The duchess had no idea how fortunate she was when he
came back and told her Lady Emily would receive her in
the library. It was not the customary location for a lady's
afternoon call, but Lady Emily had no intention of letting
the duchess see the telescope that was trained on her own
front door.

When Lady Emily came into the dim library several
minutes later, she stood for a moment in the doorway
inspecting her visitor carefully. So this was the woman
Everet had left her for, was it? Now that she saw her up
close, she was not impressed. She was not above passing
handsome, and she was very fleshy in her late middle age.
Whatever had he seen in her? Lady Emily mused as she
waved her guest to a chair. The duchess's brows rose at
her rudeness, but she made no comment as she took the
seat indicated.

"No, *doubt* you are wondering why I have *called*, Lady
Emily,'' she began. "After *all*, we have lived across from
each other all these years, and we have never even *met*.''

"I did not want to meet you,'' Lady Emily told her,
sitting up very straight, her hands folded carefully in her
lap.

"I am *here* because I am *concerned* about Miss Rosemary Barton,'' the duchess said, deciding to ignore this
less-than-gracious response. "I find it *hard* to believe she
has *left* London, with or without a *man*. I also find it

incomprehensible that she would do so without *speaking* to my daughter. They are the *best* of friends, as you must be aware.''

Lady Emily shrugged, a wintry little smile curling her lips. ''I cannot do anything about your concern, your Grace,'' she said. ''Miss Barton is no longer here. I cannot say where she is. But you have met the girl. Surely, having seen her beauty and sensuality yourself, you can understand why she might just have run off with a man she wanted. The girl was no better than she should be. Not everyone is like your exalted self, pure as the driven snow on her wedding day, you know.''

The duchess noted the bitterness in her unpleasant hostess's voice, but she did not comment on it. ''Whatever can you possibly know about *me*, ma'am?'' she asked instead.

A small grimace twisted Lady Emily's mouth. ''Perhaps more than you think. But this conversation is not productive, and I am tired of talking to you. You should not have bothered to come here. My young relative is gone, and none of your family will ever see her again. Not a single one!''

She smiled broadly now, and the duchess rose. ''I *see*. You are entitled to your opinion, of *course*, Lady Emily,'' she said with dignity. ''But I would hesitate to *wager* on that. It is *entirely* possible that the Halstons will be seeing Miss Barton again, perhaps *much sooner* than you think!'

She nodded distantly before she swept from the room. Behind her, she left a thoughtful Lady Emily Cranston, who sat on in the library, feeling a little *frisson* of unease. There had been something about the woman's last words, perhaps even a hint of a threat delivered in that light, breathless voice. Was it possible the duchess knew Rosemary was still here? Had one of the maids talked? Or that hulking bruiser of a footman that Ronald had found for her? She knew that the weakness of her plan had always been the servants, but after dismissing the newcomers, Bert and Maggie, she had had to take the risk with the others. They had all been with her for years, and there had been no other way. Still, she did not hesitate to ring the bell and send the footman running to Jermyn Street, with a request that Ronald Edson come at once, on a matter of grave importance.

18

It seemed an endless time before it was dusk and Rosemary heard Willa and Bobs in the passage outside her door. She tried to appear normal, although her heart was pounding in her breast as the maid unlocked the door and slouched in with the supper tray. As she slapped it down on the nightstand beside the bed, she said in a mocking voice, "Your favorite, milady. Boiled mutton!"

She was laughing as she went back to the door and slammed it behind her. As Rosemary heard the key turn, she reached under her pillow and took up its twin, clutching it tight in her hand before she crept to the door and put her ear to the panels.

"Up you go, Prinny, you ugly 'orse," she heard the footman say. "Time for your constitutional."

Rosemary waited several minutes after the servant's footsteps faded away. She knew she must be sure Prinny was outside the house before she left this room. Unlike humans, he would be able to sense she was not where she should be, and she did not dare risk him setting up an alarm.

At last she put the key in the lock with trembling fingers, and turned it softly. She was relieved when the door opened easily, and she slipped out and stood leaning forward, every sense not only alert but also straining. When she did not hear a thing, she hurried to the stairs. Her stocking feet made no sound on the bare wood treads. At the bottom, she peeked around the next flight. There was no one in sight, but down below she could hear some distant voices, and the clang of a pot cover as someone dropped it on the floor. Reassured that the servants, with the exception of Alvin Bobs, were having their supper, she opened the door to the main hall. It was dark, but at least she was on familiar ground here. She had planned to run along the corridor to her room for a pair of sandals and her reticule, but now, somehow, she did not dare delay. It was as if something were warning her that she must make haste or she would be caught. Hurrying down the next set of stairs and across the hall, she had almost reached the last flight when she heard voices coming from the drawing room. Startled, she pressed back against the wall.

"And I say you must take her away from here tonight, Ronald!" Lady Emily's harsh voice exclaimed. "I told you I had a visitor today, none other than the Duchess of Rutland herself. Bah! But the things she said made me very uneasy."

"But where shall I take Rosemary, dear auntie?" Mr. Edson asked, his pleasant voice reasonable. "You know I have no property in the country, and I assume you want her out of London."

Lady Emily snorted. "Of course I do! Take her to my estate in Kent. I'll give you a letter for my agent there. Then, in a week or so, you may take her anywhere you like. It won't matter then, since she will be ruined."

"I do not see why we cannot proceed as we had planned," Mr. Edson protested.

"Think, man!" Lady Emily ordered. "Although the duke has not returned from his solitary ride, he will be home soon. I cannot tell you how it has amused me to watch him every day, so lovesick, forlorn, and depressed. Observing his black looks has made the whole thing worthwhile. But if one of the servants has talked, as I suspect, he will learn that the girl is still here. Then he might well get the authorities to search the house. No, I cannot take the chance! She must leave tonight." Lady Emily's voice was full of purpose as she continued. "Make arrangements for a carriage, and I will have her drugged and ready at midnight. Why, it will be almost romantic, will it not, my boy? Escaping in the dark of the night with your ladylove?''

As Lady Emily began to laugh, Rosemary waited no longer. She started down the last flight as quickly and soundlessly as she could. Bobs would be back soon, and with him, Prinny. She must be gone!

She froze against the stairs as a querulous voice below her mumbled, ''And wot's more, I want my supper! 'Ow long will Mr. Ronald 'ang about 'ere, keeping me waiting? Not that 'e cares if I go 'ungry, not that one! 'E only cares for the wench and Lady Em's money, that I do know!''

As Rosemary shuddered, Fallow shuffled into view. She knew she could not be seen in the light of the one candle he carried, but even so, she shrank back further into the shadows. Below her, she could see the front door that led to freedom, and between it and herself, the elderly butler, the one person she had feared might interfere with her escape. She had to get by him, and soon! But as she stared at him, he put his candle on the hall table and settled down in the chair next to it, still shaking his head and mumbling to himself as he waited for Lady Emily's visitor to depart.

Rosemary closed her eyes, disappointment welling up in her breast like a sour flood. To have come this far, and then to be denied the freedom she had waited for so long. It was cruel, cruel! She began to pray as hard as she could, for something, anything, to take the old man out of the front hall.

When she opened her eyes, she saw with despair that Fallow was still at his post. But then, as she watched and wondered what on earth she was to do now, his head dropped forward until it rested on his chest. A moment later, surely the most welcome sound she had ever heard in her entire life drifted up to her in the form of a soft snore.

Rosemary did not delay another second. She picked up her skirts and ran softly down the remaining stairs. Barely breathing now, she edged past the old butler to the front door, and opened it as quietly as she could. In a moment she was outside, the door closed behind her, and she took the first deep breath she had allowed herself since leaving the attics. She looked around, but she did not see Prinny, and suddenly she was down the steps and running around the square. It had all taken so much time, she did not even dare try to go to Bread Street, and certainly not clad only in thin silk stockings. No, she must reach the duke's house, and seek sanctuary with Annabelle.

The cobbles of the road were painful, but she did not falter or slow her pace. She could see the lighted windows of the duke's mansion on the other side of the square. Quickly, Rosemary, as quickly as you can! she told herself. She pulled her skirts above her knees so they would not impede her progress. If only she had had the key to the park gates, she thought, she might have taken a shortcut. But the key was in her room along with her sandals, and she was forced to go the long way around, now that the gates had been locked for the night.

She was halfway to safety when the sound she had been dreading came faintly to her ears. Behind her, in the house she had just quit with so much relief, a dog began to bay.

As Rosemary tried to run even faster, a solitary horseman trotted into the bottom of the square. The Duke of Rutland stared straight ahead, his narrowed gray eyes cold under the brim of his hat. Suddenly he reined in his mount. The horse neighed, for they were still some distance from Number 26, and he was tired and wanted his feed bag and comfortable stall. The duke patted his horse's neck, but his eyes had gone to the large gray stone mansion across the park. Yes, there it was again, that baying, he noted. Quickly his eyes swept the square, and then they widened as he saw Rosemary Barton running toward his house as fast as she could.

He wondered if he were imagining that the dog's baying was growing even louder and more persistent. Slapping the reins on his horse's neck and digging in his heels, he set the gelding to a canter. In only a moment he was halting his mount beside a panting Miss Barton. He stared down at the girl he had thought he was never to see again, and then he leaned down and extended his arm.

"Quick!" he ordered, his voice constricted with emotion. "Give me your hand!"

She did not hesitate. Throwing a fearful glance over her shoulder, she grasped his outstretched hand. As the duke pulled her up before him and wheeled the horse, he could feel her violent trembling. He put his arm around her tightly to keep her safe as he cantered back to his own door.

In one fluid motion he dismounted, calling loudly for a footman as he did so. Then he reached up and grasped Rosemary's waist to swing her down into his arms. He took the front steps two at a time. As the door was swung open by a startled Filbert, he heard the angry barking of Lady Emily Cranston's mastiff as it flew out the door of Number 14. Then it ceased to bay, as, head down, it began to search for the scent of the girl it had been set to guard.

"Take the horse to the stables, Harris," the duke ordered as the footman hurried past him. Then he turned to his butler. "Shut the door, man! At once!"

The butler did as he was bade, and then he bowed. The duke ignored him, for he was staring down into Rosemary's face. Those dark blue eyes were shuttered by her eyelids and long lashes, and she was panting in distress. His arms tightened, as if to reassure her that she was safe.

"Your pardon, your Grace," Filbert said, at his most urbane. "The duchess and Lady Annabelle are waiting for you in the drawing room. They have desired me to ask you to come to them the moment you returned, on a matter of the greatest urgency."

Mark Halston tore his eyes from the girl he held in his arms. He looked bemused.

"If I might take the liberty, sir?" the old butler continued. Seeing the duke remained speechless, he went on. "I believe that the young lady you are holding is the urgent matter, so it will not be necessary to hurry."

Mark Halston nodded. Still holding Rosemary close, he strode to the drawing room. Behind him he could hear Lady Emily's dog begin to bay again. He thought it sounded confused and bereft, and a grim little smile curled his lips as he entered the room.

"Mark . . . oh, Mark!" Lady Annabelle cried. "You have found Rosemary! She is safe!"

"Dear boy, how *clever* of you!" his fond mother applauded. "And to think we have spent the entire afternoon in a positive *fret*!"

Behind them, Filbert closed the double doors with the most reluctance that he had ever succumbed to since he had been a green footman more years ago than he cared to remember. He was so ashamed of himself for the lapse into vulgar curiosity that his glance was even sterner than usual as it swept over his satellite footmen on duty in the hall.

In the drawing room, the duchess had taken charge. "Miss Barton, *do* speak to us so we will know you are all *right*! Mark, do not stand there *clutching* the girl, if you please. Put her down here so she might catch her *breath*."

Rosemary opened her eyes as the duke reluctantly lowered her to the comfortable sofa across from his sister's wheelchair. She looked at him briefly before her bemused gaze sought Lady Annabelle and her mother.

"I . . . I am . . ." she whispered, and then she fainted.

When she regained consciousness only a few minutes later, she was lying prone, the duke kneeling at her side, chafing her hands. Above him, the imposing figure of the duchess held a small glass of some amber liquid, and she could hear Lady Annabelle's voice in the background. "Perhaps some burnt feathers, Mama? Or a vinaigrette?"

"I don't need any burnt feathers, Belle," Rosemary told her. Her voice was weak but steady. The duke's hands tightened on hers, but she did not dare to look at him again.

"Sip this *slowly*, dear girl," the duchess ordered, extending the glass she held.

The duke helped her to a sitting position before he sat

down beside her and put his arm around her for support. He took the glass from his mother and raised it to her lips. "Do drink a little, Miss Barton," he said. "It is brandy, and it will make you feel better."

Rosemary wondered if she were imagining the emotion that made his voice quiver a little. Above their heads the duchess smiled to herself.

Obediently Rosemary took a sip, and then she had to cough as the fiery liquor burned her throat.

She closed her eyes briefly for another moment before she sat up straighter and took a deep breath. Her eyes filled with tears when she saw the loving concern on her friend's face and the encouraging smile the duchess was giving her. She was safe, safe at last.

"I cannot thank you enough, your Grace. If it had not been for you, I would not have escaped," she said formally, carefully not looking at him. She felt weak but happy and relieved, and for some reason, very tired. All she really wanted to do was sleep, sleep for hours.

"Oh, Rosemary, we have been so worried!" Lady Annabelle exclaimed. "Are you truly all right now? But look, Mama! Her feet are bleeding!"

The duke leaned forward to stare at her ripped silk stockings. One of them was bloody, and his lips tightened as he took out his handkerchief and knelt to bind up her foot.

"But, my dear girl, why weren't you wearing *shoes*?" the duchess asked. "No, do not say anything. Just sit *quietly* until you have finished your restorative and feel more the thing. Although it will be *prodigious* hard to wait. We have so *many* questions!"

Rosemary sipped her brandy. She realized it was making her feel better, for her light-headedness was gone, and the room had stopped spinning. Very much aware of the duke's hard arm around her waist, she made a little movement and he let her go and stood up. As they all watched, he walked to the window and swept the draperies aside so he could stare out into the square.

"Yes, I suspected the hunt was over," he said. "The

footman is taking the dog back to Number Fourteen. I knew it would lose the scent when I put you up on my horse, Miss Barton. It cannot follow you here, for it does not know where you have gone."

"But surely that Lady *Emily* will know," the duchess interrupted. "Might she not come here and *insist* the girl be returned to her home?"

The duke's laugh was harsh and unpleasant. "Somehow I doubt she will do that, Mama," he said.

"No, she will not come after me, especially now that I have escaped to this house," Rosemary volunteered. She frowned a little, and put the brandy glass down on the table beside her.

"Was she really holding you prisoner, Rosemary?" Belle asked, her eyes wide with shock. "I must tell you that your former maid came here today and told us she had seen you at the window of an attic room, after the servants over there insisted you had left London."

"Yes, I was a prisoner," Rosemary said. "Lady Emily and Mr. Edson drugged me at dinner, after the last time I saw you, Belle. When I woke up the next day, I was locked in an attic bedroom, with Prinny on guard at the door. I never left that room but once, until tonight."

Her lips tightened, and she frowned again, absorbed in her memories. The duchess noticed that her son never took his eyes from the girl's face and that his expression grew blacker with every word she spoke.

"Did they take your shoes away so that if you did manage to escape, the dog could be set on your trail, Miss Barton?" he asked.

When she nodded, Lady Annabelle asked, "But how did you get away, Rosemary? It sounds impossible!"

Rosemary explained how she had accomplished it, beginning with the footman's visit when she had acquired the key to the room. The three listeners sat breathless, a number of emotions crossing their faces as she told her story.

When she reached the point where the duke had put her

up before him on his horse, her voice faded, and for a moment there was silence in the room.

"But, dear girl, why *were* you kept a prisoner?" the duchess asked brightly. "I do not understand *that* part of it at all!"

Warm color flooded Rosemary's face. she looked from one to the other in confusion, not knowing what she could say.

"Perhaps you would rather not tell us, Rosemary?" Lady Annabelle said kindly. "It is all right. We understand."

"*I* don't!" the duchess insisted.

The duke came forward suddenly. "No doubt Miss Barton will tell us all about it tomorrow, Mama," he said in a voice that brooked no argument. "Right now, she is still in shock. She must go to bed—after her foot is bathed and properly bandaged, of course. I will carry her upstairs."

"Yes, do that, Mark," his sister agreed. "And put her in the gold bedroom, next to mine. I will send Patsy to help you, Rosemary."

As the duke bent to lift Rosemary into his arms again, the duchess shrugged. "No doubt you are right, my son," she said. And then she came and patted Rosemary's cheek. "Have a *good* sleep, my dear, and do not worry about a *single* thing! Somehow we will *all* manage to contain ourselves until tomorrow."

Rosemary smiled, very conscious of the duke's broad shoulders and handsome face, now she was held securely in his arms again. She wondered why she had not said she did not need to be carried at all. It was very strange! As they left the drawing room and went up the broad stairs, she hoped he could not hear her pounding heart. To her ears it was making a dreadful din. He lowered her to the bed in the room next to Belle's and she stole a glance at him from under her long lashes. His face was expressionless, but as he looked down at her, a little light began to gleam in his gray eyes. Rosemary did not know whether to be glad or sorry when Patsy bustled in, one of Lady Annabelle's clean nightgowns over her arm. The duke bade her a civil good night and went away.

In no time at all, Rosemary was being tucked into bed by the competent maid, and she fell asleep only moments later.

It was very late the following morning when she woke. She lay confused for a moment, wondering where she was before it all came flooding back. As she looked around the gracious, comfortable room, admiring the spring sunlight streaming through the curtains, she gave a deep sigh of relief.

The adjoining door opened softly then, and Maggie McGuire peeped around it. Rosemary smiled, sitting up and holding out her arms. Maggie ran up to the bed and hugged her.

After the initial excitement and conversation had died down, Maggie asked her what gown she would like to wear.

"My clothes are here?" Rosemary asked, confused. "But how can that be?"

"The duke went over to Number Fourteen first thing this morning," Maggie told her, her eyes wide. "It was so exciting, Miss Rosemary! He took two of the footmen with him, and he was armed! But there was no one there but the Fallows. Lady Emily and Mr. Edson had both disappeared, and the other servants were gone too. Even Prinny was gone! Fallow told the duke the house was to be sold, and he had no idea where Lady Emily had gone. The duke sent for me so I could pack up your clothes. I had come back here early to make sure you were all right, you see. Me and Bert were that worried when you didn't come to Bread Street last night."

Rosemary sank back on her pillows, a little frown on her face, as Maggie went to get her breakfast. She had avoided telling the most difficult part of her story last night, but she knew she could escape it no longer. As she ate her breakfast and had Maggie dress her in a soft blue morning gown, she decided she must speak to the duke alone. Heaven knew it was going to be difficult enough to tell him, but she could never tell the duchess about her husband's disastrous love affair.

She sent Maggie to beg a few minutes of his time, and when she learned he was waiting for her in the library, she squared her shoulders. As she came down the stairs, Filbert gave her a warm smile. Rosemary wished she felt more like returning it.

The duke rose from his desk as she came in and curtsied. Until the butler shut the door behind her, Rosemary stood still in the middle of the room, her eyes lowered.

"There was something you wished to talk to me about, Miss Barton?" the duke asked courteously as he came to lead her to a chair. His face was full of concern, but she did not dare look at him too closely. Already her breathing was growing shallow, just being near him.

"Won't you look at me, my dear?" he asked in a quiet voice. "After all, no matter how you feel about me, I *did* save you last night."

Rosemary made herself look into his face. He was smiling down at her, and she caught her breath. The light she had seen in his eyes last night was stronger now, but she wondered if he would still be smiling after she had told him her story.

"I must thank you again, your Grace," she remembered to say. "And thank you for seeing me, alone. I do not know how I am to tell Belle and the duchess what happened to me, and why. I wish I did not have to tell you, but you will not understand unless I do. And you deserve the truth."

"You may tell me anything Miss Barton," he said quietly as he sat down close beside her and took her hand in both of his. "It will make no difference to me, no matter what it is."

Rosemary hesitated for only a moment, and then, in a soft voice she told him everything, exactly as Lady Emily had told it to her, about the lady's affair with his father, and how it had ended. She did not dare to look at him as she did so, and sometimes her voice faltered, but he did not interrupt. She told him of Lady Emily's obsession for revenge, and how cheated she had felt when the former duke had died. It was especially hard to tell him how the elderly recluse had decided to use Rosemary to catch *him*, but she made herself do so.

"She only put her plan into action after she saw you kissing me in the park that night," she concluded. "She had made her plans long before, using her nephew Ronald Edson to help her. She promised him her entire fortune, and I was to be his immediate reward. He . . . he wanted me."

She felt the duke's hands tighten on hers, and she hurried on. "She is mad, your Grace, that is true, but I am not frightened of her anymore, not now that I have escaped."

He spoke for the first time. "I agree. Knowing her revenge has failed, there is nothing more she can do. Poor, poor woman."

Rosemary looked at him then. He was shaking his head, and that familiar frown creased his forehead. She longed to reach up and smooth it away.

He rose then, and went to lean against the mantel to stare down into the empty hearth. Rosemary watched him anxiously.

"The male side of the Halston family have brought you nothing but trouble, have they not, Miss Barton?" he asked quietly. "I do apologize, both for my absent sire who initiated the whole debacle by his cavalier treatment of a woman he must have suspected was unstable, and, of course, for my own actions as well."

Rosemary rose and put her hand out to him, but he did not see it. "I began badly, by distrusting you and trying to get you to admit to being something you were not," he went on. "I was so blind not to see how good and kind you were, a lady in every sense of the word. And then I insulted you, and made you cry. By the time I realized how deeply I loved you, it was too late. I was sure, you see, that you had left London. Oh, not with another man, as Lady Emily claimed, but to escape me, because you hated me. And I had not only hurt you, I had hurt Belle as well."

He turned then to stare at her, a tiny muscle moving in his cheek. "I suppose there would be no use asking you to marry such a fool now, would there?"

Rosemary stared back at him in amazement, feeling a glow beginning to warm her heart. He laughed bitterly. "No, I can see it would be no use at all. But even though you do not want the protection of my name, be assured that as my sister's dear friend, the protection of my house is always yours."

He turned away then, and Rosemary ran to him to grasp his arm. "It is not too late, Mark! I do not hate you!" she cried passionately. "I see now why all those long, lonely days, those dark, frightening nights, I could not forget you. It was remembering you that kept me sane. If you knew how many times I relived all your words, your kisses, if you knew how much I wanted you . . ."

But the duke did not wait to hear the end of her confession. Fiercely he pulled her into his arms, to bend his dark head and cover her lips with his own. Rosemary put her arms around him, her heart singing as his kiss grew more demanding, more intimate.

When he raised his head after several long moments, her blue eyes were shining. But still, she made herself ask, "But are you sure you really should marry me, Mark? Especially now, when you know there is madness in my family?"

He put back his head and laughed. "Not as much madness as there is in mine! For am I not mad with love for you? I do not want the empty marriage of convenience my father extolled to me, I want you, today and always. You are my prisoner now, and you must humor me, my future duchess, lest my madness grow."

"And how shall I do that?" Rosemary asked, smiling a little.

"Oh, I think you will find a way," he said in a husky voice, the last word lost against her mouth as he kissed her passionately again.

Sometime later, he put her away from him a little to

look down into her eyes. His face was serious again. "Tell me one thing, love," he said. "Did Ronald Edson touch you, force you in any way?"

Rosemary shook her head. "Why do you look that way, my dear?" she asked, reaching up to touch his face.

"Because if he had, I would have killed him," the duke told her.

Rosemary shivered a little at his cold, flat voice, until he pulled her close to whisper of his love once more.

When the knock came on the door, they drew apart reluctantly, just before the duchess came in, pushing Lady Annabelle in her chair before her. "I could not wait another *moment*, *positively* I could not!" she announced. "Come now, Rosemary, tell us your story. I was awake half the night wondering about it."

As Rosemary hesitated, the duchess asked, "Was Lady Emily intimate with my husband at one time, Rosemary?"

Rosemary nodded, and the duchess settled herself comfortably in a chair as she said, "I rather *suspected* it, after my visit to her yesterday, and from *some* things I have observed in the past. There was no *love* between the duke and myself. We shared only a marriage of convenience, so *do* speak freely."

Rosemary looked at the duke, and he nodded, smiling his encouragement. Once again she told the story of Lady Emily's madness. Lady Annabelle's green eyes got bigger and bigger, and the duchess sat enthralled.

When the story was done, and all the questions asked, Lady Annabelle put her head to one side, frowning a little as if lost in thought. Her brother eyed her with misgiving.

"Don't you even dare think about it, Belle!" he growled.

"But, Mark, my dear, what a wonderful novel it would make," she said, her eyes eager. "And no one would even suspect that it was about Rosemary, for we are the only ones who know the whole story. And I could disguise her, you know, make her a very fair blond and—"

"Belle, Belle!" the duke interrupted. "You have my permission to write anything you like about anybody in the world *except* your own dear immediate family. Do you understand?''

There was a moment of stunned silence, and then, as the duke put his arm around Rosemary and smiled down at her, his heart in his eyes, both the duchess and Lady Annabelle began to applaud and exclaim.

About the Author

Although Barbara Hazard is a New England Yankee by birth, upbringing, and education, she is of English descent on both sides of her family and has many relatives in that country. The Regency period has always been a favorite, and when she began to write seven years ago, she gravitated to it naturally, feeling perfectly at home there. Barbara Hazard now lives in New York. She has been a musician and an artist, and although writing is her first love, she also enjoys classical music, reading, quilting, cross-country skiing, and paddle tennis.